# Young Thoughts of a Man

## John Clegg

Grosvenor House
Publishing Limited

This book is published by
Grosvenor House Publishing Ltd
Link House
140 The Broadway, Tolworth, Surrey, KT6 7HT.
www.grosvenorhousepublishing.co.uk

This book is a work of fiction. Any resemblance to
people or events, past or present, is purely coincidental.

A CIP record for this book
is available from the British Library

ISBN 978-1-83615-100-5
eBook ISBN 978-1-83615-101-2

Front cover image of Titterstone Clee supplied by
a Shropshire based photographer, Alexandra Preston.
(studio details available on the internet)

# Dedication

To those lads I grew up with in Clee View, Ludlow.

Brian, Mick and Robert Woodcock.

Robert and Peter Clark.

Francis Lochbaum.

Tommy Preece.

David and Roger Pritchard.

My brother, Michael Sciville.

Also, a special mention to the gifted junior school teacher,
Mrs V Bodenham.

# Preface

This is the book I've always wanted to write, but either work got in the way or I was continually stumped by the personal nature of it. Also, I at first found it hard to capture the spirit of those times without descending into a degree of exaggeration coupled with self-indulgence, which lost what I hoped would be a simple narrative with an almost naïve charm.

Meanwhile, in an attempt to preserve a few of those treasured memories, I jotted them down in verse form, which explains the strange mixture of prose and poetry.

To keep my feet on the ground, I'd frequently ask myself, 'What would my old mate Roger Pritchard think of this?' He would tell me in no uncertain terms, and so on seeing him recently to be informed he'd genuinely enjoyed reading it, you can imagine my relief, for there stands a fair danger others will as well.

# Part One

# The opening scene c1953

"He's behind you!" came the cry from children packed in the small sitting room of the only house in the two adjoining streets to possess a television set. Watching fuzzy action on a screen no bigger than a place mat in the upper section of a large wooden cabinet, they were shouting a warning to the hero sporting a white Stetson, that a baddy in a black hat was creeping up on him. Wide-eyed at the inevitable fist-fight, the boys shadow boxed with excitement, then cheered as the baddy made a frantic dash for his horse. Spurred on by the drumming of hooves and wild urgency of music, some leapt aboard armchair crests, while others whipped the back of the sofa in the ensuing chase.

It was the post-war period, a new beginning; those years of the baby boom and streets of new houses springing up around town perimeters. The two streets that feature large in this tale, made a perfect right-angle and beyond lay meadows, orchards, ponds and streams. The ideal playground and my excitement always grew at the thought of visiting the house where my three female cousins resided, number 7, Clee View. My aunt and uncle had been incredibly lucky to gain tenancy, for although being brought up in a council house can now bear a stigma, especially when you consider how some were thrown together, these with their large gardens on the outskirts of a pretty Midland's town, were avidly sought after and occupants came from all walks of life; builders, painters, an RAC patrol man, a factory manager, volunteer firemen, plasterers, a truck driver, a school caretaker, a plumber, a bank clerk, a printer, plus even a horse trader. All of them had helped win the war; well, all apart from one, but with him marrying a local girl and eventually managing a factory on the edge of town; say what you like about the Germans, no-one had a bad word to say against Werner, for he was as much a part of the community as anyone.

It was what we now know as the 'Bulge Years' and all seemed fresh and exciting with parents toiling to create lawns, flower beds and vegetable patches while children chased in and out of the newly planted privet hedges, swarmed over the banking opposite and up into elms, standing sentinel over high hedge and orchard beyond. It was in a fact a magical time and I hope the following captures some of that spirit.

# Background details

I was born in the Isle of Man, January 1948 and lived for my first two and a half years, in a well-built, but otherwise unremarkable looking house in Crosby, a village located roughly halfway between Douglas and Peel. No more than a grey blur to those roaring at full throttle along the TT course and you would have thought something that dramatic would have lodged in a young lad's memory, but sorry, no. I have absolutely no recollection of a succession of pepper pot helmets flying past the garden hedge.

Other than the fact it's unusual for one to remember anything at all from such an early age, the meagre remnants hardly seem worthy of a mention, but for reasons later evident, I'll quickly list them. Firstly, there's the image of my mother putting jellies to cool in a small tabletop meat safe outside the back door. It gets better mind you, for then I remember a tractor breathing and rattling in the field behind the house. Yes, I'd liked the strange contraption, but didn't want to sit on the lap of the man about to crank it into action and so clung to my sister for protection.

Why do I remember a three-wheeler bike hanging from a beam in the garage, but on the other hand, have no recollection of wrestling with the family mongrel? Apparently, my sister had been petrified of the thing, but the mutt and I were inseparable.

Like many small boys, I had a yen to explore and one day managed to squeeze under the garden gate into the wide-open world beyond. What a feeling of freedom that gave and couldn't wait for the next opportunity, but something strange happened, almost as if I'd suddenly grown bigger, for on my next attempt I couldn't even get my head through the gap, never mind the rest of me. Many years later, when recalling the experience, probably checking whether I'd simply dreamt the whole thing, my mother said, no, it had been true enough, for she'd almost had kittens at the sight of me, droopy-drawered in the middle of a puddle on the main thoroughfare across the island. I'd had a fist full of gravel and realising the likely outcome of her swoop towards me, promptly sat down and for good measure, rammed the stones into my mouth. That evening, my father had been instructed to block the gap beneath the gate.

The next memory was quite unsettling, for my parents suddenly took on a different guise, as if strangers, madly shouting with looks of hatred. My mother raged down from the landing, while my father barked up from the stairs.

"Look now you've made him cry."

My father, giving me a glance, obviously thought better of continuing and I remember him returning to normal as he descended into the hallway.

Why am I telling you all this? Well as trifling as they seem, I was only two years old and these scant memories, of not only my homeland, but of my father back in 1950, I've hung onto ferociously, keeping them inside to be cherished. I'll divulge the reason later and yes, I would prefer to have remembered the TT races, but no matter what age you might be, you can't choose your abiding memories.

Many years later, I took my family back to the island and the sight of Peel harbour jogged another recollection; my father descending a long flight of stone steps to a neat white boat on green water. I recall a sense of happiness, with all waving at his departure, but for me it was quite unsettling. Was he leaving for good? Not an unreasonable concern after all that shouting.

Also, people did seem to come and go somewhat. They'd be like new best friends, making funny noises in your face one minute and then that would be it, you'd never clap eyes on them again.

Now here's another thing that perplexed. You could be praised to the heavens for doing a simple act one day, for it to be deemed unspeakably horrid on another. One just didn't know what to do to be right.

The poo in question, I'd been quite proud of, for it had been a splendid effort, but my sister sharing the same bath, had leapt to her feet shouting, "Gusting!"

In fairness, my mother tried to make light of it, capturing the brown flotilla in a pot as the murky water eddied away and now I think about it, I had been right to feel concern at the sight of my father's jaunt across Peel harbour, for one day something happened that changed my life for ever.

This I remember vividly, for there was an incredible sense of urgency; panic almost. Of course I'd not been told what was going on, but always having had an ability to sense moods and atmospheres, I watched with concern as clothes were being rammed into suitcases, but then to cap it all, I realised I'd not seen my golly being packed. Shocked at the thought of it, I checked and he wasn't in his usual place. OK, I might have been small, but I tell you what, I certainly made my feelings known.

Being hauled down the stairs I heard, "You don't want that old thing! I'll buy you a nice new one."

I didn't want a nice new one, I wanted golly and was even more enraged when my sister, a bossy seven-year-old, described him as old and smelly. It was probably round about that time I first got the notion, boys and girls might have a tendency to think differently. To be honest, I was absolutely seething, for my beloved golly might have been nothing more than a bundle of rags, but seemed like part of my very being and there she was, sounding so judgemental and grown up. How dare she dismiss him with such disdain! Plus, neither sister nor mother explained how my dad would be able to find us. They probably thought, given time I'd forget him or he'd appear as if nothing more than a figment of imagination. But they weren't fooling me. I didn't forget him and knew he'd been an actual person in my life. Also of course, at that age I wouldn't have known a word like disdain, but you don't need to, to know what it feels like.

# England

Next thing it was England. Alright, I obviously wouldn't have realised that immediately, but in the fullness of time, began to get the drift. Also, even though the first birthday I recall was my fifth, logic tells me, that when I first saw that lady in a blue frock, looking dwarfed by a pair of black doors far side of a busy street, I must have been two and a half and also as my new nanna smiled, spreading her arms in welcome, instincts hinted she and I would be getting along famously.

Initially, it was all very confusing, but the way she bustled and fussed, cheered me up no end. Not as much as when first meeting cousin Jennifer mind you. She just had the edge on me age-wise, in fact was a full four months older and hadn't wasted a single second of it, getting up to all sorts of tricks, leaving me quite breathless. Attempting to keep up with her was initially frustrating, but as I felt coordination improving, was able to assist in serious tasks, such as carrying glass bottles down to those huge black gates mentioned and we giggled together, listening to their cheery progress, rattling and clanking down the pavement outside. They were beer bottles, for I now lived at the Compasses Hotel, roughly halfway up the slope of Corve Street.

I don't remember being told not to roll bottles down the street, it was more a matter of there not being sufficient room one day, to actually squeeze them under the gate. In fact, there was only just enough room for a one-eyed squint, for on certain mornings, if I lay on my side, I could just make out the quick-scissor flurry of hooves drumming across splatter, plus the odd skip at stick-thwack and guttural shout. The pub was located on the main road through town and the weekly auction was held in the large expanse of corrugated iron sheds and steel pens down near the train station. Sometimes, when the sheep were driven through it sounded like the sudden onset of heavy rain.

My mother told me, that I would often beg to be taken there to peer over the brick wall at the cattle packed in the pens, but to be honest, I have no recollection of it. Not the slightest glimmer. It seems you can't choose memories any more than you can decide what to dream.

One day, the milkman gave Jennifer and myself a ride in his delivery cart. We were helped up onto the metal step, then through the small door that was clicked shut and we sat together, beyond the churns, on a neat little side seat. I remember the immensity of the horse, its not unpleasant odour and as we jerked forward, how its broad back with everything in motion, swayed from side to side and yet the cart whirled along in a perfectly straight line. The rhythmic clipping of hooves echoed in the lanes and we felt like the most important people alive. Not surprisingly, whenever catching sight of the nice Mr. Tilt, even though wagging fingers and serious reproaches warned us not to pester the man, we wanted to climb aboard at every opportunity.

On another day we were taken for a picnic at Wigmore Castle. I know that's where it must have been, for I distinctly remember the grassed banking rising steeply above where cars were once allowed to park, at the lane end, opposite a muddy farm. I have no recollection of the ruins across the fields, but didn't forget that grassed banking, for on it was some dried white poo to which cousin Jen laid claim, piping up brightly, "I just did that."

Was there any end to this little minx's abilities?

Alright, I'd been rather naïve, just like when a massive low-loader truck rolled past one day in Shrewsbury. I was living there at the time, but won't go into that just now, other than say the odd-job man who lived in the same residence, told me the vehicle was for scribing red lines down the margins of writing paper. It seemed an awful lot of rumbling equipment for such a small task, but I trusted Old Bill and so it wasn't until sometime later I thought, 'What a load of old dog poo! That truck was a tank transporter!'

Swiftly moving back to those early Ludlow memories; on market days the pub used to be heaving. It was fascinating and I'd watch all the activity as it unfolded below my secret vantage point, a tiny glass paned window at the turn in the stairs. Hanging above all, was a light haze of tobacco smoke and men in light brown coats stood in huddles or leant on the bar, as a never-ending supply of glasses full of brown liquid, went from the cranking pumps to awaiting hands.

Above the general hubbub of conversation, the odd voice would ring out, followed by guttural laughter and amongst all my mother would fearlessly wend her way, emptying ashtrays, collecting empty glasses and wiping tables. My grandfather, known to us as Uncle Stan, (I'll explain later) seemed to be the main pump-puller, with sweat gleaming on ruddy brow, but also my mother would occasionally lend a hand at one of the mechanisms that kept the liquid flowing.

I remember one day a cheer ringing out, as my grandmother, with a white cloth of action draped over a shoulder, sailed amongst all to deliver an urgent demand. I was later told, she had given Uncle Stan strict orders to clear the men from the gents' toilets, an outside facility with its entrance just beyond where she'd been slaving in the kitchen. She had grown heartily sick of the singing.

This tickled me no end, for that witnessed from my vantage point already went way beyond the behaviour expected of everyday, sensible adults, who I'd noticed seemed to find things in the bar far funnier than life normally encountered, but now came the news, some even went outside to linger and sing in the gents' toilets. I was probably, only about three at the time and so was quite puzzled as to the cause?

Then one day, sitting there minding my own business, I realised I'd been spotted, for an angry face snarled up and a stick was prodded in my direction. Truly frightened, I retreated to my room, but then thought, 'He really has no right to do that!' I reasoned, it was my grandmother's pub and she was quite happy for me to sit there.

Plucking up courage, I crept back to peep down into the bar once more, but there he was, waiting and my whole insides jumped as he approached to snarl and wave his stick. Back in my room I was truly shaken and felt deeply troubled, worried regarding the safety of my mother working amongst such monsters. How could she seem so blithe and untroubled, using just the odd flick of a tea towel to keep them at bay?

On quieter days, I'd sometimes venture down to the bar and without really inviting it, would receive a fair deal of attention and the odd small gift, but I always checked first to make sure that man was not there. Even on the occasion when he sat on a stool smiling, all his ruddy hatred dissolved and my mother coaxing me not to be frightened, for he'd only been joking, I still wouldn't go near him. He could smile all he liked, but he'd had his chance and it troubled me not that he now looked sheepish.

Of course, I wasn't allowed beyond the main doors of the pub, but was free to wander into the yard out the back, where I always felt rather overshadowed by the massive stone wall on the northern side. I wouldn't have known it then, but it is a remnant of the town's mediaeval defences and the Compasses pub stands on the western side of what would have been the Corve Gate.

There wasn't much to do when out there on my own, the chickens in their coop being only of passing interest, but then one day, beckoned by a cheery call, I looked up to see my sister and a friend had somehow climbed onto a parapet running parallel with the kitchen roof. Now this seemed more like it, but how had they got up there? My admiration was tinged with mild frustration of not being able to join them.

During opening hours, folk would use the pub yard as a shortcut between Linney and Corve Street, marching straight through where I was playing and sometimes boys roughly my age, accompanying their mothers, would stare as if I happened to be some sort of local curiosity.

With them merely passing through, my efforts at friendship were at most faint-hearted, but being stuck there on my own, I'd sometimes give it a go. First, however, it was important to establish their age and after a brief exchange I'd put this question to the mother. I don't know why it was, but even at that age I thought, 'Why don't they ever give a straight answer?' What did, 'Four in December,' mean to a young lad who'd not yet learnt to count and certainly didn't know the progression of the months?

Even so, I would politely say thank you and as they continued on their way, back it up with a nonchalant whistle, leaving them in no doubt as to my credentials. Sometimes a moon-faced boy would look back in surprise, but I'd think, 'Why do so many faces seem so dull?' Very few I met in those early days made me come alive like cousin Jennifer did.

So, the fact I could whistle, means I was probably approaching four years old.

Now, before I continue, I'll have to take you back a bit, before that moment of shock and exhilaration, when that first perfect note had escaped my lips. I remember feeling really fed up one day, for I had nothing to do, could find no-one to talk to and even my mother seemed to have disappeared. Everything was deadly quiet, exceedingly dull, almost as if the very air had become too heavy to raise itself from the dust in the yard. I called out for my mother, then for my sister, but the reply I got shocked me to a standstill. Looking up, I spotted two girls atop the high stone wall and they were not only pulling faces, they were mimicking me. I certainly wasn't going to run from view and so had to suffer those whiney voices, daring to mock me. I couldn't help it,

I blushed, for I simply wasn't used to this sort of treatment. Admittedly, there had been that man with the stick and of course I'd had the odd admonishment, but generally people seemed glad to have me in their company. So, who were these weaselly girls with faces as nasty as cod liver oil laughing down from their vantage point? I chose to withdraw to my room, for if there were more creatures like those lying in wait, I needed to give serious consideration to that world outside.

At intervals during the day, the bells in the tall church tower, looming just beyond the high stone wall, played a tune. Every day a different melody chimed, floating out across the town and these seem to have etched themselves into my very soul and still bring a pang of nostalgia whenever I hear them again. It's not hard to imagine myself, back in that yard, chickens scratching and pecking and washing billowing on the line. Winnie, the maid, would sometimes be out there, heaped basket at her hip. She lived in the small cottage located halfway down the yard, was always cheery to talk to and although never sounding her H's, talked to me properly, rather than as if to someone who still needed a pram. Yes, Winnie and myself got on quite well, although I did happen to have one uncomfortable meeting with her, but more of that later.

On some mornings, a line of cars would be parked out in the yard. Their interiors had polished wooden dashboards and deep, lived-in looking upholstery that gave off a rich aroma of leather. The doors opened backwards and below, either side, were running boards, terminating at the front in large polished mudguards that swept up in an arch with headlamps on top. I would sometimes peer at these exotic machines, amused by the distorted reflexions. It was always worth waiting for the leaving procession, for when the engines rattled into life, I'd watch fascinated as they carefully edged their way, sending out plumes of fumes, down the tunnelled exit to the main road.

Looking back now, I suppose their occupants would have been company representatives or those who had taken rooms on race day. Cars in the yard meant an uncomfortable night was in the offing, for my mother and grandmother having given up their beds to guests, would squeeze themselves into my bed.

If I heard my nanna's cheery, "Oh, he's kept it nice and warm for us," I'd think, 'Oh no! Not again.'

One day, I was taken by my mother to meet a man in a room that was up some stairs in a house at the bottom of the hill. I didn't care for this turn of events at all, for I sensed a change coming, one I might not be entirely pleased with. Although he seemed friendly enough, I didn't like my mother's distant look as we ascended the hill back to the Compasses. Not only did she not answer my questions, she seemed in a completely different world.

Sometimes, on a quiet day the man would appear in the lounge bar of the pub. That's where he gave me a stick of pink rock. Sweets were still on ration and so this was an incredible luxury. I'd never tasted anything like it and gnawed my way as far as the label, that apparently showed a seaside town whose name was written down through the rock, but of course those symbols meant nothing to me.

I had been warned not to eat it all in one go, for it could make me sick. Disregarding his advice, I crunched away, down past the label that now looked as sticky as I felt and it was only near the end that I realised I could be in trouble.

Fortunately, my mother noticed my change of colour and rushed me outside, where I gazed down at all that rock once more, in tiny pink and white shards, spattered on the downspout and grid of the drain. I immediately felt better, but also rather sheepish, for it seemed such an act of ingratitude after having been gifted something so special.

In fairness, he told me not to worry, but his raised eyebrows said, 'I did warn you.'

Like I said before, I get these feelings and somehow knew things were about to take a momentous turn and therefore sought a quiet place to sit on my own and think.

'Who was this smarty-pants who knew I was going to be sick and where was my dad?'

Looking back, I must have been four when one summer's day, my mother took Jennifer and myself to Batty's Island. I had been there before, but with having a kindred spirit aboard, this particular day stands out. The boat keeper was old Mr. Stewardson, who as usual beamed with delight at our approach and also as usual, confided we could keep the boat for as long as we liked. I used to think, 'What a nice man,' but it was years later when looking back at old photos, I realised why his face always lit up at sight of my mother.

Aunty Rita, Jennifer's mother had given us a small gift, a triangular paper bag containing pear drops. Not to be eaten until safely aboard. This was more like it, for on a previous occasion I'd been gifted a packet containing tiny pieces of coloured plastic, pressed into the shape of racing cars. Of course, I'd said thank you, but it had seemed a strange thing to accompany a boating trip.

It was always cool below the trees shading the old green boathouse and I always felt a surge of excitement at the sight of water slowly flowing beneath the boards of the walkway, gently tugging the long slender skiffs to the end of their tethers. Mirrored in the broad expanse, before the waters slipped down the curve of the weir, was the mighty image of the castle. What drama as we were helped aboard, with Jennifer and myself carefully picking our way over seats and decorative metal to share the perch in the stern. It was enough to bring on an excited drumming of heels on the hull.

Mr. Stewardson carefully fed the long oars out to my mother, untethered the craft, urged it into the flow with his boathook and waved us on our way. Jen and I waved back and then trailed a hand in the cool water, feeling its impact wobble our fingers as we gathered speed.

My mother had become quite well known locally for her rowing skills, to such an extent, an American officer stationed in town during the war, had once challenged her to a race. With him being an accomplished oarsman back home, he'd offered her a head start, but she declined and much to his annoyance, beat him. If it had been a courting gambit, it had failed dismally. Also of course, by the time the Americans were on the scene, she would have been a married woman, but more of that later.

Back in those days, a far more generous portion of the river was made available for boating, right up as far as the gravel shoals at what is called Batty's Island. Even though it had long ceased to be one, the old water course could still be traced by following an indented curve in the meadow where forlorn willow trees still clung to the banking, leaning forward as if eternally mystified as to where the water had gone. On the downstream point of what locals called Battys, enough of the old river course remained to form quite a sizeable harbour, long enough to accommodate boats pulled up from the ooze, to loll like a line of feeding piglets on the banking. In summer, the water was warm and that inlet was the perfect place for children to splash and play.

This was where most local children first learnt to swim, as there was no swimming pool, seaside holidays were rare and a trip to somewhere like the Isle of Man, seemed as far flung as going to the Bahamas today. So, families flocked here for a picnic, a swim and pleasant day out. In fact, if you told strangers, you were holidaying this year at Batty's Island, it actually sounded quite exotic.

Years later I wrote the following in memory of my mother, whose ashes are scattered there. It had been a day when just the two of us had embarked, with me like a figurehead, perched on the tiny triangular seat in the prow. I had those tiny plastic racing cars in my pocket. Well, all except the yellow one.

# Batty's Island

I remember the walk down to the river,
Two small steps to my mother's one,
Her dress was pretty, redolent of flowers,
To me she seemed old, but photos show young.

Trees; cool respite, mirrored in water.
Life's soup; fish rings; struggling fly;
Enigmatic edifice, castle towering,
Moving gently against the billowing sky.

My aunt had gifted, small plastic race cars,
Each half the size of a rationed sweet;
Liked all but the yellow one and dropped it idling,
Down between landing-stage boards at my feet.

The old boatman smiled as we rocked aboard;
Steadied the sharp prow, before we knifed upstream;
Trailed fingers wobbled, cool in the bow wave;
Sun-pins through leaves lit a dappling dream.

Riverbed patterns flickered up through branches,
Creaking rowlocks, the only sound to rend,
The stillness, 'til passing family reflected;
White hats and smiles, sailing down round the bend.

Mother, aiming towards the low-banked harbour,
Scoured riverbed shoal, ducks clattered, were gone.
Our long hull lolled in its oozy mooring;
We dined in the sun, 1951.

The inlet's now dry; no farrowing boats;
Just lambs and silence, and to escape life's pace,
I and my children still visit the shrine,
Batty's Island, a secret last resting place.

# Things moving on

The random nature of memories can be peculiar. A few can be scary and some, no matter how enigmatic, give a strange nostalgic glow even though the event remembered might not have been particularly important at the time. Also, one wonders, would those hazy recollections represent significant clues as to how a personality was forming; foundations for the person most would eventually recognise as being typically you? If that's the case, I suspect analysts would have their work cut out forming a character sketch from the above and the motley assortment immediately following. Obviously as one matures, more is remembered and there evolves a threaded connection, more of a life story, but meanwhile all I have left from those early years is more like an ancient moth-eaten tapestry.

I can't remember it ever having rained back then. Strange when you think about it. I do remember being freezing cold mind you, even when muffled in a coat and wearing my new dungarees on a brisk walk along the path running below the castle to Linney, where looking down on a rough patch, you could see goats tethered. The grim edifice of the castle; gaping windows and grey walls rising as if to the heavens, brought a shudder at the thought of anyone living in a place so cold.

Below, the river reflecting day's last light, curved like a band of burnished steel and icy gusts down the valley buffeted the gaunt trees lining the path into sudden insanity and stung my face as if the wind had whips in it.

"Nearly there. Soon be nice and warm." Soothing words from my mother. She almost made it seem like a game, where everything would be alright as long as she said so. She never failed to tuck me in at night with a kiss on the cheek, which gave a cosy feeling and reassurance when embarking on that trip through darkness.

It must have been about that same time she took me up the road, yet again on my insistence, to where shop lights cast a warm glow on the pavements and where all the people looked so cheery. We would stop at my favourite window, where a small Father Christmas tapped on the glass with a stick. It would have been from there, my sister and I were bought new shoes and she proudly showed hers off to our visiting cousins, Pat and Jennifer.

Seeing their marvelling looks, I proffered a foot and said, "And I have." It didn't have the same impact, but at least I'd managed to bask in a little of the glory.

Residing in a popular town hostelry gave insight to people's reactions when something of importance happened. Generally, I didn't know who or what they were talking about, but one day there came a breathless announcement that Jim Penny had died. He was a jolly faced man who lived up the street and so for once I could follow the thread.

I heard things like, "Are you sure? He can't be! I was only talking to him yesterday." The questions and avowals of disbelief continued all morning, the throng swelling until the place was packed, as if the Compasses was the only place to go for latest news. Large amounts of that brown liquid were consumed, a few tears were shed and judgement passed on the wife who'd survived him.

It was the first time I heard the saying, "Why is it only the good die young?"

Around about this time the stomach aches started. I know pain threshold isn't very high at that age, but these were truly agonising, like trapped jagged glass. Whatever I did brought no relief and so I'd just limply sit, until eventually it melted away and my temperature returned to normal.

When really bad, I'd roll around in bed almost crying with the pain and when sick, it felt like the spasms would never end.

A doctor visited, felt my stomach and forehead, before declaring it was nothing to worry about.

"Huh! Easy for him to say," and to make matters worse, I then had to swallow a regular dose of sour tasting red medicine.

Anyway, for some reason the pain finally abated and I began to feel normal again, descending to a changed world. My grandparents were no longer there and my mother now ran the pub, occasionally helped by that man we'd visited at the bottom of the hill. I must have been told where my nanna and Uncle Stan had gone to, but with not having a clue where Shrewsbury was, it didn't mean a great deal.

I didn't like the way things had a tendency to suddenly turn themselves upside down and I also didn't like the first film I was taken to see, Alice in Wonderland. The fact that you could be big one minute, small the next, I found most disturbing and when a pack of playing cards came to life chasing Alice down into a vast vortex, I clung to my mother in terror, not consoled in the slightest by her reassurance, it had all been nothing but a dream. It was at a time when still upset that my dad was no longer with us and as yet, hadn't worked out where my grandparents had disappeared to, so I certainly didn't appreciate a film that scared the living daylights out of me.

Strangely, I don't remember any of my first Christmases. Not the actual day that is, but I do remember the amazing gift of a blue peddle car. I loved sitting in it, turning the wheel, making 'Brmm, brmm' noises, but still needed to grow a little before being able to peddle the thing.

I must admit, I don't remember this being the case, but before being able to put it into motion, I suspect my sister Ann would have become heartily sick of being the power source.

Sometimes, if I thought I could be missing something of interest, I'd hold off doing big jobs for as long as possible. Sitting down helped, but thankfully it was only a passing phase. While on the subject, however, when up town with my mother, I'd occasionally be in desperate need of a wee. Well of course I was too young to go right round the far side of the Town Hall to the gents and so she'd take me into the ladies. Please understand, this is an explanation given with hindsight, for at the time I thought it was quite normal to be taken into a cubicle where my mother would assist with the necessary. That was until the day she pushed the lavatory door open and I saw a young woman, knickers round her ankles, crouched within like a startled young bird. It gave me a strange feeling in the pit of my stomach that was hard to explain.

As said, nothing seems to remain the same and in the pub, grand works were being undertaken. Furniture would often be draped with white sheets, which were perfect for hiding under and there was constant hammering accompanied by plumes of dust. The builders seemed happy to answer my questions and when approaching I'd hear comments such as, "Hear he is. Come to help again." One even showed me the remains of a petrified rat he'd found in a wall being demolished, which puzzled me rather, for why would a creature go to such lengths just to die?

My friend Winnie, of course drew plenty of attention and was playfully chided when skinnying her way through stacked up furniture and debris, to lead me away to where, yet again, my mother would tell me not to pester the workmen. I couldn't help it though; I liked my new friends.

Periodically, however, I had a reoccurrence of that stomach pain I told you about. I wasn't putting it on or making a meal of it, as I much preferred to feel well and was always eager to see what each day would bring, but it was back with a vengeance as if having been stabbed in the side. Along with it came a temperature, throat ripping vomiting and terrible nightmares. The doctor must have visited again, for the next cure-all was jelly in a jar and whatever ailed me must have briefly gone into remission, for I remember flicking a teaspoon of the stuff to bounce off the far wall. Thoroughly bored at my lengthy confinement, I set to work flicking the lot, aiming at the lampshade, wardrobe and window, until none remained.

When my mother came in, her greeting smile froze into one of incredulity and she said, "Oh that's really naughty. It was meant to make you better."

I doubt she believed in the stuff either and of course, I might have been young, but knew she couldn't be too cross, not with me being ill.

Her regular visits alleviated the boredom and if the burning inside subsided, I'd go to the window and watch the world outside. There were fascinating things like an oil tanker revving back and forth to gain entry to a tiny lane opposite, stopping traffic in both directions. Some might ask, how would a three-year-old know what a petrol tanker looked like? Well of course I didn't, but remembered the shape until I did. Also, while on such matters, I know the castle didn't really move against the clouds as described in the above poem, but to a tiny lad, the optical illusion made it seem that way.

Anyway, in the end that pain somehow seemed to just glide away and my builder friends almost gave a cheer at my reappearance. I noticed there were a few fresh faces, men who didn't seem to hear when asked about certain details. They soon softened, mind you, to became part of the gang and in fact, the one who had initially seemed the most remote was the one I eventually got along with best of all.

Then one morning, when hurrying back to the domestic side of the hotel, having visited them as usual, I ran straight into Winnie, who recoiled as if from an explosion and the pain felt in my chest was indescribable, as if somehow my skin was on fire. She had been mounting the step into the room carrying a jug of boiling hot water for the builders' tea. If I hadn't been tall for my age I would have been disfigured for life. I remember Winnie, hands to face in horror as my mother scooped me up and I was taken, almost at a run, round to the nearby cottage hospital, up by the church.

The ward was full of grown-ups who of course stared with great interest at the infant, naked to the waist, being unceremoniously upended for further stripping. Whatever those nurses did for me, it was a whole lot better than anything that doctor had done regarding my internal problem, for in seemingly no time I was able to sit up and talk to the two ladies in the nearest beds. I'd initially felt a bit embarrassed, knowing they must have seen my willy which believe me, was of far greater concern than the scalding. My mother's quick reactions at hearing Winnie's scream, had saved the skin on my chest.

She of course, popped in regularly to see how I was getting on and later told me, it broke her heart each time she had to leave her little boy, looking so lost in such a big bed. Strange thing is, I don't remember feeling particularly little, let alone lost and in fact, once over the mortification of having been exposed to the ward, got along quite well with those ladies either side.

I don't know why it was, but I seemed to find grown-ups easier company than many children my own age. That's why the kindergarten, a small facility run by a French lady, known to all as Mademoiselle, came as rather a shock. I think the problem was, with me being tall for my age, all thought I was older than I actually was, when in fact I'd have almost been the youngest there.

Our day consisted of drawing, singing, playing in the back yard and finally, sitting cross-legged to listen to a story. All the children seemed to know the routine and two older girls were given small duties which were undertaken with a grand air of authority.

It was all very puzzling and I had not one clue of when to stand or sit down, which drew unwanted attention, but nothing like the derision when one of the boys noticed my hair. Mother had restrained my rather long locks with one of her hairclips.

"He's a girl!"

All the children laughed, I went bright red and then was surrounded by the boys, chanting, "He's a girl! He's a girl!"

How was I to know, only girls used hairclips? This was my first full encounter with a room full of children my own age and it came as a nasty shock. They seemed to relish any slight blunder and at going home time, laughed when I did my coat up the wrong way. Children's macs and coats in those days, had optional buttoning, left for girls, right for boys and of course I'd not learnt my left from right. I soon figured it out, however, for when envisaging punching one of my tormentors, it told me which was my right hand.

As you can imagine, I wasn't keen to return to Mademoiselle's, but my mother, a believer in tough love, told me I'd soon get used to things and to stand up for myself.

In a way she was right, for by the third visit I didn't seem to be in the way as much, but was still thoroughly confused by the French songs and at playtime, stood alone, bemused as the boys either chased one another or played trains. Having been kindergarten regulars they'd formed into two separate groups. The chasers seemed to whirl about without rhyme nor reason, while the train gang, fastidiously chuffing and hooting, rotated their arms like pistons, even putting the action into reverse when backing into tight places. Wherever I stood, it seemed I was on one of the imaginary railway lines and they'd shout, "Get off the track!" if I tried to join in.

The girls, meanwhile, either leapt about over a skipping rope with skirts tucked in knickers or played at mums and infants, where the two smallest girls were led around, staggering on their haunches while making goo-goo noises.

I stood amongst it all feeling totally lost and so when the gang of chasers beckoned, I gladly joined their rush up the yard. At their jeering and half-hearted pushing against a wooden door, I thought it high time I showed them what I was made of. My look of shock when the door swung open, was matched by that of the occupant, a girl called Jaqueline, who was desperately trying to pull up her knickers. Sadly, not quite quick enough, for the gang pointed and taunted mercilessly, before triumphantly running off to tell Mademoiselle what I'd done. I felt really sorry for the poor girl, but my confusion left me dumbstruck.

So, on receiving a severe finger wagging, to be told I had been a thoroughly dirty boy going into the girl's lavatory, I mutely hung my head in shame and desperately prayed mother would return to deliver me from the nightmare. Goodness, life was tough without her, but there again it wasn't all bad, for there did come one unexpected bonus, Jaqueline occasionally smiling at me. This brought that strange funny feeling inside, the same as felt once before in the Town Hall lady's toilets.

You'll be glad to know, I did eventually find my feet at that kindergarten and also became acquainted with the location of Shrewsbury. It was at the end of a long thirty-mile journey taken, either by bus or train and it broadened my scope beyond belief, for if someone now said they had travelled from, let's say, Liverpool or Cardiff, I could say, 'Phew! Is that further than Shrewsbury?'

At hearing, 'More than twice as far,' I could reply with another meaningful, "Phew!" and if, 'Much, much further than that,' I'd look thoroughly impressed and utter something I'd heard Winnie say, "Evans above!"

I of course didn't know who Evans was, but for some reason, it never failed to raise a smile.

At the end of that long trek to Shrewsbury, a bubble of comfort awaited at the White Horse pub, up by Lord Hill's Column. It was run by nanna and Uncle Stan, plus they'd made friends with a host of new people. Loads of interesting folk from all walks of life. Of course they were customers, but it felt more like a large family.

On arriving at Shrewsbury, we would board a Midland Red bus taking us up near the Column, but there was always that final stretch, where my mother, walking so fast, would drag me along and I was forever stumbling, grazing a knee and being told, not to be so clumsy.

'Bloody knees and cursed for it!' There was no doubt she was a caring mother, but occasionally gave a glimpse of a far tougher, warrior side.

I of course, relished the train journeys to Shrewsbury and back, but not the bus trips. Something about the rumbling and swaying had the tendency to make me feel sick and on hearing that doleful cry of, 'Mummy,' my mother would rush me down to the back, asking the conductor to open the door and let some fresh air in. The bell would be pressed for the driver to pull in at the next stop. Didn't always work, but I can't have been the only one, for a small stack of newspaper was kept stored ready in the compartment beneath the stairs.

They were wonderful when you think about it, answering my mother's profuse apologies with, "Don't you worry, madam. Lots of little boys are sick on buses."

I suppose we went by bus, winding its way around village lanes, because it conveniently departed from right outside the Compasses and in Shrewsbury, we could step from one to the next, taking us up to the Column, thus saving the walk from train to bus station.

In comparison, the train journey was more like an adventure and with my mother always attending to last minute duties, we'd almost have to run down Corve Street, so as not to miss it. As the mighty engine rolled past, hissing and clanking, we'd hurriedly buy tickets from the man behind the glass window in his little kiosk, before hauling ourselves aboard to sink with relief into the carriage seats. On the walls were pictures of enticing holiday destinations which I'd been told, were quite a few Shrewsbury's away and most glass panels of sliding doors on corridor trains, bore the sign, 'NO SMOKING.'

Of course, my mother had to read this to me, as she had done with amusement on some of the buses, 'NO SPITTING.'

Return train journeys always seemed to be at night and at each stop the guard would call out place names, which gradually I learnt by heart. When putting my forehead against the glass and cupping my hands to block out the ghostly mirror image hovering out in the darkness, I could see the station signs and longed to be able to read them. There were all those books full of stories I couldn't wait to delve into, but meanwhile had to rely on my mother or sister to read to me.

Of course, most were not corridor trains and with head pressed against the glass I could watch people hurrying past, huddled against the night air, plus on occasions the guard would wheel a bike to an awaiting man with protruding shoes and trousers looking comically tight around the ankles.

Those carriages had a cosy feel; conversations would soon strike up and it would bring a sinking feeling when people with fascinating tales to tell, gathered themselves to alight at their destination. I'd eye newcomers warily, wondering if they'd be as interesting as those just departing. The carriage door would be pulled shut with that unmistakable slam of security, a parcel or small suitcase might be slid into the overhead luggage rack and the newcomers would then make themselves comfortable.

As we all sat in silence, a muffled cough might be heard from an adjoining carriage, a distant door slamming, maybe a cheery exchange from up by the small station building, before a sharp blast of whistle preceded the gentle jolt into motion. Then once underway, the busy fussing of the engine could just be discerned along with the clickety-clack, diddly-dum, diddley dum and occasional whoosh beneath a bridge.

Given a reassuring squeeze, I might hear, "Craven Arms. Not far now. We'll have a nice bowl of hot soup when we get in."

As said, my mother had a knack of making you feel safe and secure. Even simply straightening the sheets and plumping up the pillow, when I was ailing with a cold, had the magic effect of making me feel a whole lot better, but because of pub duties, she was not always at hand. It was then, a local lady called Mrs. Preece, looked after me. Preecy, I called her, or thought I did, but apparently, what I actually called her was Peecy. She and I got on famously and I was told years later, she would proudly walk up town with me as if I'd been one of her own. If still on duty at night, she was the one to tuck me in with a kiss and would often return to check I was alright.

On one occasion she'd heard, "Peecy, tuck. Peecy, tuck."

She'd replied, "I've already tucked you in."

On her next visit, the same happened.

It was only when my mother gave the final check of the night, I was at last liberated from where I'd slipped, to become stuck between bed and the wall. I'd be lying if I said I remembered the incident, but it amused my mother, who often repeated it.

I can't recall my fourth birthday, but was aware I'd reached that momentous landmark and shortly after, remember a day of absolute deathly silence. Hardly a sound, apart from the incessant tolling of the church bell. It went on annoyingly all day and by late afternoon, when having had enough of it, I started imitating the sound in mockery, "Boyoing, boyoing, boyoing,"

My sister was outraged and stamping a foot said, "How dare you! The King is dead!"

It was the first time I'd realised there had been someone important enough to be called a king. But king of what? I'd heard, 'I'm king of the castle and you're a dirty rascal,' but nobody had explained about nations, kings and queens.

Having said that, I must admit, I had heard of Prince Charles, whoever he might have been, for I would sometimes hear ladies say, "Isn't he handsome. Just like Prince Charles."

Really? Anyway, moving swiftly on; with my knowledge of the world only stretching as far as Shrewsbury and back, I had been completely unaware of the importance of King George VI. My sister, however, a rather precocious young lady of the world, gave strict instructions that we were creep about like mice, making no noise at all. With this obviously meaning so much to her, I apologised for my transgression and did as instructed, for having now taken all the new information on board, realised this was probably the most significant event to have happened during my lifetime. Jim Penny suddenly dying had made a sizeable impact, but all things considered, this felt a good many Shrewsburys ahead of that!

# Waterloo

I don't actually remember moving from Ludlow, out into the country, I just remember one day being there. The only thing to even remotely resemble moving, was when someone we referred to as Uncle Bob, delivered a small van load of possessions to our remote location, an outpost beyond a succession of lanes and stone track, where the grand old house commanded a hill as if a bastion against the wild lands beyond. His arrival stands out, largely because his bronzed face had brought such cheer and laughter into the hallway. "Never thought I'd ever get here. And that old clock of yours!" With a shake of head, "Ears are still ringing. Damn thing chimed at every bump in the road."

Many families had close friends known to the children as aunt or uncle. Of course, the word uncle, said with a sly nudge could imply a bit of something going on, but generally it was an honorary title. It would seem quite quaint and old fashioned these days, but this was an age where a little charm and respect went a long way.

Of course, you can't hold back time, for customs, words and phrases change and I don't want to become too deeply immersed, but have to admit, not all was better back then. For instance, some people were openly racist, many women were downtrodden and homosexuality was outlawed. Oh, on a lighter note, gay meant happy back then and to make love meant no more than flirtation.

So many 'with-it' words and phrases are the height of 'hip' for one generation, only to be considered 'so last week,' by the next. For example, that last sentence would have brought looks of puzzlement in 1955 and by 2030 will seem so awfully fin de siècle.

Can you imagine a scene in a current movie where an actor bursting in, blurts in panic, "Hide that reefer the rozzers are coming!"

The audience would either be puzzled as to the meaning or erupt into laughter at it sounding so outdated, but back in the early 60's, words like rozzer and reefer were cutting edge.

I won't go on; well just one last example, bimbo. Fairly recently it implied dumb and blonde, but back in the 50's it was a hit song, where the opening line of, 'Bimbo, Bimbo, where you gonna go-eeo?' was answered by, 'He's going down the road to see his little girl-eeo.'

Just as I said, not everything was better back then.

Anyway, the Georgian stone farmhouse we rented was known locally as Waterloo, but was officially Waterloo House, so it stands a chance its foundations were laid in 1815. Proudly commanding a terraced garden, it gave off a grand air of faded glory and today would be worth a tidy sum, but back then was considered remote and lacking in modern facilities. The only heating was a Rayburn stove in the living room, or on special occasions the fire was lit in the sitting room and the only lighting was by candle or oil lamp. There was a copious supply of spring water from a spout out in the back yard, a primitive system of lead piping and strangely, in a cupboard beneath the stairs, was a telephone. That latter facility might well have saved my life.

Below the front terrace was what once would have been the farmyard. To the left, when looking out, was a clapboard barn on stone foundations and directly below, a stone barn with triangular openings for doves. The lawns atop the stone terrace were on two levels and to the right of them, a path ran between stone walls down to an ancient grey gate beneath walnut trees. High, to the rear of the house was a large vegetable garden, plus fruit trees, which meant, by careful storage, salting or bottling, we never ran short of cooking apples, damsons, runner beans or potatoes.

Directly behind the house was a large tank for collecting rainwater and far side of a flagstone path were two sheds, one used for holding the garden tools and the other, smelling of musty oil spills and paraffin, was the winter fuel store. There was a stone building containing a cider press and another we used for further storage, perched high and dry above our water supply. The property would be highly sought after today, but to us then was only a stop-gap measure until our turn came for a Ludlow council house, with all the latest facilities.

I know. Were we mad?

Rising opposite the house was a high wooded ridge, that returned an instant echo and in the immediate depths beyond the common was a farm from which the usual farmyard noises drifted up. There was the occasional duck squabble, cock crow, Mrs. Griffiths calling, "Bessy, Bessy, Bessy!" to the big fat sow and if the breeze was in the right direction, even the bell-like chorus from foraging chickens could be heard bringing a sense of comfort.

Behind the house, lay wild untamed tracts of Herefordshire and our only way back to civilisation was down a stone-rutted track, bottom right of the house, which led down past orchards and common to a narrow lane that wound down through woods to a ford. There was a raised footpath to the side of the stream, but all vehicles had to negotiate a lengthy crossing, whether picturesque in summer, or a brown torrent in winter. Each Saturday, a bus arriving far-side took locals to Ludlow, but during the week the only way out, was by catching the regular service, which made a stop at the Dun Horse pub, located far side of the main road, a mile further on.

Returning to the grand old farmhouse, it sported majestic Georgian windows and within was a distinctive musty aroma, almost aromatic, like snuff and I bet if you led me there blindfolded, I would be able to tell you exactly where I was.

Apart from the fact I was often rather lonely, the place was ideal for a young chap growing up. Initially, however, my sister was there every day, meaning we must have moved sometime in July, during school summer holidays and that man I told you about; the one who gave me the stick of rock; he was there as well. All seemed to slot into place and at that age, as long as you're looked after and everyone's happy with the arrangement, you tend to just go along with it.

When I think back, mind you, my mother was not in an enviable situation. She was still legally married to my father and a quick bit of reckoning, tells me she must have been pregnant at the time, carrying my brother Michael and that man who had gifted me that memorable confection, was obviously his father. Not such a big deal these days, but back then it would have been considered scandalous. Is that why we were living out in the wilds, with no electricity and an ancient water system?

Also, a child's mind doesn't always comply with what adults expect, for on the day my mother called me to the phone cupboard beneath the stairs for me to say hello to my daddy, on hearing his voice I replied, "That's not my daddy!"

I was told, he was now and that my real father was dead. I admit, this piece of news was broken rather more gently than that, but it still brought a deep feeling of sadness. It wasn't that I could remember much about him, it was more the fact that from now on, the dream of what he would be like was over. I took the live coal of internal pain to a quiet place alone and mentally going over those scant memories of the Isle of Man, realised things would never be the same again. That's all I'll say on the matter, however, for far, far worse things have happened to children over the years and in fact are still happening.

You would be justified in wondering; how could my mother still be legally married to my dead father? All will be explained in good time.

I loved it when my cousins came to stay, with laughter ringing through house and gardens and I bet the old place enjoyed it too. An Irish cousin, Cathlene visited for a while and even though she and my sister were many years my senior, I still went exploring with them and didn't feel excluded.

Another visitor was my mother's Aunt Winnie from Liverpool. She just seemed to materialise one day, neat in coat and hat, silhouetted in the grand Georgian doorway. With a smile and glasses glinting, she bent to give me a hug and we became instant best friends. She was obviously of advanced years but exuded a feeling of, forever young and I couldn't wait to show her some of my favourite haunts.

Her visit must have been in late August, for the first of the blackberries had ripened and I made her promise not to tell mother I'd been eating them. I had been warned not to, on account of them supposedly giving little boys worms.

Aunty Winnie's face crinkled into a conspiratorial grin as she put a finger to her lips.

Of course, my stepfather's parents made regular visits and mother and I would have to trek down to main road to meet their arrival by bus. By the time we finally made it back to the house, I would have slogged four miles, quite a distance for a four-year-old, but not considered that remarkable at the time.

I must be truthful and admit, I didn't much care for this new nanna with the powdered bony face I had to kiss. Her husband, however, known to us as grandpop, was a lovely old chap who told me interesting things I'd never heard before on our rambles through nearby woods.

He even knew the story behind the impressive wooden cross standing amongst the trees behind the house. The man we rented the house off had had it erected in memory of his wife who had died young. I was mesmerized, almost as if I could sense her spirit and left the dappled glade feeling quite saddened.

35

My mother left us one day. Well that's how it felt as I'd not been given a reason for her departure. My stepfather cared for me at night, but each morning, delivered me down to the homely welcome of Mrs. Griffiths at the smallholding in the valley.

I was told my mother would be back soon and meanwhile had ducks, chickens, sheep and the big fat sow, Bessie to keep me occupied. I found the ducks comical and was amazed the way Bessie would follow Mrs. Griffiths about and roll over on command for her vast pink belly to be given a good scratch. Even so, I often felt hollow inside and as much as that kind lady tried to cheer me up, her words often fell between us, lost, as if wasted on a fading spirit. When feeling at my worst and wanting my mummy back, 'really badly,' her cheeriness could actually become annoying.

In the evenings I must have pestered my father with, "When's mummy coming back?" so incessantly, it revealed another side to him, for he'd snapped saying he didn't know and warned me not to ask again.

If you notice, I just referred to him as father, which in fairness he became, looking after me as if I was actually one of his own and on realising he'd been rather harsh, gave my hair a ruffle and said, "Be brave, old son. She'll soon be back."

One morning when dropping me down at the farm, he left as usual on his bike and took the steep rise to the main track standing on the peddles, eliciting the murmur of admiration from Mrs. Griffiths, "Like a young man," which gave me a slight feeling of pride.

If poor weather kept us indoors, she would entertain me with the fact a monster dwelt in the bedroom above the kitchen. With not having encountered any monsters, I imagined it to be similar to an ogre in the Jack the Giant Killer stories my sister read to me. It was alright for Jack to nonchalantly eat his Cornish pasty before his next encounter, but I was actually terrified and eyed the door to the stairs, ready to run at the slightest hint of the thing suddenly storming into the kitchen.

After a while, I assumed she was simply teasing and would creep to the door and even made it to the first wind in the narrow stairway, but never dared venture further. Of course, I wanted to know what it looked like and stared back in horror as she described its massive ugly head. Why would she want such a thing in the house and each time she ventured up there, I'd listen intently, to the lifting of the bedroom latch, her footsteps on the floorboards and when the low groaning started, expected to hear savagery and ripping of flesh. But no, Mrs. Griffiths, head still intact, would calmly reappear carrying an empty mug or chamber pot and I'd ask, "Doesn't it frighten you?"

"It was asleep."

"But I heard groaning."

"It has bad dreams," she said laughing.

So there really was a monster up there! OK, she had laughed it off, but remembering how she'd urged her dog, kneeing it almost gleefully to attack something in a sparse stand of nettles, it sent a chill through me, for the dog had re-emerged with a massive rat dangling.

Yes, I lived in the country, but wasn't used to its ways.

At least the lavatory wasn't up in the monster's lair, but even so, the only available facility encouraged perseverance and I'd hang on in the hope of making it back home before an accident. Of course, when just needing a wee, I'd use the nearest hedge, but for matters more serious, it meant a trip down the garden to a smelly little shed at the end of the path. Inside, yawned an oval hole in a plank seat, scraps of newspaper hung on a string and half-finished cigarettes lay browning a saucer. When asking about the latter,

I was told they helped sweeten the air, but they certainly hadn't whenever I'd had to use the place.

I've just realised, I've not told you what my temporary guardian looked like. Mrs. Griffiths was a round jolly woman whose girth raised a faded cotton frock and apron to just above wellington height to reveal a glimpse of beefy red legs. I could tell she liked me, even though I had declared her to be a man-lady when spotting facial whiskers on our first meeting and once getting to know her better, I liked the way she treated me like a young man rather than an infant. I detested the way some people would make silly noises, as if I was retarded.

By the way, the second I spotted a smile freeze on my mother's face, I knew that utterance of mine to have been a mistake and I was given a good talking to as we walked up the path back to the house. There again, when mother next met up with my Aunty Rita, I think it must have been her attempt to explain the shock and embarrassment at me declaring Mrs. Griffiths to be a man-lady, that caused their side-aching laughter as they held each other up like bookends.

I'll digress a little, for I remember, even when my time in her care was over, I'd sometimes wander down to help Mrs. Griffiths feed the chickens and ducks and one day she even asked my mother if she could take me apple picking. It was at a farm on the main road, about two miles distant and with being given regular rides on the tractor and told I could eat as many apples as I liked, it seemed like heaven. As the tractor was quite a small grey machine, it was probably a Massey Ferguson and the fact the apples were ripe, plus I'd been given a freer rein than ever before, means it must have been mid-September 1953, the time when things were taking a decided turn for the worse back in Waterloo House.

But anyway, back to those first few months of happier times out in the country and of course the way my heart absolutely soared at the sight of my mother's return, entering the hallway as if blown there on a fragrant summer breeze. I had noticed prior to her leaving how she had taken to wearing loose fitting clothing and when my new dad gave her a squeeze of rapturous welcome, I commented, she had even grown slightly taller than he was. Also, she had a more upright stance and would sometimes stop and wince, with both hands pressing the small of her back.

When she started taking afternoon naps, I'd play with my Dinky Toy tractor and trailer at the top of the stairs, for there were rails remaining on the oak boards, where a wooden safety gate had once slid, forming a perfect lane. I think my sister was staying with cousins at the time, my father would have been at work and so it was just mother and myself in that large house. She used to praise my patience, playing quietly while she rested, but when deeming her to have had quite sufficient sleep, I'd take her a glass of water.

Eventually I was told why she had become so much bigger and when my sister returned, she informed me in that smarty-pants way she sometimes had, she'd known about the baby for ages and on the morning in question, we both went down to Mrs. Griffiths' farm to await developments.

When my dad finally appeared, all smiles and told us, it was a boy, we fairly ran up the most direct path through the trees, to have a look at him.

My mother lay there, pale and exhausted, but quietly happy and in her arms, swaddled in a crocheted shawl, was my brother. As she pulled the cover back to reveal a tiny red face, she asked, "What do you think of him?"

"He's very small."

"All new baby's are small!" retorted my sister.

It was alright her being such a know-all, but I hadn't forgotten my mother telling me, when Ann had been my age, she'd looked up from her prayers, to enquire, "Mummy? Do angels wear knickers?"

# Random memories

Some of the memories from this time are hard to put an exact date to, but they all happened in a period between the summer of 1952 and late summer of 1955, when my freedom came to an abrupt end, with enrolment at last into an institute of education. I should have gone to the local village school two years prior to that, but for reasons best known to my mother, I didn't.

Immediately following the birth of my brother, there came the time of breastfeeding and stinky nappies, but also, probably early the following year, my friend Preecy came back into the scheme of things, there to help out in general and keep an eye on Michael at times when it was imperative that my mother should be elsewhere.

The year Michael was born, August 1952, my sister performed a small miracle and passed the entrance exam to Ludlow High School. We actually lived just within the Leominster catchment area, but with my father, Eric, travelling each working day to Ludlow, common sense prevailed and it was deemed a better idea for Ann to go there with him. Best of luck trying to do the same these days.

One murky evening, she was told a surprise awaited at the first post supporting our phone wire.

"Nothing horrid and slimy is it?"

"Just go and have a look."

She reappeared, with smile gleaming, pushing a bike and each weekday morning, she and her stepfather would disappear down the track and cycle to the main road. The bikes were left in a shed at the Dun Horse pub and they'd catch the bus to Ludlow.

As winter wore on, mother and I would await their return and in the dim light of the oil lamp she'd tell me fairy stories. Mike would be tucked up in his carry-cot and we'd have ears cocked for the sound of the front door groaning open, night air howling into the passageway, before two faces flushed with health would appear in the front parlour.

Now, before going on with various other memories, I must tell you this bit. On the 2nd of June the following year came the event that held the nation spellbound. Princess Elizabeth was crowned Queen of England and we were all invited up to the White Horse at Shrewsbury, for near there a valued customer and close friend of my grandparents, possessed a magic box, which would portray images of the amazing happening for all to see. It was my introduction to such a wonder and so brimming with excitement, walked with the small party to Dr Wilson's house, to witness the event of the decade.

We were welcomed and shown into what they called, the television room, where a large wooden cabinet commanded the far corner. The doors in the top section were opened; a black knob was turned and the air felt electric as the set warmed up. When moving pictures flickered across the tiny screen, all craned forward and I watched mesmerized as soldiers, sailors and airmen from all corners of the Commonwealth marched in fuzzy black and white phalanxes. The royal coach was like something straight from the Cinderella story and the minute I saw the Queen's Lifeguards, mounted and majestic in their gleaming breastplates and helmets, I decided there and then, that's what I wanted to be when I grew up.

Back at Waterloo I drew pictures of the coronation on any scrap of paper or cardboard I could lay my hands on and stomped around the garden with a stick across my shoulder, as stiff legged as I'd seen the soldiers marching on parade. I remember asking my dad, "How do they march up steps?" and on trying to ascend from the lower lawn without bending my knees, saw his face break into a broad grin.

My other passion at the time was a toy farm. I didn't yearn to be a farmer, but with all the farming going on around, it was only natural I should take an interest. Each birthday and Christmas, family and relatives added to my collection, until I had a farmhouse, painted lead animals, farmer and wife, a muck-spreader, two tractors, a trailer, a land rover and the prize possession, a yellow vertical loader. All vehicles retained their bright colours, whereas, I noticed in reality, farm equipment tended to end up in a less savoury state.

One lead animal, a brown cow, suffered an unfortunate accident and on trying to straighten its back leg, broke it clean off. My sister asked why I'd left it in the play box and I replied, I wasn't having a three-legged cow spoiling my farm.

She couldn't help but interfere and propping it against the farmhouse said, "There. Now it's perfectly alright."

With shake of head, I placed it back in the box. In my mind, the game was reality and who ever saw a three-legged cow leaning against a farmhouse? Also, it occurred to me, some girls never seem to understand.

However, when I think about it, she was marvellous, showing me how to make papier-mâché masks, painting hard-boiled eggs at easter, cutting out patterns on the back of cereal boxes and folding them into houses, inventing short theatrical pieces we performed on the oak windowsill, which had the added drama of weighty curtains as if in a real theatre. So, when I accused her of firing my pop-gun at me and she hadn't, the guilt has left a scar to this day.

Now, with her being at the big school, there came an interesting development, for vivacious young friends would occasionally be invited back for weekends and even though they were much older, I could still imagine and dream. The beauty of one particular young lady, left me almost lost for words.

On a walk up the track in the woods opposite the house, she bent to pick up what lay like an attractive chain in the grass. It moved and at a screeched warning from my sister, we all fled down the path at such a pace, I didn't make the turn at the bottom and ended up in the bracken.

"He came out faster than he went in," said the girl to my mother, once reaching the safety of the house, which made me absolutely glow with pride.

I had of course been warned to look out for snakes, to stay clear of bulls and cows with calves and never to accept sweets from strangers. I didn't quite understand why strangers' sweets were a danger, but it was so ingrained I wouldn't have dreamt of not complying with it.

A joy in those days was Uncle Mac's Children's Favourites on a Saturday morning, opening with, "Hello children, everywhere." Popular requests were, Run Rabbit Run, Teddy Bear's Picnic, Big Rock Candy Mountain, Sparky and the Magic Piano, Bimbo and a song by a German school choir that was like a healing balm so soon after the war, The Happy Wanderer. I'd sometimes whistle the tune whilst patrolling the orchards.

At a quarter to two in the afternoon, came Listen With Mother and I'd be glued to the radio, listening to the story. I didn't whistle the opening tune to that particular programme as it simply went, 'Dingy-doo, dingy-doo-------ding! Ding! But I could energetically whistle the signature tune to Children's Favourites. A fat lot of good that would do me when eventually starting school.

When young, one can have the strangest fears. I knew it wasn't likely there was a tiger under the bed, but even so, I didn't risk it and would take a running leap at night and then before getting up, would have a quick peep beneath. Also, why would robbers sneak in and take me away in the night? You never know, though and I'd often check in the murk of the morning, to make sure I was still actually in my own bedroom.

The night I dreamt I could fly out over the gardens and common with such nonchalant ease, it had been so realistic, when arising next morning I fully expected to be able to run into the garden and launch myself aloft. It proved a bit tricky, however, not helped by my mother laughing at my arm flaps and little leaps trying to get airborne.

I took the trouble to explain, fully expecting her to give some sound advice on the matter, but all she said was, "You'd better go and look for your wings, then."

I thought, 'I'll show her,' and marched outside, thinking a bit of a downward slope or leap from a step might do the trick and so her mocking, "Found them yet?" when later hanging out the washing, I found particularly irksome.

As regards flying, considering our remote location, we seemed to have more than our fair share of planes roaring up the valley. It was only years later I realised, back in those early days at Waterloo, a war was still going on and the jets had possibly been using the topography as practice for the real thing out in Korea.

They used to fly that low, they'd scatter the sheep on the common and I'd run to the highest point of the garden hoping to get a glimpse of a pilot. When told there were much bigger planes that carried passengers, I asked how it could be possible and how big were these planes? On being assured they were bigger than a house, I thought about it a while and then drew a dwelling with little faces at the windows, but instead of a roof, added a similar building on top. Some think it easier to humour a child rather than take time to explain properly, but believe me, it can lead to some strange notions; for each time I was told, 'No, much bigger than that,' I'd add another few apartments until in the end I'd drawn something resembling a skyscraper, bent like a banana. Not even I could imagine that taking to the air.

The answer came, not long afterwards, when given a picture book full of planes whilst in Shrewsbury Royal Infirmary, but please be patient, I'll provide the details a little later.

First there was the cow I forgot to mention. It belonged to the farm in the valley, but had freedom to wander and graze wherever it liked, until an adder bit it and it died. Those snakes were a constant danger and I didn't need much in the way of warning, for I always kept to the short sheep-nibbled expanses, rather than venture into long grass or bracken. Even so, you still had to be wary, for they often lay curled up basking in the sun. Our pure white Persian cat, Candy, once brought one back for her kittens to play with. I never actually saw that particular trophy, it could have been a grass snake, but whatever variety, it got chased out at the end of mother's broom. Whenever our cat had kittens, she'd bring home various offerings; mice, voles, or even lug in rabbits bigger than she was. On one occasion, my mother thought there'd been a miracle extra birth, but it was a baby bunny, which she carefully released out on the common.

If there were any stale crust leftovers, they'd be saved in an old powdered milk tin, for offering to the sheep that often grazed the old farmyard patch below the house. One in particular, which we named Martha, would rear up against the stone terracing, neck craned and huge limpid eyes checking for danger, as she nibbled crusts from hand. On bearing twins, she appeared in the yard as if showing them off and I remember, as they butted her underside, their long tails quivered.

"They do that to produce the milk," my mother explained.

Next spring Martha seemed to be no more and also, I heard deafening squeals piercing up from the depths. I ran to investigate and from a vantage point saw strange men at the pigsty and piglets fleeing in noisy distress, blood running down their back legs. It horrified me that men could come especially to harm piglets. Much worse was to follow mind you. On the morning poor, faithful Bessie had the knife plunged into her heart, the din of rage and terror made me cover my ears and I ran back to the house horrified. The old sow, that had followed Mrs Griffiths about like a pet dog now hung upside down, ready to be cut to bits. Was it to feed the monster in the bedroom?

Talking of bedrooms, I had one to myself until Michael was old enough to join me in his cot, but he was a sound sleeper and rarely woke me. Some early mornings, when peering out through the leaded glass panes, my teddy and I would see pheasants on the lawn or rabbits hopping and nibbling. Before going down to breakfast, I'd clap my hands to frighten them off. We regularly dined on game my father shot, but call me a bit of a softy if you like, I enjoyed seeing wildlife below my window and didn't relish finding my morning visitors hanging up in the larder.

My mother was the same when it came to foxes. As a young woman, up on the Wirral where her family originated, she'd had one as a pet. That's until it eventually did what foxes do and had to be destroyed. The way she laid into the hunt one day when the hounds came loping over the fence to bound across our lawn, made me think she'd not got over the loss. Striding up to the fence in quite a magnificent manner, with one hand raised she said, "Don't you dare! Not one of you is coming across this property."

They reined in and the lead huntswoman asked haughtily, "Have you seen the fox?"

"Do you think I'd tell you if I had? Now be off! The lot of you!"

As they turned and picked their way back through the silver birch copse, she said, "The very cheek of them!" and I asked, "Mummy? Why did that woman have such a strange voice?"

"Oh, that type tend to have a plum stuck in their throat."

I remember thinking, 'She'd be better off seeing a doctor, rather than chasing poor foxes about.'

I mentioned the larder earlier and although small, it was probably the most important room in the house. Few houses had fridges in those days and so a cool room on a north facing wall was essential. It kept, milk, eggs, butter and vegetables fresh; there was a meat safe and in autumn, bottled damsons, gooseberries and raspberries, plus jars of salted runner beans stood to the back of the stone slab and on the shelves above were jars full of chutney and numerous jams made from apple, blackberry, damson, plum and blackcurrant. In the autumn there were walnuts; potatoes were stored in the dry shed above the water spout and up in the attic, cooking apples were kept, individually wrapped in newspaper.

As said before, it was cosy in the kitchen during dark winter evenings, but when my sister returned, with the fresh smell of rain in her hair and face alive with stories, I began to feel trapped, wishing I could start school. It all sounded fun and I wanted to be able to relate what teachers and schoolfriends had done, or how a squirrel had leapt off Ludford bridge to sail down to a branch just above the waterline. I wanted to be on a bus that ran over a snake, or had hit a rabbit that the conductor collected to be taken home for supper.

Sometimes on those winter evenings we'd have homemade toffee as a treat or potato cakes cooked on the hotplate of the Rayburn. My brother didn't care for the texture of the latter and looking disdainfully down from his highchair, held one out to dangle limply, sending my mother into a fit of laughter.

For me, it was walnuts. I'd initially loved the flavour, but after a surfeit one autumn, returned to the house, lips black from biting off the casings, feeling thoroughly sick. Never liked them since. I relished the greengages, however, within reach on an ancient lichen covered remnant in the old orchard above the farm. The gnarled apples ripening there, although on the ugly side, were the sweetest in the area and in late spring, delicious, tiny wild strawberries could be found on the banking to the right side of the track leading down to the lane.

These days, most damsons are left to rot where they fall, but back then were a precious resource and so when my dad caught me throwing moulding windfalls up into a tree at the back of the house, trying to dislodge fresh fruit, he yelled that loud, it made me jump.

"Just what do you think you are doing?"

I replied in a worried voice, "All these have fallen down and I'm trying to stick them back on again."

He gave that narrow-eyed scrutinising look he was good at, but left it at that. A little later, I heard him relating the little episode to my mother and was glad to hear them laugh. I'd noticed the atmosphere changing of late, didn't know the reason why, but was definitely glad of anything that thawed the ice forming between them.

# The trouble returns

I deliberately have not gone on about it, because it would make me seem like a bit of a whinger, but occasionally that awful stomach pain returned, so bad at times, I was confined to bed. Once again, ghastly medicine was avowed to be the cure and my parents were told it was just a passing ailment.

One morning, however, I was carrying a plate downstairs, dropped and smashed the thing and was sick everywhere. Sitting limply in a heap, I remember thinking, 'Now I'm for it,' but to my surprise, mother appeared like a gathering angel to wash and provide me with clean pyjamas, before I was carried in a bundle and tucked into bed.

Next thing I remember, a doctor I didn't recognise, appeared and later that day came the realisation I was no longer in bed, but in the back of an ambulance heading for Shrewsbury. My mother told me later, she'd been so incensed at being fobbed off by the family doctor, she'd used the phone beneath the stairs, to demand a second opinion. Without that phone I could well have been a goner.

She came with me of course and held the bowl as I retched, what felt like my throat lining, into the phlegm. Even though there was nothing left to vomit, the compulsion wouldn't leave me. I was absolutely drenched in sweat and her voice came floating, almost as if in a dream, explaining the doctors were going to cut a little hole in my side to make me better.

For some reason, I remember the ambulance bell echoing as we raced beneath the black girder bridge of the old Much Wenlock railway line. Strange what sticks in the mind, when rather concerned about having a little hole cut in one's abdomen.

Then came the memory of being briskly trolleyed into a large ward and for some reason, my bed had a screen around it. A small glass of water was left on top of a grey metal cabinet, my temperature was taken and the nurse left closing the screen behind her. Thankfully, although not quite myself, I at least didn't feel sick any more, but still had a burning in my throat. On reaching out for the water, my hand must have been shaking, for most of it spilled onto the cabinet. Worried regarding the consequences of such clumsiness, I sank back on the pillow and waited.

The nurse returned, saw the mess I'd made and with nothing more than a, "Oh dear, never mind," wiped it up and left, leaving me thinking, 'I could get to like this place.'

I can't recall much detail of what immediately followed other than the rattling noise of being pushed along corridors to a brightly lit room, where a team of people awaited all dressed in strange clothing.

With rather a sickly smile, a man showed me the needle he was about to use. Seeing me recoil, I was assured he would stop the moment I said it hurt.

The man must have been deaf and also, when now looking up general anaesthesia, I can't work out why a needle came into the scheme of things, but it definitely did.

Next thing I knew, it was morning and I was back behind the screens with a jagged pain in my side. Tentatively checking for damage, I fingered the edges of a massive plaster covering my tummy. A nurse swished in, smiled and after asking how I felt, took my temperature, wrote something on a clipboard hanging on the end of my bed and left again. Later, she was back to do the same. Next time it was a different nurse, then a small group led by a man in a white coat.

Later that day, like a pleasant dream come true, my family arrived and Ann was almost in tears explaining how worried she'd been. I felt truly touched. It was strange to be the centre of so much attention and they'd even remembered all those questions I'd asked about planes, for I was given a picture book full of them. When a nurse had time, I'd be read a few descriptions below the images and one nurse, the one that made me feel tingly, assured me that the Sunderland flying boat, shown banking over the Suez Canal, could really land on water. It captured a wonderful feeling of freedom and of course, no-one knew then how pivotal that canal was soon to be in our countries' history.

The following morning, after a nurse had briefly led us in prayer, breakfast was rattled round, but it didn't look appetising and I didn't feel hungry. Lying there, awaiting further developments, more out of boredom than anything else, I pressed my foreskin right over the end of my willy and let it crimple back of its own accord. It felt comforting. When the nurse in dark uniform marched in, I must have looked startled, for eying me suspiciously she whipped back the covers.

We both stared as the crumpled skin slowly retracted, to reveal a tiny pale-pink grin, nosing into view.

"Dirty boy," she snapped and covering me up, marched out. With memories of the kindergarten incident returning, I huddled low fearing the consequences. She'd probably tell the whole hospital and even those nice nurses would now view me differently. It seemed that something innate deemed me to be, not a very nice boy at all and feeling doomed, awaited developments.

"What are you doing hiding under the covers? Come on, I can see you."

It was the prettiest nurse of them all and she even tickled me under my chin. The relief felt at my reprieve was immense. She was the one who would playfully chide when straightening the sheets and plumping up my pillow, which almost made it a pleasure to be in slight disarray.

Once the screens were wheeled away, I was able to get to know the man on my right. I didn't bother with the one on the other side as he had a face like a tortoise and spent much of the time snoring. When he was taken one night, another man was wheeled in, completing our little group to such an extent, others would join us when allowed out of bed.

I had more family visits, which must have taken an immense effort when you consider the remoteness of our house and them having no car. Ann told me, the reason I'd been put into an adult male ward was on account of the children's ward being full and as it had been such an emergency, I'd been given the only bed available.

A few days later came an ominous sign. The screens were rattled back around my bed and the small group entering included a serious looking balding man in a white coat. He politely asked, could he take a peep at the plaster covering my stomach. As he picked at a corner, I winced, but giving a reassuring smile, he said soothingly, "I only need to see THIS bit," ripping the whole thing off. These days one would be tempted to say, "You bastard!" but being nought but a little boy and fearful lest my skin had also been ripped off, I took a tentative look. The gash across my stomach, resembling a badly stitched up leer left me feeling horrified, but a little comfort, even if mixed with disbelief, was gained when he said, "Good. That's coming along fine." The scar was covered by a long plaster, they all left and the screens were wheeled away.

I began to feel much better as the week progressed, to the point I'd dare sit at the bed end pretending I was driving a tractor. A man at the ward's far end kept an eye out for sister, that stern nurse who had called me a dirty boy, to warn if she was imminent so I could quickly scramble back beneath the covers. One day was gloriously sunny and patients were allowed out onto the balcony overlooking a broad sweep of the River Severn. I longed to accompany them, but only when two ward-mates assured sister they'd keep me out of mischief, was I allowed to join them. Having hair blown in the sunshine and needing to squint when looking into light reflecting off the water, brought the balmy feeling of instant cure. I think my candid observations and laughter must have helped the general sense of well-being and encouraged by their obvious amusement I became even bolder.

It was the jumping up and down on a chair that did it. The nurse was horrified and taking me straight back inside, summoned sister.

"You silly boy! Look, you've got yourself all hot!"

She was right. That night, my feverish body soaked the sheets and I came out in boils.

My mother was up in arms when she next saw me, but I insisted, it hadn't been the sister's fault, it had been entirely mine. An early lesson to take note of; 'Calm down, for it will only end in tears.' In fact, for some strange reason, sister and I got on far better from then on and sometimes she pretended to be cross when we both knew she wasn't.

Then one evening, having put on my best little boy lost face, I watched the bustle around each bed as visitors chatted, handed out fruit, drinks and reading material, but not a single soul came to see me. Visiting time ended, the lights went down and I slid beneath the covers feeling very sorry for myself. When I asked why I'd been forgotten, the night nurse explained I'd be leaving next day.

Sure enough, my mother and Uncle Tony arriving the following afternoon, brought liberation. I gave the ward sister a friendly kiss farewell, but not the nurse I really liked. I think I'd fallen for her to such a degree, I felt sure my mother would have noticed and have felt betrayed. Hopefully, this explanation of such peculiar reasoning might help mothers understand certain strange things their sons might do. Even now I can see the hurt look on that young woman's face and feel deep regret for my behaviour.

Uncle Tony, in his debonair way, raced the train on the way home, but it didn't lift that feeling of guilt.

I remained bed bound until the boils subsided and had to amuse myself, drawing pictures or firing arrows out through the window. It was more fun than trying to get the suckered ends to stick to the glass.

When my mother finally flung them back on the bed and said, "Now look! I'm fed up with this! I'm not fetching them again!" I knew it wouldn't be long before being back in action.

# Cousin Jennifer and other memories

Occasionally, my cousin Jennifer would come to stay, which never failed to lift my spirits, as she was someone you could really talk to. Someone who really understood how you felt. With both now being quite grown up, we were allowed to explore the woods and orchards and seemed to enjoy all the same things. With her being a girl, however, there were bound to be a few differences. Like most curious souls when growing up, we discovered the obvious ones, but I won't dwell on that. It was things such as her attempt to revive a dead mouse, I found pointless and frustrating. It was up in the storeroom at the back of the house. It served as a playroom on wet days, but with it being a fine day, I wanted to be outside, playing. She wouldn't listen, however and fuming, I waited as she went to the trouble of procuring the cat's milk to carefully prod the rodent's lifeless nose into the saucer. "Now," she said, "We both have to remain completely silent and only creep about."

Well, I wasn't having that in my own playroom and marched around stamping on the wooden boards.

"You're cruel and horrible!"

I thought, 'How soppy!' for even though I could be a bit of a softy myself sometimes, I certainly knew a dead mouse when I saw one and felt no sadness, having become hardened by the sight of all the corpses arrayed by our cat each time she had kittens. Even dead game in the larder no longer aroused emotion, provided I'd not had to witness its demise.

One day, when Jen and I were in deep discussion, perched on the front wall of the lower lawn, I received a stinging blow to the back of the head. It really came sharp. I picked up the missile, a small

Dinky toy and looked around for the guilty party. The only possible culprit was my brother Michael, sitting impassively above us in his pram.

Rubbing my burgeoning lump and expecting a little sympathy, I pointed and said, "It was him!"

"Well you have to admit it was a good shot," said Jennifer, chortling merrily.

I was going to have to keep an eye on master Michael.

In his very early nappy days I can't remember much about him, other than he'd sometimes let me give him a brotherly hug, but at other times, would scowl and push me away.

My Aunt Ronnie from Ireland would go into fits of laughter at that scowl of his and although attempting it many times, never managed to capture it on camera. Uncle Stan was highly amused at the way he cried, not a harsh screeching or wailing, but a rather melodic, "Boo-hoo."

Well anyway, I have a secret to confess; I became quite smitten by one of the young district nurses who visited to weigh him and carry out various other duties. The only one I confessed this to was Jen, who demanded to see what this supposed nursing beauty looked like.

On visiting day she suggested we wait in the barn and view her approach through a crack in the door.

"Perhaps she'll ask you to go and stay with her."

That gave my spirits a lift, until I heard, "Then you won't need me to play with, will you!"

Our patience was rewarded by the approach of a car rocking up the track, tyres pinging out the odd stone. My heart sank as a rather stout woman emerged from the vehicle.

"Is that the one?" Jen whispered.

I hissed back, "No, it's nothing like her."

"Why, what's wrong with her?"

"I bet she's got an eggy one."

Jen held her sides, laughing helplessly, eyes almost cascading stars. When finally gathering sufficient breath, she gasped, "John, you really shouldn't say things like that," before succumbing to laughter once more.

Although I had grown enough to be proudly introduced by my Shrewsbury nanna, as her young man, there were of course still strong traces of infancy remaining, such as having to check for the tiger beneath the bed and never failing to tuck teddy in at night. Plus, I had peculiar notions, such as thinking trains ran on what I called railway lions and also thinking fire engines were wicked machines for making such a racket and into the bargain, setting everything alight. Why else would they be called fire engines?

Also, because my sister now attended high school, I imagined her having to scale a huge ladder up into some sort of educational top room. It seemed an awful imposition and was probably the reason she now had to wear huge navy-blue knickers.

This was at a time when aertex vests became all the rage, a welcome advance on the liberty bodices that had once bound me. There were also aertex knickers and a pair of my mothers' must have been mistakenly put into my chest of drawers. When I staggered through to her bedroom one morning, struggling and saying through a leg-hole, "Mummy, I can't get my head through," she went into convulsions.

Like most small boys, I adored my mother. It was she who had made my teddy bear. He was just the right size, soft to hold and wore a very patient expression. She even crocheted his shorts and cardigan. If ever we went to stay with relatives, he was never left behind and I never once lost him. Not like my brother. When he left the third one on a bus, my mother gave up making, or buying them for him.

When you consider how close I was to my mother, it's not surprising I was beside myself with worry, the day an ambulance arrived to take her away. It must have been in the early days, because Preecy was there helping out. I wasn't told what the problem was and on seeing my mother, looking so pallid, being stretchered from the house, it brought a compulsion to run down the path and tell her I loved her. The very least I could do was wave her off, but my sister and Preecy held me down on the lawn and to make matters worse started tickling. I've never laughed such rage before or since. The more they tickled and thought it funny, the angrier I got. How could they laugh when I might never see my mother again? I decided the only option was to bite. Which I did, deep into Preecy's arm and managed to reach the track just in time to give the departing ambulance a wave.

My sister was enraged, "Look what you've done to Mrs. Preece's arm!"

I didn't care. How could she not understand the importance of supporting the main person in my life? What would mother think of me if I'd not made the effort to wave her off? When she eventually returned, looking pale and worn out, I explained why I'd bitten Mrs. Preece. All she said was, "Come here," and gave me an all-enveloping hug.

# Visits

In the early days we were visited fairly regularly by my stepfather's parents, arriving all the way by bus from Clun. No easy feat actually. Years later, when describing that particular nanna, my mother had dismissed her as, 'A drop of vinegar on a razor blade,' and so you can imagine, even though grandpop was a genial old soul, the visits tended to have a rather tense air about them.

At one point they must have been looking after Ann and myself for a short while, for I remember my sister being reduced to tears.

"How dare you go into our bedroom!"

"Sorry nanna, I was just dusting. Trying to help."

"You had no right!"

Well, other than it being our house, she might have had a point. I know they must have been caring for us briefly, for had my mother been there she'd have waded into action with a few things to say. The put down of being daughter of a publican, however, she rose above, not dignifying the remark with a reply, but did post an old newspaper cutting to Clun, which emblazoned the fact her father had been in charge of the construction of the iconic Liver Building in Liverpool. Can you imagine, being put in charge of such a project at the age of 21?

Money was lost in the 30's financial crash, he died young, which left my grandmother to fend for three of her four girls. Auntie Ronnie was safely ensconced in Dublin, but the others, ex-convent girls, had to all muck in helping run a pub in Ludlow. The war was on, soldiers were billeted in any building available, so you can imagine the rest, but more of that later.

The year of Michael's second Christmas, we visited the nice nanna in Shrewsbury and on Christmas morning I went through to see what gifts Santa had left him in his baby's booty. I was quite excited by the thought of his surprise at my unhooking the sock from the headboard and handing it to him. I was amazed, for he'd beaten me to it and was already sorting through the contents. On seeing my surprise at one so small taking all in his stride, he just gave one of his looks, as if saying, 'Well, what do you expect, it's Christmas.'

The following Yuletide was the Clun year. My brother and I shared a room and one glance at the fire grate told me, as miraculous as Santa might be, not even he could gain access via a thing so small. This was worrying, made worse by the fact a huge cooking range blocked any access to the kitchen. So how would he deliver our presents? My credulity had already been stretched, for back at Waterloo, the note to Father Christmas written by my sister, hadn't even made it beyond the large open fire in the front room.

Watching it burn and shrivel I asked, "How's he meant to read that?"

"He just will," said my sister. "It's magic."

'That's all very well,' I thought, 'but how will he know we've gone to Clun?'

Then when thinking about all those children living so many Shrewsbury's away and Santa visiting all those chimneys in one night without even getting his suit dirty, I began to have serious doubts about the whole Santa Clause idea. Fair enough, I'd seen the crumbs from the mince pies left him the previous year on the plate in Shrewsbury and been shown the empty sherry glass, but who's to say my parents hadn't scoffed the pies and downed the sherry? I thought it would be best, however, to keep quiet and await developments.

It must have been about five in the morning when, reaching out yet again to see if he'd been, I at last felt the lumpy stocking at the end of the bed. My rustling in the dark woke my brother, he found the tom-tom he'd been gifted, but enthusiastic thumping brought his dad onto the scene, for the lot to be confiscated and we had to wait for broad daylight before finding what else Santa had left. I knew there'd be an orange at the bottom of the stocking, but could hardly get back to sleep wondering what the other gifts might be.

Breakfast we took that morning, was on the frosty side, but things had thawed sufficiently by lunchtime and I was allowed to wear the best present I'd ever received, Indian buckskins. I was even allowed to don the war bonnet that dangled down behind, but did wonder how an Indian chief managed to sit at the dining table without crushing his feathers on the back of the chair?

Another visit that remains in the memory, was one taken on foot, an invitation for afternoon tea at a large country pile, located on the right-hand side of the lane leading to the Maidenhead pub on the main road. Ann and I wore our best clothes and mother was attired in a pretty frock, light cardigan and mules with raised solid heals, comfortable and sensible when walking such a distance. With it being just the three of us, it must have been in the early days before Michael was born.

We were greeted by a pleasant lady, of pretty countenance and slender build who clasped her hands tight together and almost wriggled with excitement at first sight of us. Ann and myself felt rather superfluous as mother and our hostess chatted in the large dining room and as neither of us had eaten much since breakfast, being told it might spoil our appetites, tummies rumbled. Mother looked relaxed and quite serene, whereas latest news and family details being exchanged, seemed to send the lady of the house into quite a state of excitement and animation. She struck me as being rather nervous and although obviously having had the good sense to have the plum removed from her throat, I still detected a lingering trace of it. The conversation dragged on for such a length,

I began to get that fidgety feeling and on exchanging a look with mother, realised I wasn't alone in my judgement of proceedings, for she sighed. The lady trilled on, however, as if completely forgetting the reason for our visit.

Then thankfully, with a loud clap of hands she turned to Ann and myself and said, "Goodness! Silly me! You two poor things must be starving."

She opened a door and there almost within reach, on a large kitchen table were plates upon which neatly cut sandwiches had been arranged and on others, dainties stood arrayed. The sight left us at a bit of a loss regarding what to do next, stay put, or help her carry the food through, but her shrill insistence and shooing of arms, had us walking to the far end of the room to stand and wait.

A nearby hatch clattering open made me jump and when the hostess bent to pop her head through and chime, "Here I am!" had Mr. Punch suddenly whacked her on the head, my sister and I couldn't have laughed any louder. It was a struggle to return to where we'd previously been sitting, without dropping the food. Mother chided, telling us to behave, but once children find something comically ridiculous you might as well talk to the wall. Obviously, the house sported a service hatch and the woman was determined to make the fact known.

"Goodness," said mother, once back in the lane and out of earshot. As we walked home, I wondered where the woman's husband might have been, for the house had a strange empty feel and even though we laughed at the experience, I couldn't help feeling a tinge of sadness, but didn't know quite why.

Visits Ann and myself always relished, were the rare Saturday trips into town on the bus. Mother was always late and we'd be instructed to run down beyond the ford and ask the driver to wait. We'd go single file beside the stream, which flowed a fair way before disappearing down a culvert and gasping for breath,

Ann would call up to the driver, that mother was close behind. They were anxious moments as we waited and I never dared sit before catching sight of her.

"Here she comes." The driver would give a reassuring wink at the sight of legs, frock, then framed by the trees, my mother's slightly windswept look materialising as she descended the final slope to the path beside the ford. I had noticed her fuller look and radiance, but was too young to know the reason why. Don't forget, this was back in those early days and unbeknown to me, my brother was also riding along with us on that bus.

The little dilly was always moderately full and shortly after heading back towards tamed territory, it would change its mind and head for the hills, taking a sharp left into a lane hardly wide enough for a car, let alone a bus, but with branches scraping windows and gearstick vibrating madly, it would whine its way up the ascent leading to the Goggin. Many passengers lugged baskets of produce aboard and it wasn't unusual to see a chicken's head appear, to gawp about with a puzzled look.

The bus was also a delivery service, occasionally stopping to offer parcels into grateful hands, but the newspapers, rolled tight and bound with brown paper, were simply wanged by the conductor, to land left or right on cottage lawns. They were good newspaper lobbers, making their job almost one to envy, but it was way down the list compared with Queen's lifeguard or train driver.

One morning, Ann pointed at a caterpillar, like a tiny green mobile bridge, inching its way up a woman's back. We both sniggered, but actually burst out laughing when spotting her later in town, for the caterpillar was vainly stretching to gain more height atop a grey curl. I imagine, someone must have finally told her, as there was no sign of the grub on the way home. People seemed far jollier on the return trip. Going to town they were like a tiny congregation awaiting the vicar's arrival, but heading home, a few resembled red-faced revellers after a christening and I puzzled as to the reason why.

Some trips to town must have been on weekdays, for it was just mother and myself and the walk to catch the bus at the main road seemed endless. She was a fast walker and took some keeping up with. There again, if you missed the bus, the walk back would have seemed twice as long.

"It's alright, we're in time. I can see people waiting."

The bus, although only a single decker, was massive compared to Saturday's transport. I liked the Shrewsbury double-deckers best, where I could climb the stairs, rush to the front and pretend to be the driver. For a special treat in Ludlow, mother and I would occasionally go to DeGrey's café, a splendid glass fronted haven, given an enticing look of seclusion by the dramatic way the upper floors cantilevered out over the walkway. Before entering, I would be asked to spit on a hanky for my face to be wiped clean and we'd enter to the delicious aroma of freshly baked cakes, spiced buns and homemade jam. The staff, in their black and white outfits, would make a fuss of us and we'd always have a pot of tea along with éclairs, muffins or whatever happened to take our fancy, for as yet. the craze for coffee was way ahead in the future.

Another visit fondly remembered, was to Ludlow's Clifton Cinema, where Ann was part of a dance display, high on the stage. There was a short ballet performance, various other forms of dance and I remember, as they did a rendition of the Can Can, a woman's voice saying, "Disgusting."

"What rubbish!" retorted my mother.

After the show, the girls seemed so animated and thrilled, you could almost imagine them flying from one to the other like excited fairies. I was so proud of my sister, but also longed to be part of a team production, playing football, putting on a school drama, or at the very least, a game of cowboys and Indians in the playground.

The nearest I got to fulfilling such a wish was when going to stay with my cousins in Ludlow. The prospect thrilled to such an extent, I'd hardly be able to sleep the night before. The neighbourhood swarmed with children, many being my own age and each day seemed like an adventure. I of course didn't know the rules of the games they played, but even so I was included and cousin Jen was there to explain.

One morning, I was awoken by her loud banging on a drum as she ascended the stairs, calling out, "Wake up! Nobody sleeps while I'm awake!"

There came deep, stern words from Uncle Tom in the main bedroom, to which she chortled a, 'See if I care!' sort of laugh and then started singing, 'Take me back to the Black Hills, the Black Hills of Dakota,' which in fact was quite apt, as it was written for the 1953 musical, Calamity Jane.

Although, all seemed exciting, it was also testing, as I'd never freely mixed with so many children before and had not learnt what they considered to be right or wrong. Also, strange as it may seem, I'd never climbed a tree before and got stuck in the fork of the holly tree, growing in the hedge directly opposite my aunt's house. Luckily a neighbour was close at hand, Mrs. Pritchard, who cheerfully announced she'd found a little monkey and reaching up, lowered me to safety.

One day, when playing in the orchard directly opposite the houses, all the children suddenly ran screeching, Bengry was coming. I hadn't a clue what a Bengry might be, a bull, or bogey man maybe? Later, cousin Pat informed me, "He's the farmer, of course!"

We played in the long grass behind the houses, where trails had been made and in one clearing a secret camp had been set up. It all seemed like a dream come true, especially as one pretty girl whispered, "Yes," she'd show me hers if I showed her mine. "But wait until we're alone."

On first being delivered there by my mother, my Aunt Rita had given me a severe warning. On no account was I to go down the lane at the bottom of the road. It was an inviting trail running between hedges, but apparently it was dangerous. I asked, why was it dangerous, "Are there wolves down there?"

"No. It's just dangerous, that's all!"

In the end Pat said, a young boy had been abducted by some strange man, who had left him wandering in deep distress, way over by Morgan's pond.

This was of course was a deeply disturbing piece of news in such a paradise. 'Why would a man steal a young boy?' It was like my night fears of robbers coming to reality.

Out of interest, I did wander down to inspect the entrance to the lane one day, but didn't dare enter it. When a young boy on a trike came peddling close, I thought it was the least I could do to warn him not to go any further.

"Why not?"

"My aunty says so."

Naturally this didn't make much of an impression and so as he tried to peddle past, I restrained him. He might have been smaller than me, but had a temper and so when he swung an elbow, I gave a slap in return.

Abandoning his bike, he stomped up the hill making a frightful din and I was alarmed to see him running up the path directly next door to my aunt's house.

Instincts told me I'd made a big mistake and I avoided returning there for as long as possible, hoping, with time the matter might be forgotten. It wasn't. The atmosphere almost crackled with vexation.

"Here he is!"

Aunty, marching into the kitchen, to bend over me, demanded, "Did you hit little Mervyn?"

"Yes Aunty Rita."

"Why?"

"He was going down the lane."

"You had no right to do that!"

"But you told me it was dangerous."

"You had no right to stop him," sneered cousin Pat. "He plays down there all the time."

"And why ever did you hit him? Wait until I tell your mother!"

"He hit me first, Aunty Rita."

"What, a little thing like that! You ought to be ashamed of yourself! You great big bully!"

It was all so confusing, especially when I later found out, dear little Mervyn had been the boy who'd been kidnapped. Life seemed so difficult without my mum there. I had trouble sleeping that night, felt shame at being called a bully, was worried about strange child stealers and none of it was helped by the mournful wailing, sometimes heard drifting up from the rail track that ran through town. Not long after, The Runaway Train, sung by Michael Holliday, became popular and the notion of the occupants being doomed to travel for ever more, probably helped inspire the following, written years later.

# Night Train

I remember years ago, trips to my auntie's
New house in a street; young hedges, neat gardens.
So many children, so many games.
Butterflies in the sun, whispers in the long grass.

Cars rarely seen, TV's only dreamt of;
One bag of sweets was a treat for the week.
At times, the street emptied for a play on the radio,
A room full of people sitting listening in silence.

Before going to bed, we'd change behind the sofa,
Then goodnights all-round to grown-ups in the warm glow.
Upstairs was cooler, smooth in a strange bed,
Then drifting to sleep, thinking of the morning.

Sometimes at night, I'd waken and listen.
Was someone in the room going to take me and kill me?
Straining my eyes, a man's shape mizzled forward,
Looming in the black then deflating once again.

With sheet around chin and eyes staring wide,
Holding my breath, heart throbbing louder,
I'd quietly pull blankets over the pillow,
And nestle curled up in clammy security.

I'd pray in the night for crow of a cockerel,
Or birds' dawn song and purple light of morning,
Until first sun's stab splayed light from the hilltop
And friendly sounds drifted, like whistle of the milkman.

But until morning light, world belonged to demons,
Claws grabbing ankles if venturing from bed,
Feelings of loneliness, sadness and fear,
Were things that troubled a small boy's mind.

Then often wailing, forlorn in the blackness,
A long dreary whistle, iron racing wheels,
Rolling closer and louder, drumming and drawing
Away down the line, a long box of light.
So, what souls were doomed to ride evermore,
Facing each other so pale on the night train?

The Mervyn incident must have soon been forgotten, for my
mother never mentioned it and before I left for the wilderness
of Waterloo once more, Aunty Rita took the trouble to walk with
me down the lane of such danger. I found it fascinating, for boys
had made a camp in a hazel thicket, there was a stile leading
to lush meadows and we came across a band of older boys
sporting home-made bows and arrows. They had a small campfire
smouldering and on hands and knees, blowing the embers, one
said something I didn't quite catch.

"Hey! Dunner get steppin' on m'jacket," was a Shropshire form
of parlance that as yet, was foreign to my ears.

Plus, it was a second too late, for I clumsily trod right in the
middle of where it was spread on the grass. His groan and
exasperated shake of head, brought broad grins from his friends.
I wouldn't have welcomed the outcome had my aunt not been
there. I didn't know it at the time, but these same boys would soon
figure very large in my life. I had a lot to learn.

Talking of which, I could now count to a hundred and knew the
ABC, but precious little else. Meanwhile, my parents were
breaking the law, not sending me to school. My mother had said

she would let no son of hers go to a rough village school where boys impaled birds on the railings. Thinking back, my stepfather must have been quietly petrified, for if news had leaked out a child directly under his care was not being sent to school, he could well have lost his prestigious job. For with him being chief assistant to the Ludlow Town Clerk, what sort of example was he setting?

From up in my bedroom at Waterloo, I couldn't hear any evidence of discord drifting up from the depths, but moods were becoming decidedly icy.

# Waterloo. Final memories

A constant in my life seems to be, recollections of so-called grand occasions fading with time while quite simple things, not thought to be that stupendous, could settle in as abiding memories, bringing a sense of nostalgia. If it's the same for everyone, it begs the question, why go to such great expense when years later that warm inner glow will more than likely be derived from something costing virtually nothing.

As said, I don't remember many of my early birthdays or Christmas's, but for some reason floating my toy lifeboat down the flow of the ford and running along the path to catch it before it got swept down the culvert, still sparkles in my mind like those very waters. I also remember vehicles edging through in winter, with a bow wave in front, then wet tracks being left to glisten up the lane.

My mother told me, that one evening when alighting from the bus, there had been a pretty girl playing far side and obviously intent on making an impression, I'd ignored the path to splash upstream in shoes and socks. I only have mother's word for it, as I simply don't remember.

Just beyond the ford, even though it was on the tame side, there was an outpost of wilderness where the witch lived. Well, that is what Ann and myself called her, for she always wore black, the cottage was barely visible in the tangle of trees and cats swarmed everywhere.

We'd dare approach the gate, but if catching any hint of black movement, would run back towards the cottage overlooking the ford. Kindly Mrs. Plant who lived there, would not have minded if we'd taken refuge in her garden. Ann was probably old enough to know the poor old dear in black was not really a witch, but still relished the game.

I enjoyed our walks up echo hill opposite the house and mother working in the garden once told us, she could follow our progress from the chatter and laughter ringing back from the woods. Emerging into sunlight to stand in the tiny thread of lane at the top, we'd stare in awe looking across the broad patchwork sweep of valley farms to the prominent outline of Titterstone Clee. Ann told me, she'd had it on good authority, a rail line ran to the summit and knew for certain, cars drove over a road near the peak.

Gazing, trying to imagine such a thing, I vowed to myself, 'One day I will climb that hill.'

In those remaining months at Waterloo, brother Mike became more of a bosom pal and joining me in my vehicle in the front room, we'd travel to all sorts of places. The six high backed, barley-twist dining chairs, were the horses, Ann's skipping rope the reins and the cupboard to the right of the chimney breast was our carriage. I had to lift him onto the shelf, where he would patiently wait if I needed to stop and ask the way, feed the horses or untangle the reins. He loved it if the horses started without me and almost bounced with excitement as I rushed to scramble aboard before the robbers caught up with us. Wide eyed, he'd help urge the team into a gallop. Peering back around the cupboard's side, I'd yell, "They're still after us!" but after a sufficient spell of careering full pelt, the horses would be slowed to a trot.

A little voice would ask, "Are we safe now?"

"Yes, we've lost them," but taking a further look behind I'd shout, "Oh no, here they come again!" He loved it.

Obviously, I had grown a fair bit, but did tire of the fact it was constantly being remarked upon. What else did they expect me to do? Also, being regularly compared to Prince Charles began to grate, the same as he would have felt if in my shoes.

"Mater, who is this John Clegg, being constantly referred to?"

I had been able to reach the pedals and rattle around in my car for quite some time, but the terrain limited the activity to paths and lawns and so for anything more on the wild side, I had to set out on foot.

On sunny weekend afternoons I liked to wander down to the gate barring the way to any sheep fancying a wander off the common. People exploring our realm by car, appreciated it being opened and then closed behind them and would usually hand me a small amount of coinage. This would go into my red money box, saving to buy family Christmas presents. When heading for town, other uses would of course spring to mind, but mother kept the key.

The families usually picnicked sitting around a blanket and played games in the sun. Their laughter brought slight envy, for I wondered, why my family wasn't like that? Things had taken a serious turn for the worse and I didn't know why.

The couple living in the bungalow directly below the gate, were friendly and often invited me in. I would be regaled with stories of army life, not fighting, but peeling huge mounds of potatoes and how at Christmas the pile of presents for the troops could be high as a house. When stationed abroad, there had been such ferocious summer heat, wealthy people seeking respite would head for the hills and although not understanding how going nearer the sun could be the cooler option, I didn't doubt my friend for one minute.

There was one boy who lived not too far away. Billy was two years my senior and had the misguided notion, that catching bees by hand using grass to protect him from stings, would impress my sister. It didn't and at the sight of him pulling claws off crayfish, she told him what a heartless monster he was.

Talking of monsters, I at last found out, Mrs. Griffiths didn't really harbour such a thing upstairs in her cottage. It had been her poor husband all along, burdened by a hideous growth on his head that eventually killed him.

Anyway, back to the charming Billy. I happened to be down at the farm on a day Mrs Griffiths had guests and with two being brother and sister, slightly older than myself, I was of course glad to meet them. They wore, what appeared to be Sunday best, the girl in a colourful summer frock, plus ribbon in her hair, the boy in a loud zig-zag striped pullover and hair slicked down. We got on instantly and I was told, they loved the country and that Beermigum was a doomp. We played by the duck pond and I was just taking them to a little glade I loved, when Billy showed up.

He wasn't long in challenging the boy to a fight and when this was declined, he waded into attack, scragging him to the floor, to rub his face in the dust. I must admit, I didn't much care for the boy's choice of pullover, but felt as guilty as if I'd attacked him myself. With the girl screeching outrage and condemnation, Billy departed up the track, but before disappearing from view, he turned to give a triumphant fist shake to accompany, "We showed 'em!" I watched as the girl, giving me an accusing look, helped her brother back down to the farm. I wouldn't have known the phrase, tarred by the same brush, but certainly knew how it felt.

The strange thing is, whenever Billy turned up to play at Waterloo House, at the sight of my mother he was all sweetness and light. She didn't mince words, however and warned him; any sign of roughness, and he was going straight back home.

He could actually be good fun and when playing pirates, I followed him, climbing to places in the barns I'd never dared attempt before. We even found a way, right up beneath the roof ridge, edging our way from one barn to the other like intrepid explorers. We roamed further than I'd ever been before, out beyond the birch wood, creeping in case the imagined enemy spotted us, ranging across wild country to where a cottage stood alone in its garden. The only access seemed to be a trail winding down through woods and Billy told me it led to his house in the lane; the one that ran down to the ford. I suddenly realised my location and also, who lived in the cottage. When down by the stream, at the marshy spot where the tang of wild garlic hangs heavy, I would occasionally hear the children returning from school, hooting and hollering while wending their way home. I was very much in enemy territory, near the lair of those bird impalers.

Washing blew on the line and billowing full-cheeked, were a splendid pair of pink bloomers, biggest I'd ever seen in my life.

"Better not let her catch us looking at her britches," said Billy and we withdrew.

Sometimes we'd walk down to the ford, water always attracts, and race sticks in the flow, but one day I froze, for a gaggle of children approached far side and I instinctively knew trouble was imminent.

"This is the one who laughed at your mum's drawers," called Billy.

The biggest youth, who was well into his teens, ran up, swung a fist in my face and then pummelled further as I curled up for protection on the floor. Once satisfied I'd been taught a lesson, they left for the woodland path, with jeers of triumph echoing and I remember through the tears, seeing Billy's mocking laughter. Needless to say, I never played with him after that.

Back at the house, things had become frightening, not because of rancour and violence, it was the days of endless silences, hanging like a pall over everything that brought fear and dread. My stepfather had taken to sleeping alone with his rifle and my mother now said things like, "Ask your father if he wants another cup of tea."

Long gone were the days when he would return from work looking truly happy, ruffle my hair and ask, "So what have you been up to today?" And long gone were the days when mother would attain an overall tan on the front lawn, clattering for cover in sandals if hearing a car groaning up the track. Remembering the evening when they'd trundled a treadle Singer sewing machine up the path to the house with such mutual elation, I wondered if those days would ever return. Also, now I think back, how had they managed to transport it from the Orleton auction? I don't remember any delivery vehicle and they can't have pushed it through the ford and up the lanes. I told you memories can be strange things.

At the time of receiving the lesson in treachery from Billy, I must have been seven, meaning that those silences would have started two years earlier, when I was five. One time when we returned from Shrewsbury, Eric, my stepfather had not been with us and so Mother and Ann shared the load of Mike's carry cot. I remember his face as we entered, looking as thunderous and black as if carved from ebony. I'm not exaggerating, it was what could be described as murderous. Talking of which, all six of Candy's kittens had disappeared and it was heartbreaking to see her worried, wide-eyed search for the playful little balls of fluff.

Looking back, I now realise, for some reason that particular day had heralded a frightening turning point, but at the time didn't know why. Thankfully, there had been glimmers of hope in those final years at Waterloo, like the time of the damson anecdote, but they'd been false dawns and Ann and myself often crept about the house with worried looks, hardly daring to speak. Of course, I sided with my mother, but one day, when helping my dad wrap a transistor radio he'd bought for her birthday, my heart bled for the man, for it was flung back at him.

# Around the Column

On top of the column, one of the tallest Doric columns in the world, stands the 17-foot Coade Stone figure of Lord Hill, a military tactician of remarkable genius during the Napoleonic wars and instigator of the 1840 postal reform, when stamps were first introduced. Just beyond, when heading from town, lies the White Horse pub, run at the time by my grandparents and in a street nearby was St Giles school, the supposed answer to my lack of education.

I don't know why, but even from the outset, the teacher seemed to dislike me, but thinking about it, the fact I was illiterate could have had something to do with it. All my classmates had had two years education and I sat there day after day, so puzzled as to what was going on, I might as well have been in a foreign country. Not one single effort was made to teach me reading, writing or arithmetic and the only way I could make it seem as if making progress, was by trying to commit to memory the words that went with the pictures, as each page was read aloud. This was obviously prone to error, leaving me open to ridicule from the teacher I began to hate. I had so looked forward to school, but now dreaded every day. The only things I could excel at were drawing and running.

This must have irked, for on sports day, when lining up against the boys I'd already easily beaten in practice, my teacher plucked a toddler from a watching mother and planted him five yards from the winning tape. I stood no chance and had to watch the tot being held aloft in triumph.

Nothing I did seemed to gain any favour, but with luck I'd only be there for a year and so during class time, simply switched off. During play and lunch breaks, I got on well with a boy called Barry and strangely, even though I was the class dunce, one of the brightest girls seemed to like me, plus I mustn't forget a boy called David, a natural comedian whose antics often had me in stitches.

My grandparents were of course very good to me, but it didn't help the hurt from missing my family and mother in particular. I'd often sit, staring out of a bedroom window that overlooked the car park and imagine her striding into view from around the corner.

That friend, Barry and I would sometimes walk to a railway bridge where we could watch trucks being shunted in the large goods yard beyond. I found it fascinating, until realising having seen it once you don't really need to see it again, but Barry became a complete devotee, saying it would stay in our memories for life. He was right there I suppose.

Also, I bet if still alive, he's never forgotten a mad idea of mine; standing on the rail of a trackside protective barrier as an express train hurtled past. I'm surprised our hair didn't turn white and slumping from our perches, we stood juddering like a pair of road drills vowing never to do such a thing again.

Another friend, Alwyn had a trike with a metal carrier slung on the back. I would rattle around in my pedal car and using a huge haul of bottle tops, we'd play banks. The car park was perfectly flat and so it mystified me why the game was called, 'banks,' but I thought it wise not to ask.

I loved helping my Uncle Stan, doing grown up stuff, such as lining up beer bottles on shelves behind the bar, or tossing empty beer crates up into tall stacks and was always disappointed when such tasks were completed, asking, "What can we do now Uncle Stan?"

I think we all called him uncle rather than granddad, because he was my grandmother's second husband. Her first, the Liverpudlian architect, held in such high esteem, had died from septicaemia in the early war years and as explained earlier, when hearing of a pub becoming vacant in Ludlow, a place safe from bombing, she took a train south to weigh up the opportunity. It must have been winter, for seeing snow on the Stretton Hills, she had regaled her daughters with the exhilarating notion of traveling through 'Little Switzerland.'

When they finally made the move, the snow had melted, the hills looked as drab as their feelings and with winter not yet over, they entered a run-down establishment on the northern edge of a small market town, thinking their world had come to an end. Can you imagine, three ex-convent girls, having known the high life up on the Wirral, now having to pull pints and muck-in at the Unicorn Inn, surrounded by locals they could hardly understand? They soon adapted mind you, seeing the fun side of where life had taken them and with Ludlow brimming with military personnel, word soon got about and they did a roaring trade.

Thinking about it, if it hadn't been for Herr Adolf, I would not have been born. My mother would have had no reason to leave Cheshire and my father would not have left the Isle of Man to enlist in the army. He was posted to the grand metropolis of Bromfield, acting as assistant quartermaster of the munition depot on the racecourse, within easy cycling distance of the Unicorn Inn.

The pub became such a success, my grandmother, plus Uncle Stan, who had now been welcomed into the team, were offered the Compasses, up near the centre of town, that place I described in the third chapter. There are many more details, such as my two aunts joining the WAAFs, but that will suffice as background detail for now.

Uncle Stan was actually a very accomplished engineer and could turn his hand to anything. He was very concise and diligent, making it a pleasure to watch him, even the neat way he ate, leaving his plate perfectly clean.

I suppose helping him, acted like an antidote to feeling such a failure at school and I always looked forward to our days at the allotment. All the weeds were dropped into a huge water butt that had a tap outlet. The green brew, trickling into a watering can would not have been to everyone's liking, but the plants loved it and grew almost to the point of us having to stand back when administering the potion.

It was there one day, we'd had to avoid stepping on a Great Dane, sprawled asleep across the path. Between its back legs were two strange, very prominent bulges with an almost a liquid look, like the sheen of mercury.

As they seemed so huge and alien, I asked, "Uncle Sta-ann?"

"Yes."

"What are those?"

After a moments' pause, he said, "Oh, that's just part of him."

He'd have been unaware, I later overheard the little incident being related and at the sound of his infectious laughter, it suddenly dawned on me what part of the dog those whopping great dollops were.

A character known as Old Bill helped with odd jobs around the pub, sweeping the yard, emptying smelly ashtrays and cleaning out fireplaces. He had been a soldier in the Boer War and was interesting company, even though a bit doddery at times. One day a ferocious gust of wind got hold of his baggy trousers, nearly blowing him off his feet whilst attempting to cross the road down at Abbey Foregate. Perhaps it was divine retribution for telling me that whopper about the tank transporter being responsible for scribing red lines down the margins of writing paper.

There was a maid called Sacie who helped with morning chores, such as washing glasses, wiping tables, replacing sodden beermats and mopping the floors. Where she worked, always seemed filled by her bright and breezy manner and the ring of her singing. When bending to sing me the first two lines of, How Much is that Doggy in the Window and jabbing my tummy at the two dog barks, I would go bright red, but her rendition of This 'Ole House I enjoyed, for it fairly bounced along. I was sometimes invited to her house for tea, which was extremely kind of them, but when leaving the family atmosphere, I'd have a yearning inside for mine. Things had moved on a pace, by the way. People must have become far more affluent, for I remember they owned a television set that had a screen much bigger than that first one I'd seen the coronation on.

My life was given a lift when Jennifer's younger sister Susan came to stay, for we seemed to have an understanding that brought the realisation I'd only been making do with some of my local friends. One day, I remember her looking very strange, almost as if in another world. Next thing I knew, she'd been rushed into hospital with something so serious, a priest had been called to administer last rites. While he and my aunt and uncle were fervently praying, Susan opened her eyes. What a miracle!

The hotel car park was often packed and when coaches pulled in, both bars would be heaving. My grandmother organised food preparation and seemed to glide around like a small ship, tea towel draped over a shoulder as she oversaw quality and efficiency. Often, when in the thick of it, Uncle Stan would perspire freely and I noticed how much weight he'd gained. Years later, mother explained, constant beer fumes had largely been the reason, but by that time I'd reached an age when I could form my own opinion.

The clientele differed from that remembered in the Ludlow pub. I suppose the Compasses must also have had its mix of tradespeople and other professionals, but my most prominent memory was when seeing it packed on market day. I of course would not have known the professions of the White Horse regulars, but just knew them to be different, for I never once saw a customer in brown dairy coat and wellies during my stay there.

The family dentist was a regular; the one that had put a ghastly rubber mask over my face, sending me into such a wild state of dreamland. The local doctor, whose TV we'd watched on coronation day, was often there. I was befriended by a local artist, Mr. Holt and taking note of his helpful instructions I'd cover every scrap of paper and cardboard I could find. I drew and painted pictures of cars, lorries, planes, people, animals and buildings. When drawing the latter and adding another, slightly smaller, behind, then another and another, he was amazed, telling me I'd stumbled upon perspective. I didn't know the meaning of the word, but did realise the discovery gave my pictures depth.

After closing time, I had free reign to use the bars and corridors for the rest of the afternoon and I'd roll my fastest Dinky car as far as I could manage. On retrieving it from beneath upholstered seating running the length of the lounge wall, I found coins that had been accidently dropped there. With my toy forgotten I went prospecting further, gathering quite a handful and giving thanks to the fact, Stacie was obviously better at singing than cleaning, made a point of regularly doing the rounds. Nothing matched that first haul, but it was still worth the effort.

When Jennifer came to stay, she marvelled at the bounty I'd gathered and was keen to join the search. It was the time when section by section, the pub was being redecorated and so we had the added fun of hiding beneath the dustsheets, sniggering at those wondering where we'd got to.

Uncle Tony was also there at the time and there was just something about him that children instinctively felt drawn to. Before having to go to bed, we'd beseech him to chase us again.

"No, not tonight."

"Pleeese Uncle Tony," we'd call down from the landing. Then seeing a dark shape slowly ascending the stairs and occasional cigarette glow, we'd flee in a state of gleeful hysteria.

When begging him yet again, only to hear that that was enough, for he'd got a bone in his leg, we knew the game was over.

He and Aunty Ursula had recently returned from two years in Malta, looking tanned, glamorous and adding to the mystique were leather suitcases emblazoned with exotic labels. Uncle Tony was an amusing raconteur and had us hanging on his every word when recounting their adventures.

I had been quite looking forward to welcoming young Nigel, their son, as I'd not seen him since his early nappy days. He was roughly the same age as my brother and I remember years before, my mother and her sister brightly chatting, each holding a baby bundle whilst reclining together in a double bed. Both suddenly stopped to frown and sniff and my mother asked, "Is it mine or yours?"

On the day of their arrival, looking as unflustered and urbane, as if having merely stepped ashore from a ship docked up by the column, a huge welcoming spread awaited and as we all tucked in, I noticed Nigel turning imperiously away from anything offered. In the end, probably feeling rather embarrassed, Uncle Tony picked up one of the discards and saying, "Pity to waste it," ate one of the quartered sandwiches.

"Daddy's eating my tea!" wailed Nigel in floods of tears and bubbles of snot.

Everyone agreed, that he must have been tired, but looking across at my brother, who was now old enough to convey words without saying anything, I received the narrow-eyed judgement, 'That's no way to carry on.'

For his brief stay, we shared a bedroom and that's when I realised, he now had a little friend, who he called Bundy. I enquired, regarding the shape of this Bundy, "What does he look like?"

With a look of incredulity, he replied, "Like Bundy of course!"

Even at such a young age, I could detect Michael's character forming and although intrigued as to how Bundy had made his way to Shrewsbury, was left to assume he must have somehow hidden himself in the luggage and come by train. Meanwhile he'd taken up temporary residence in the linen cupboard near the bed. One morning I asked, "Has Bundy come out to play yet?" but received a sigh, along with a frown that said, 'Course not. You'd have seen him if he had.'

We were jumping about on the bed one morning, when I had an unfortunate meeting with the footboard, catching me where it hurts most. On hearing my cry of pain, mother came in and asked, "What's the matter? What have you done?"

"I've hurt part of me," I groaned.

Having made sure I was alright, she departed and I could just make out the fact she was relating the unfortunate incident to Uncle Stan, for at his sudden outburst of laughter, I realised he'd probably just been told what I'd said. He had the most infectious laugh of anyone I'd ever met and even though still in pain, it had me ruefully grinning to myself.

Nanna never did tell him how old she really was and I noticed he and my mother got along, rather like conspiratorial siblings.

Just briefly, I'll list a few other memories of that year in Shrewsbury. For a start, there was the long climb up to the top of the column. The man who took payment also kept the steps swept, saying he had to work from bottom to top, for if going the other way, the updraught made it impossible. I could describe the view from the top, but I'd be making it up, because infuriatingly, that particular memory has slipped away.

My nanna sometimes took me on shopping trips, proudly calling me her young man and I remember Bertram Mills circus coming to town, with the huge elephant blimp drawing everyone's attention. It was the year of massive flooding and I gazed in awe at the brown torrent swirling beneath the Welsh Bridge and at the houses along the embankment at Frankwell, half under water. A special tour bus, packed to the limit, drove out to Atcham, where all gazed in wonder at the flooded fields, the hedges like weirs and sheen of water as far as the eye could see. I was taken to Wellington market, where Uncle Stan bought me a toy Winchester rifle and to Cosford airshow where an attempt was made to break the sound barrier. I saw the jet, but as hard as I looked, could not discern the barrier mentioned. Down at the Welsh Bridge crowds flocked to see a dead whale on a lorry and I was stunned, not only by the size of it, but also the smell. The fact I'd been to Wellington market on a school day didn't help regarding my tepid relationship with the teacher, but I had reached a stage where I almost relished the way she fumed. The visit to the circus was in the evening and I remember the man on stilts towering over us as we approached the big top; the clowns throwing water at one another, rather than at the tiny building on fire; lions and tigers snarling as they entered the ring; pretty girls urging the elephants forward, looking like warrior queens flowing with each stride and the way Uncle Stan stood to applaud those same girls in their skimpy costumes and exotic plumage, when negotiating the circus ring, brightly smiling atop massive silver balls. To me, it seemed the least interesting part of the show, but to Uncle Stan, it must have been a highlight, for he applauded as enthusiastically as any of the other men, arising to roar approval. I haven't gone into further detail, for how can you tell whether you're describing that particular circus or one seen years later on television? I did wonder, mind you, how the jabbing of a skimpy chair would help, should one of those giant cats decide to leap on the lion tamer.

Now we come to the visit that topped my list; Wroxeter Roman city. The thought of all those people wandering the streets and occupying the buildings so many centuries before, had me mesmerized. For the most part, only foundations are on view, but in my mind it became a bustling metropolis. I was full of questions, such as, 'Who were the Romans and where did they go to?' and realised I needed to become literate; and quickly.

A large group of family friends, or maybe they were related in some way, would pay regular visits and I'd have to listen to them marvelling, yet again, how much I'd grown and them asking, yet again, was I going to be a policeman when I grew up? I'd told them I wanted to be a Queen's lifeguard countless times, at which they'd marvelled, but for some reason never seemed to remember.

The other thing is; for some reason one of them would always grab hold of me to start tickling, making me laugh to such an extent it was frightening, for I couldn't breathe. When one of the ladies said, "Careful, he might wet his pants," it gave me an idea.

Seeing them all bustling into the dining room one afternoon, I nipped to the kitchen, downed a few glasses of water, then returned to the throng. It's actually incredibly difficult to wet your pants when forced into side-aching laughter, but persevering, I did at last feel the warm release and saw the man's trousers darken.

"Well I did warn you," came a woman's voice and he never tried tickling me again.

Another visitor was Uncle Stan's brother Wilf and his beautiful dusky Malay wife. He was handsome, tanned and told amazing tales from the Orient and I could hardly take my eyes off the lady at his side. Now you'll have to take my word for this, as I didn't mean to burst in on her as she arose like Venus from her bath, but before she'd grabbed a towel, I'd seen my very first bare-naked lady. I'd seen my mum of course, but that hardly counts. The reason for my rude intrusion was, having had it dinned into me by my grandparents to always turn the taps off properly, the sight of water gushing into an outside drain prompted me to do my duty; race upstairs and stop the flow. The unlocked door bursting open brought a piercing shriek and red-faced with embarrassment I fled the scene.

I wanted to apologise and explain, but it would have sounded ridiculous and anyway I was too ashamed to go near the lady. Sometime later, when I was forced to join all in a stroll, she made a point of turning to give me the sweetest of smiles and although I blushed, you can imagine my relief.

About this time, there was a flying saucer mania. Everyone was talking about them; people knew people who had seen one and there were artists impressions of them in the paper. Early one morning when staring out of my window, I espied in the pale blue distance, an interesting light. It didn't seem to move, but I was convinced it must be a flying saucer. Down at breakfast, other than humouring me, my amazing sighting was ignored and I was not even told I'd been staring at the real Venus, which although not an alien craft, would have still been fascinating.

Undoubtedly, the best thing I ever witnessed, from an upper window of the White Horse Hotel, was something I'd often imagined and prayed for, my mother striding into view. My feet thundered down the stairs and bursting out across the small patio onto the carpark, I threw myself into her arms. It was near the end of that dreadful school year and she made me feel like a whole person again. I hardly left her side all that day.

I suppose I'd grown out of most of my clothes, for I remember trips into town for shirts, shorts and wool; mother always knitted our socks and pullovers. One day when returning to the hotel, I remember talking to a very pleasant lady on the top deck of the bus and in fact, we got on so well, I thought it best to advise her to say, horses and houses, not 'orses and 'ouses. The look on my mother's face was enough to tell me I'd erred.

While planning the next move in their lives, my aunt and uncle remained at the hotel and with my mother briefly there, it made for quite a party atmosphere. Uncle Tony was forever creating things, like amusing devices constructed from the Meccano set Uncle Stan had bought me and he worked diligently on marquetry pictures that brought great admiration. He was even on the TV show, What's my line? where Wilfred Pickles denied him the prize by guessing his woodworking hobby on the twentieth and last possible go.

There was an electric train set, supposedly for Nigel, that dominated the function room and talking of Nigel, he'd mastered to perfection, the art of being a little monster until finally getting his own way. To any onlooker it was obvious what his game was, but instead of a firm hand, he was mollified by a seemingly endless supply of Penguin chocolate biscuits, with me not getting the merest sniff of one.

Well anyway, by the time of my mother's brief visit, the chocolate had finally done its job and cousin Nigel was well and truly bunged up. He did sit and strain but it must have been like trying to pass sea urchins. Having witnessed a few days of this and become sick of the sound of his bawling, plus the sight of her sister rocking back and forth wailing, "I just don't know what to doooo!" my mother said, "Give him to me."

After gentle application of Vaseline, Nigel was plonked to sit wide eyed on the throne, that thundered to such an extent, you could have well imagined the poor lad having to clamber onto the seat for safety. Luckily, I was near an open window.

On the day mother was due to leave, suddenly remembering my haul of coinage, I proudly showed it to her. It didn't receive the reaction I'd expected, for unbeknown to me, someone with light fingers had been at work in the pub till and what I now held with such elation made me prime suspect. I was quizzed in the gents' lavatory, but the place where I'd often gone to whistle on account of the acoustics, now rang to my mother's voice demanding to know if I was a thief?

I was hit with, "Your father was a liar, now I want you to tell me the truth. Better to be a thief than a liar!"

Some comfort! But then it got worse. You know what they can be like, for it all came out. Even how I'd lied, saying I'd not been eating blackberries, when stains around my mouth made it obvious I had.

In the end, I took her on a tour of where I'd found the money and luckily, discovered a penny on the floor. "See, Mummy. I didn't steal it." Calming down, she finally believed me.

When later, seeing her making preparations for departure and still reeling from the way someone I had always trusted had doubted my word, I couldn't help it, I burst into tears.

"Come here. Whatever's the matter?"

"I don't want you to go away again."

She gently explained that I only had to wait a short while longer and I'd be back with her and the family again.

# Part Two

Clee View is the name of a road on the eastern edge of Ludlow, which at the time had nothing lying between it and the majestic granite outcrop of Titterstone Clee, other than a distant B-road, winding lanes, a barely used rail track, tiny villages and farmland. The perfect adventure playground for those growing up in the late 50's.

Looking back, our moving there must have been largely thanks to my cousin Susan. She made a full recovery from whatever it was that had nearly killed her, but my aunt and uncle were advised to relocate to the sea-side where the air would be fresher and less likely to cause a relapse. Knowing the Midlands air, with its tendency to be damp and muggy could endanger his child's life, my Uncle Tom urgently sought another job and to his relief was offered a transfer north. Therefore, once they had decamped to the majestic sweep of Morecambe Bay, we moved into their vacated council house, fourth door up at number 7.

I still held that earnest desire to climb to the summit of Clee Hill and on a clear day, with it seeming close enough to almost reach out and touch, I was thrilled by the prospect. The puzzle of how cars and trucks managed to surmount such an impressive barrier, was explained by the fact the road only traversed the less dramatic slopes south of the peak, but even so it could be treacherous during winter and we often heard stories of vehicles not able to make the gradient or being abandoned in snowdrifts.

This still left the puzzle of how a rail track somehow made the ascent to just below the peak and also the question, had the stern looking protrusion once been a volcano? It certainly had the look of one and so would I find a crater when finally reaching the summit?

It felt wonderful having a fresh start, with family now reunited and children seemingly everywhere; up trees, in the road and across the fields exploring endless countryside. Tea chests full of belongings remained stacked in the hallway for quite some time and our small front room was a temporary store while we worked out where everything was to go. It all added to the excitement really and with my stepdad taking a pride in the garden, we soon had a plentiful supply of vegetables, plus gooseberries, currants and raspberries from the bushes my Uncle Tom had planted. Fresh flowers always livened the house and I secretly prayed that my parent's new honeymoon period would last. A raised voice at night, would have me sitting up, holding my breath while I listened. Only when hearing sounds of cheer, or laughter, would I dare breathe a sigh of relief and go to sleep. Still tucked my teddy in at night, by the way.

Down in the hallway, leaning in the lefthand corner, was a yew wood bow. My mother had once been a member of an archery club, but now promised the bow would be mine the day I could string it. With it beside me upright, I could already reach the horned tip, but ownership still seemed a long way off.

Our portion of Clee View comprised five semi-detached houses on a gentle rise and running at right angles, bottom of the hill, was Riddings Road that had the entrance to the famous lane that ran east as an ancient continuation. Two roads ran parallel behind Clee View and Riddings Road, but with all back gardens being so generous, the occupants of those houses rarely featured in our lives. The geometry of the set-up, meant that where the two roads met, there was a vacant square to the rear of the first four semis and what had once been a small meadow, now held allotments and a row of garages. To the rear of all, completing the rectangle, was a massive recreation area, with swings and a slide in the furthest corner and enough space to host cricket and football matches.

Directly below Riddings Road was Ludlow Town football pitch and by virtue of a well-worn gap in the hedge, we could watch the matches for nothing. There was a groundsman, we called Spike who collected entry money at a green hut, far end of the field, but he wasn't that quick on his feet and we easily gave him the slip.

Opposite our house was a slender field and with it having four apple trees, it was called the Orchard. Beyond was a large sloping meadow, which on account of its size, was named the Big Field and immediately beyond lay two small fields, belonging to another landowner, a kindly old gent by the name of Morgan. So of course, these pastures, with a pond between were called, Morgan's.

All the hedges at the time were at least 20 feet high and by virtue of the gate at the top of the Big Field, one could gaze beyond the Ludlow/Clee Hill road, across to the wooded scarp slope of Whitbatch, or even further to the prominent bulge of Brown Clee. Although not looking like it, this hill is slightly loftier than its southern neighbour, but because of its dramatic outline, it was always Titterstone Clee that drew our attention.

There were actually two gates at the top of the Big Field, leading to a pair of slender fields sloping down to the main road; the one on the left being of little interest, but the one on the right, with a deep groove and sudden dip before the pond, was known as the sledging track. Off to the bottom right lay the hamlet of Rock Green, where Mr. Morgans farm and the Nelson pub were located. I say, were located, but of course the pub is still there, even if completely swallowed by the advance of modern developments.

Out of interest, the old lane we so often played in is actually the surviving section of an ancient trackway that led up to what was the Portcullis Gate in the Ludlow town wall. Even that remnant is now much shorter, having been truncated by the town by-pass. To the south of this ancient relic, lay vast acreages owned by the Bache family and beyond the football pitch was land owned by the Smalls.

We would often cross these fields to reach Ledwyche stream, another favourite adventure destination and beyond was the massive Ledwyche pool before the steep rise up to the Iron Age hillfort, Caynham Camp. The present pool is only half of what it was back in those days and the word Ledwyche is locally pronounced, Lettich.

The semis we lived in were called Airey Houses, which most thought, was on account of them being drafty, but in actual fact they took their name from the designer. They were rushed up in the 50's to help combat the housing shortage and consisted of an iron frame, sheeted with tinfoil, topped by abrasive pebble-dash slabs, mounted shingle fashion. Interior walls were simply fibre board, roofs were conventionally tiled and rainwater goods were of cast iron. There were two main bedrooms, plus another with just enough room to squeeze into, beside a single bed. The bathrooms, with their 50's carbolic smell, were considered quite modern and the small kitchens, with sink, gas cooker and pantry cupboard were adequate. There was a main living room with its cosy Rayburn stove, a smaller room usually reserved for welcoming guests and a fairly large hallway bottom of the stairs, boasting a front door that was rarely used.

Entry to all the Clee View houses was usually via the kitchen door, referred to as the back door, even though it was actually on the gable end. Opposite this was an open coal house, plus small enclosed lavatory facility and left of all was the wash-house. This held the meter for the town gas supply, plus whiffy evidence mixed with the smell of boiled washing. For some design reason, the kitchen doors and outhouses along Riddings Road were on the back of the dwellings. All had only been given the expected lifespan of 20 years, but all be it with substantial alterations, they still stand there today.

Our bathroom was immediately top of the stairs, Mike and I shared the first bedroom off the landing, our parents had the master bedroom next door and Ann had the small room at the end of the landing. Below her bedroom window was the columned flat-roofed porch and as it also spanned the front entrance of next door, the feature gave all the Clee View council houses an unexpected hint of grandeur.

The prerequisite for a families' eligibility regarding rental possession of one of these properties seems to have been children.

They swarmed everywhere and for me it was like a dream come true. In fact, trying to make sense of it all, brought what would now be termed overload, for there was obviously a hidden structure regarding who played with whom and rules to their games, but with not having the slightest clue it was hard to join in. Also, being the new kid, who I suspect spoke in a rather posh manner, brought with it a sense of suspicion and even slight resentment.

For instance, first week there, Peter Clark, roughly my age, who lived around the corner, challenged me to a race.

"Bet I can run faster than you. Race you to the willow tree."

There were many willow trees, but the large one in the hedge running behind the goalmouth of the football pitch was **the** willow tree. I beat him fairly comfortably, which I could see rankled and I had to watch my step as the fact he had an elder brother gave him a disproportionate amount of influence.

This same reasoning posed a problem when 5-year-old Robert from up the road, whacked me in the ear with a stick he'd prodded in cow muck. My dilemma was not only tempered by the Mervyn incident, but also by the fact he had two brothers, one a year older than me who was strong and rangy, backed up by another four years my senior, who had a definite mean streak.

So I didn't grab the stick and return the favour, I wiped my ear clean with grass and spoke of the incident to my mother.

"Goodness me! He's much smaller than you. Don't be such a baby!"

It was no good explaining the political side of life in the street and so I now had to nurse wounded pride along with a throbbing ear, while trying to think of a solution.

Unfortunately, sport was not the answer as I'd never played football, rounders or cricket. I was last to get picked in a kick-about and no-one would pass to me when I finally was. Then when trying to take a catch offered from a lofty swipe from bat, I was dismayed at the sight of them all falling about laughing. When one blurted, it looked like I was performing some weird arms aloft rhumba, I had to suffer his smug look along with the fit of tittering from the girls who had taken an interest. It wasn't just basic schooling I'd been missing out on.

Shortly after our arrival, my mother walked with me to the junior school. I felt so embarrassed with all the children staring at the new boy needing guidance from his mum, but in the large main schoolroom I was introduced to the homely looking Mrs. Bodenham who took immediate charge and during the course of the morning set me a simple test.

Having looked at the result, she didn't comment, but took the trouble to walk me up to the infant's school, where she then explained, I'd be given the basics to cope with lessons in her class, later that year. At seeing me looking utterly crestfallen, the blow was softened by her confiding it was the best solution and that the few months would soon pass.

My spirits sank further when eying the head teacher I was entrusted to, then further still at first whiff of the remedial corner I was put in. She wasn't actually bald, for she had a white wispy bloom on a pink scalp, but I still didn't like the look of her and the boy she told me to sit beside stank of urine.

A darker side of the educational regime gave hint of why there should be such a nearby smell of humanity, for of course, any child repeatedly whacked with a twelve-inch ruler was bound to piss his pants. Even those from other classes were brought in for the same treatment. There was no sex discrimination, for all was meted out quite fairly on an open palm until the pain forced sinews to contract, causing the last blows to rattle the knuckles. All those witnessing winced in sympathy and not wanting the same treatment, I soon made myself familiar with Janet and John and once able to master more interesting literature, felt myself moving beyond range of the ruler. Then on having got the hang of adding and subtracting using cowry shells, I quietly helped Robert, him with the pissy gusset, attempting to save him from further savagery.

Very early on I'd learnt that if I managed to remain unscathed through the morning, there was little risk of harm in afternoon sessions of drawing, sticky paper patterning or taking part in music and movement, especially as the latter was overseen by a different teacher. At break time we sometimes played football and with all the boys being my age or younger, I soon improved and in the rounders matches occasionally organised for the afternoon, rather than the single team-sash, I wore the captain's crossed-braids and felt such pride, didn't want to take them off.

There were three attractive girls in the top group and if my luck was in, I'd be invited to play with them. Not girls' games, for I was the doctor and they acted as either nurses or patients. Although my role didn't stray into the realms of inviting a thrashing with a 12-inch ruler, the game still offered a certain stimulation. Also, we sometimes walked around the grounds on stumpy stilts, or did somersaults on the climbing frame, with them pretending not to notice what I couldn't help taking a glance at.

They had a certain something that set them apart from other girls and Roger Pritchard, back at Clee View had become so besotted by the one called Kathlene, he'd forgiven an earlier transgression of mine, being avid for any information I could pass on. With him attending the junior school, the only glimpse he could gain of his heart's desire was by lingering at the entrance to our school.

It wasn't unusual to be grabbed by the scruff to be asked, "You wanner playing doctors and nurses again was yah?"

I had begun to decipher the local way English tended to be spoken thereabouts and would answer, "No Roger, they don't always ask me to join them."

"You better not be lying!"

"I'm not lying. They were busy doing girls' things and I played football."

My first meeting with him hadn't gone at all well. In fact, in the early days, I got on better with his older brother, David, for with Roger giving the impression there had somehow been a powder keg in his making, it caused me to give him a wide berth.

The incident in question came about following an invite the new boy in the road received, to play on Pritchard's back lawn. You have to remember I was fresh from the country and at the time, not only knew nothing about football or cricket, I also had not the faintest clue regarding the dynamics of camping. I could hear boy's laughter coming from beneath the canopy, but on approaching, tripped on a guy rope. Alarmed by the noise erupting I took a step back and became so entangled in a taut support, it caused the front end of the tent to sag. Then on hearing what was in the offing for the idiot responsible, it caused such alarm I stumbled over another guy rope, to leave the campers furiously wrestling like puppies in a sack.

"Might be a wise move to make yourself scarce," suggested David, barely able to talk through laughter. "Come on. I'll show you the gap through to the orchard."

David was actually known to us all as Copper, on account of his mop of red hair and I felt quite privileged that someone four years my senior should bother to come to my assistance. Never occurred to me, it could have been on account of him fancying my sister, so when Roger crashed in chasing me round bushes and trees, my plea for help was answered by him appreciating my predicament, but that didn't mean he was prepared to fight my battles for me. Even on the next circuit beseeching him further, he answered, I had to learn to stand up for myself.

All very well, but his brother was blessed with extraordinary strength and when riled could do immense damage. Luckily, I was a bit nippier than he was, but even so, couldn't keep dodging around bushes all day.

He snarled at me across a thicket. "You canna hope to keep this up! And when I catches holt on ya, you'll wish you wanner born!"

As he made another lunge, I yelled over a shoulder, "I'm sorry. I couldn't help it!" and arching my back just managed to evade clutching fingers. It was on the next circuit, the change of colour in Copper's face became evident, his laughter having sent it from freckled pallid, to as red as the hair on his head.

"Can't you do something?" I pleaded.

"No, you'll have to learn to look after yourself."

Both Roger and myself were now panting, me looking like a hunted fawn, him seething like a minotaur. The predicament wasn't helped by the tale I'd been told. One day, when having had a difference of opinion with his father he'd flung a stone that had made a perfectly round hole in the topmost pane of the kitchen window, which was then immediately matched by the one in Roger's scalp, from a stone flung in return.

An ambulance was called for, but like a wildcat, he'd fought off all attempts to get him inside, screeching, "You're not taking me to any fucking hospital!" Even when Mr. Pritchard lent a hand, he still wriggled free and only when a neighbour rushed to help, did the four bruised adults manage to wrestle a wild six-year-old into the back of the vehicle.

Now here he was, much bigger and older, threatening all sorts of horrors, if only he could lay his hands on me.

I had a fair turn of speed in those pre-teen years, but I'd also been blessed with stamina and so somehow did eventually manage to make it back home unscathed. The experience obviously shook me, but I reasoned, if I avoided Roger for a while he was bound to calm down and also, if I successfully negotiated such teething problems, the locality held everything I'd been missing.

I of course had to decipher their way of speaking and when in polite company, avoid some of the words they used, but all in all I was absolutely thrilled by the situation I found myself in. Regarding swear words, I must point out much of their discourse was peppered with them, but it would become tedious to faithfully copy what was said, so instead I'll just pop the odd one in as a reminder and leave the rest to the imagination.

It wasn't long before I could climb the easier nearby trees and from one there hung a rope to swing on, which no-one minded, but even though fascinated by a camp built down the lane with a fire crackling outside, I was told, only those having helped in the construction were allowed to enter.

I longed to join them trekking off for adventures across the fields, for when regaled with tales of being chased, or amazing things discovered, myself and other juniors had to be satisfied by being nothing more than awestruck listeners. On account of his strength, Roger was allowed to join them, Mick Woodcock and Pete Clark would sometimes be taken along, but there seemed to be a certain extra required, before the likes of myself would be accepted. Of course they didn't want to lumber themselves with a liability, plus there was something that had to be earnt first; respect.

Meanwhile there were two living next door, roughly my age, I could play with, but when those I yearned to join departed for the wild beyond, it left the street feeling decidedly tame.

Young girls slopped around in their mother's old high heels and frocks, often leading infants round like little chimps on their haunches, or sat in huddles, with dolls and tea-sets beneath a blanket held up like a tent. Others skipped, played Jacks, made mud pies, or for some reason ladled dust onto plates or into plastic cups, using teaspoons. Tiny boys rattled around on huge black bicycles. When on a ladies' bike, the saddles prodded the mid-back region and to master a gents' machine they rode slightly askew, using one leg beneath the crossbar to reach the far pedal.

Boys and girls often played cricket or rounders in the road, hopscotch on the pavement and at night beneath the lamppost near the end of our front path, games such as Old Grey Mare, Grandmother's Footsteps or Jack, can I cross the water. In the closing stages of the latter game, the colours blue and white became prevalent in the hope the girls would have to show their knickers before being allowed across the road.

While still finding my feet, I often played with the two boys I mentioned, one a year older, the other a year younger than myself. We made a camp on top of their tool shed and clattered down the road in our pedal cars. Both Anthony, the eldest boy and myself had outgrown the vehicles and needed to rest our legs on the bonnets, relying on gravity to provide the motion. If we then pushed the vehicles along Riddings Road, we could descend further, bouncing and rattling down the concrete slabbed road as far as Rock Lane, a continuation of that ancient drover's road mentioned. Momentum took us past the derelict cottage where Dirty Dan slept, but we never lingered or ventured further as beyond lay forbidden territory.

The dwellings along Sandpits Avenue and Rock Lane had been built many years before our houses had even been dreamt of and youths living there strongly resented the newcomers moving into what they considered their patch of territory. Apparently, rabbits had abounded and somewhere in the scheme of things there had been a sizeable pool. Children of the first colonists came under regular attack, to the point they found need to construct a barrier across the end of the lane, a redoubt they could defend when under a hail of stones. By the time I appeared on the scene, things had calmed somewhat, but when listening to tales of epic battles told around the campfire I almost longed for another flare-up.

As it was, however, these were calmer days, where those poaching rabbits were allowed free passage through to our fields and we were tolerated when passing through their territory to collect offcuts from the wood yard or coke from the gas works. Never alone though. Only a fool would risk that and it was years before I saw what the very end of the avenue looked like.

The word avenue, by the way, must have been a planner's idea of a joke, as it conjures up an image of tree-lined bliss. There were no trees and certainly no bliss. We were told by the rent collector, all the problem families tended to be put far end, so as not to cause too much mayhem for those living nearest Briggs's, the local shop. Apparently in winter, doors were often chopped up for firewood and coal kept in the bath. I believed the firewood part of the story, but did suspect the coal in the bath notion could be what we now call an urban myth. But when folk come home fighting drunk, let their lurcher dogs roam everywhere, chuck all sorts of mess out into the front gardens and leave sofas to rot in the street, others have a tendency to believe anything said about them.

In the fruit picking and spud-bashing season, old army trucks would collect and take them to the fields, children included, leaving numerous classroom desks abandoned and years later, many of the gypsy words they used became common parlance about the town. Chav, by the way, originally meant child and so if this was sneered in one's direction, it implied milksop or greenhorn; and gorger, which gradually evolved to mean, divvy or dope, originally meant non-gypsy. In other words, when calling someone a gorger, it was loaded with absolute disdain for those supposedly their betters, to the extent, they actually considered themselves superior to those having to slave away in their sensible lives.

As an interesting sidenote, many of the families living in the famed street were remarkably fecund, but one amazing lady outdid the lot of them, giving birth to twenty-two children, eighteen of whom survived.

The pronounced slope of the hill we lived on meant the neighbour's kitchen window at the lower end of our semi was way above the path and as I played with the Owen boys their mother's face would often beam down as if from a television screen. The slightest thing would send her into hoots of laughter and so it was hard to imagine her ever being anything other than cheerful.

Brother Michael pulling up their antirrhinums one bright morning put paid to that notion. He thought he'd help the neighbours by doing a little weeding and when Anthony, the eldest boy, tried to stop him, he sent him sprawling into the flower bed. I was astounded that a four-year-old had managed to upend a very solid nine-year-old and just wished I'd been there to see it, but I did happen to be there when Mrs. Owen stomped round in such a fury to deliver an unbroken tirade aimed at the region just above my mother's hairline. At the tightening of folded arms, her ample bosom swelled to bring such intensity, the blast could have removed a hairpiece. There wasn't much logic but a theme eventually emerged along the lines of, it was bad enough for the flowers to be pulled up, but what really rankled was her AnTHONee, as she called him, being pushed into the remnants. She actually fizzed with indignation when calling my four-year-old brother a bully.

"Goodness! He's less than half your son's age. I apologise for the flowers, but quite honestly, I do think you are being totally ridiculous." With that, mother quietly closed the back door.

Michael was of course reprimanded, but for some strange reason got away with disfiguring a section of wall in the newly decorated sitting room. Mr Owen from next door was a top-rate painter and decorator and even constructed alcove bookshelves and a mantlepiece. The wallpaper pattern had been carefully matched, the smell of fresh paint hit as you opened the door and there, down to the right was a scruffy patch rubbed through to the pink of the plaster.

I called out, "Mum, there's a hole rubbed in the new wallpaper!"

"I know. It was Michael. He was only trying to help."

"Help? How?"

"Doing a bit of polishing."

I wouldn't have given much for my chances had I done it. But in actual fact, years later, when Mike and I had both left home, mother looked upon that little patch with a sad sense of nostalgia.

Even though it was convenient to play with the two next door, my heart yearned for adventures with the other local boys. Trouble was, abandoning those who had helped me through the teething phase of living locally would have seemed like treachery, but how was I ever going to be accepted and taken on wild adventures if I continued playing with those who didn't even mix with them?

We did ambush the Post Office van once, causing it to screech to a halt in the road. We fled with our bows to the bottom of the orchard and when I dared return to the house, recoiled at the sight of a policeman walking along our path. Much later, having plucked up enough courage to return for tea, I was told, the officer had merely called to collect a handbag my mother had found abandoned at a social function.

That incident and a walk to the bottom of Angel Bank in my first attempt at scaling the western face of Titterstone Clee, were the highlights of my time with the Owen boys and I puzzled how I was going to slip away and join those permanently living on the wild side. A football was the answer, but more of that later.

In the final weeks of remedial studies at the infant's school, I could hardly wait for my time of enrolment at East Hamlet Junior School where I would meet up with Mrs. Bodenham again. I know I'd only spent half a day with her, but instincts told me we would become as close as if she had been a favourite aunt. My reading ability had improved beyond all measure, but I still remained at my original desk in the dunces' corner alongside pissy Robert. The very one I'd often helped when he'd struggled with maths. It was here I learnt a vital lesson; some people never forgive a favour. Following a minor misdemeanour, he raised his hand and reported the matter to the teacher and I waited apprehensively, thinking my first and only meeting with the 12-inch ruler was imminent.

Miss Holland looked at me long and hard, then simply said, "Don't do it again."

Thus came another lesson; we all make mistakes, but some are allowed to get away with them.

In the last house, bottom of the road, lived a fairly ordinary couple, who you couldn't even envisage craftily lifting a buttock to pass wind, so imagine how shocked I was to hear Aunty Rita relating to my mother, how she had called one day to find a smiling Mr. Brown totally naked, but for a cat on his lap for decency. Declining an offer to stroke the moggy, my aunt had taken her leave, saying she would return when Mrs. Brown was back in residence.

The relating of the tale had the sisters doubled up with hoots of laughter, heightened by the revelation, not only did the Browns occasionally play strip poker, Mrs. Brown had once walked around the block stark-naked for a dare.

They were a very private couple and apart from Mrs. Brown, with her congenital hip problem, jerkily walking down to Briggs's shop, pulling her wicker shopping trolley, you rarely saw either of them. So imagine how surprised I was to see a smiling Mr. Brown on the flat roof of our school, lobbing down balls that had been lost up there. He'd been the school caretaker all along and I'd not realised.

Just up the road from us lived the weatherman; always leaning out of his bedroom window when the sun shone, but as soon as my mother and sister ceased sunbathing on the back lawn, he'd instantly disappear. Both he and his wife came from large families and so fairly regularly there came the need for Saturday, weddings', births' and deaths' outfits, but whatever the venue, by the time they'd made it up the gradual rise far side of the hill from us, the man's choice of bad-blood bitter and his wife's tipple of shrieking sherry would have them fired up into such a blazing row, on cresting the hill we'd receive full benefit, but once behind closed doors things became relatively muted, sounding more like a bargee couple quarrelling over kitchenware.

We had our fair share of ordinary, everyday people and directly round the corner, bottom of the road, lived the Williams's. All the folks in the two streets tended to visit one another, but I'd not heard of a single person who'd ever been inside their house. Mr. Williams was a plasterer who parked his ex-Post Office van at night in the end of the lane and his wife had a habit of hoisting up her bosom to scratch beneath as she talked to a neighbour with a voice like a corncrake. Their only child Bernard, was probably in his early 20's and regularly used the street lamp near the entrance to the lane to shed light on his motorbike maintenance. He had a vast collection of war comics and also those booklets where the naked ladies stand coyly holding a beachball over the most interesting part. Either that, or the negative had always been altered to show just a blank triangle in the pubic area.

I don't know what need he had of all those thoroughly bland books, considering he had a fiancée who regularly rode pillion? In fact it was one of those long South Shropshire engagements that never did end in marriage. Meanwhile, I remember us yearning, wondering what it would be like to have a job from heaven? Being a photographer for a nudist magazine.

# Junior School

It was well over half a mile to East Hamlet Junior School, but we thought nothing of walking it. Just as well, for other than for business, very few owned a car back then, and the same applied to telephones, for the Clarks in Riddings Road were the only family to have such an appliance, being essential for running the print business crammed into the front room.

It brought a slight sense of elation to be at last walking into the massive main schoolroom, for now feeling confident enough to cope with lessons, it was almost like arriving at a stage of my destiny. I still wasn't brilliant at spelling, but the teacher made little of it and as regards my habit of adding e's to the end of words for good luck, she simply laughed and called me Johnee Cleggee.

I don't care what method of teaching one might subscribe to, for a certain few manage to transcend all latest fads by innate ability alone. Mrs Bodenham possessed that gift, making it seem effortless. The classroom held over forty pupils from all backgrounds and she reigned supreme as if conducting an orchestra. Children wanted to succeed for her. She had a way of bringing the best out of them and I for one managed to work my way into the top group, glowing with pride when she read some of my stories to the class.

To maintain the drive for excellence we were divided into four teams, red, yellow, green and blue, with any work of merit being given a coloured star, whether mental arithmetic, spelling tests, writing short stories or painting. Each team had a captain for the month, cajoling members to do their best and when I had the privilege of being the red team captain, we won with numerous stars to spare.

There were two educational sides to the school: A, being possible Grammar and High School material, then B containing those destined for the Secondary Modern and annually the various years of both sides played each other at football up at that recreation ground I mentioned. The night before, I could hardly sleep and must have checked my kit at least three times. I'd been given an Arsenal shirt as a birthday present, had a pair of red woollen socks and with the blue shorts being a remnant of my stepfather's playing days in Devon, they needed rolling over four times at the waist to prevent them tripping me up.

We all clumped to the pitch in leather-studded boots and when the whistle went, all but the two goalies swarmed after the ball, trace of passage being marked by the fallen. Taking a short break from the melee, I discussed with two classmates the fact this wasn't the way to play the game, but seeing no immediate alternative, we re-entered the fray.

Following a frenetic period of hacking and kicking in our penalty area, the ball finally squirted free to take refuge beyond our goal line. I remember trudging back to school feeling as disconsolate as if we'd just lost the FA cup.

Mrs Bodenham broke off conversation with another teacher to enquire, "How did you get on?"

"We lost, Miss. They kept shinning us."

They both found the word, 'shinning,' highly amusing, not realising what a crushing blow we had to cope with, followed by the ignominious helplessness when enduring the jibes later.

Now here's a surprise. One bright afternoon when all were engaged in painting, last lesson before home time, we had a little visitor.

110

# First day at school

Late-afternoon, first year at Junior School;
Up with the big kids, an infant no more.
Two per desk, packed forty with ink, nibs and blots;
All turned towards small silhouette at the door.
"Who's this then?" Teacher offered a welcoming arm;
His face glowed with health, "Come to see my brother."
Large serious brown eyes searched the room for me.
"Walked all that way, did you tell your mother?"

First question, he nodded, second, shook his head.
She thought for a while, then had him sit by me.
"No phone to ring home? Stay paint a nice picture.
John can walk you back, have you there for tea."
Then quietly reasoning, although now a big boy,
Four years old and of course welcome to stay,
"Promise you'll never go wandering again;"
What staggered her, was how he'd found his way!

She took from him, "What a weight!" my old torn mac.
Laughed at extraction of rocks from pockets.
"Lucky stones," he explained desk top rockery.
When asked, "What's the painting?" Dark frown, "Rockets!"
They all made a fuss of him. Told, "Simmer down."
One's such days recalled by most as a rule.
Can't remember mine, yet patently clear,
Won't forget my brother's first day at school.

As regards 10-year-old David, aka Copper, you might have
wondered about the adult way he spoke and you were right to
wonder, for he had a bit of something about him that got him into

the Grammar School, which so shocked his family, they bought him a drop-handlebar racing bike from Downs's shop in Old Street. The whole area was proud of him, for looking as if he'd made it in life, he would rattle through the derailleurs when creaming around the corner to go racing off down Riddings Road, or cycling the other way, could effortlessly glide to the summit of Clee View, by simply clicking down a gear.

A number of local girls had hopes of emulating my sister and passing to the High School, but most of the boys couldn't wait to leave school, get a job and earn some money. Going to the Grammar School meant playing Rugby rather than their beloved football, plus none wanted to be split up from their mates. When I earned a reputation for having my head buried in a book, I'd often be told by one of the wise elders, "Don't know what you want all that edumacation for. Never did me no good."

I'd already found one benefit, for when Mrs. Bodenham asked for volunteers one day to take part in a classroom play, I swiftly read the script and volunteered for the part as the peasant. The lovely tousle haired Kathlene was the princess and I relished the chance of kissing her at the end, for the peasant was the real prince in disguise.

The thwarted prince-pretender was of course put out, but nowhere near as much as David's brother Roger who was still madly besotted by Kathlene and when news of a certain kissing reached him, he grabbed me by the scruff to demand, "You didn't bloody-well kiss her did you?"

"Couldn't help it Roger. It was part of the play."

"You better not have done!"

"Don't worry, it was only a dress rehearsal."

"What d'you mean?"

"We've got to do the real thing tomorrow."

"If I gets to hear you've bin kissin' her again, I'll bloody-well throttle yah!"

After brooding for a while he asked, "What was it like?"

He and I had started to get on a little better of late and I could feel a bond building, but meanwhile still felt indebted and tied to the Owen brothers.

Roger's brother David, continued to amaze, winning the Grammar School's under 15 cross-country. Never before had a first-year student ever done this and I doubt it's ever been done since. I viewed his achievements with awe and slight envy, for by passing the 11+ he'd done the educational equivalent of slipping through the eye of a needle. The catchment area for the Grammar School was huge and each year only about 32 were accepted. Even though I felt confidence building, helped of course by Mrs. Bodenham, I could still sense the pressure mounting. Somehow, I had to pass that 11+ exam, but it seemed like a mountain to climb.

Now this is where a football came into the scheme of things. It must have been a Christmas present. A proper case ball. The thing we had been using had been stitched-up countless times; its bladder had patch upon patch; when wet it was like kicking a stuffed bag of suet and anyone daring to head it risked a sodden braining.

One day I was mildly surprised to see Copper walking along our path, for someone so much older than myself arriving specifically to request my presence down at the football field where many of my elders awaited, left me rather awestruck. It was when he added, I needed to bring the football, I began to get the drift.

I felt rather bashful walking past the Owen brothers.

"Aren't you going to play with us?"

"Yes, as soon as the game's over."

"Don't bother," sneered Anthony. "You only wanted us when you had no-one else to play with."

I did squirm rather at such perception and even more when Copper said jeeringly. "Don't know why you bothered with those two drips anyway!"

Roger and Mick Woodcock, a year ahead of me at school, were still younger than most of the boys there, but had enough natural flair to hold their own. Meanwhile, although I'd improved, in reality my presence was only tolerated on account of me owning the only decent football in the whole area.

I had detected a little resentment manifest itself in certain unnecessary remarks and so had mixed feelings when days later I was invited to join them in a foray over towards Bluebell Wood. Something didn't feel quite right. Too many smiles and it was all too friendly. Somewhere in the region of Shaky Bridge, was where they bolted, hoping I'd become hopelessly lost amongst shrubs and brambles. Of course I felt betrayed, but wasn't going to let them get the better of me and so took off after them. When catching up with the two ring-leaders I asked, "What are we running from?"

They returned a searing glare and so were even more annoyed, when having run off again, I overtook the stragglers to breeze up to where they were both bent double, fighting for breath. The eldest Woodcock, Brian, actually looked in pain, wheezing like a punctured organ, while the other, who was eldest of the two Greenhills, wore such a sneer, his utterance of, "You fuckin' lanky bastard," seemed almost laughable by comparison.

I might not have matched them at football, but I could run and so held on to that tiny shred of comfort without replying.

The next little incident happened in the eastern goalmouth of the town football pitch. The downside of owning the only decent football, was the fact it was difficult to depart once you'd had enough. We had played all morning, to the point my muscles and groin ached and when fresh arrivals demanded I join them all for an afternoon session, my heart sank. I had enough sense not to let them take possession of the ball and so reluctantly forced myself to take part, even though every muscle below the waist felt locked solid. With tea-time beckoning and seeing one lad dangling from the crossbar singing, "Lady of Spain I adore you. I'll pull down your drawers and explore you," while three other survivors of the marathon, lay sprawled on the grass, I told them I was taking my ball home.

I heard, "That's what you think," and found myself wrestled to the ground, with even Copper joining in the playful jabbing. I was let go, then thrown to the ground again with the jabs becoming more vicious and after about the fifth time of being toyed with like a mouse, I have to admit it, I started to cry. When they'd finally tired of their game, I got to my feet and when safely from range blurted, "I'm telling our mum!"

Well you can imagine the impact that had. They all burst out laughing. Deep throated laughter from pubescent boys.

My mother appreciated my distress, but said she couldn't fight my battles for me. "Go down there and hit them back!"

"But they're much older than me!"

"I'm sorry dear, but you'll just have to learn to look after yourself."

"How can I? There are four of them."

"Then hit the biggest!"

I tell you what, I was so mad at the injustice of it, I marched back down with tears of rage glinting and waded in with fists flailing. Copper got special attention for his treachery and they were all so shocked they backed off.

Yes, there was a bad patch to come, but I didn't get picked on by that lot again.

Fights at school were often the highlight of school breaks. The cry of, "Fight! Fight!" would have most boys running, usually towards the playground meant for exclusive use of the B side of the school. After a few swings, most encounters ended as a scrabbling battle on the floor until one was able to sit on the chest of the other and with fist raised ask, "D'ya give in?" A couple of noteworthy scraps, however, were like proper boxing matches, fists punching like pistons until the one with the bloodied nose, or swollen eye closing like a clam, retreated to the classroom.

Mr. Williams, the only male teacher known to all as Daddy Williams, would sometimes intervene administering slaps about the head and it wasn't unusual to see him armed with a cricket stump, chasing a miscreant, to only give up when the boy had fled towards Sandpits or onto the Dodmore estate.

In the front playground, the A section of the school, there was a smooth tarmacked section ideal for sliding on frosty mornings, but most of the rest had ample craters where marbles could be played. Not a genteel rolling, for the rough terrain only allowed something akin to aerial bombardment, made all the more dramatic if the marble-pit held rain water.

One lad said to me, "Came to school with just three marls, now look at this." He used both hands to squeeze the huge bulge in a pocket of his shorts.

The marbles were of coloured glass, with the jacks being four times the size of those in the ring. Some boys brought ball bearings to school, but had such an unfair advantage the cry would go up, "No baldies allowed," which of course didn't refer to a crestfallen little man.

The terrain was ideal for marbles, but if unlucky enough to take a tumble or get flung off the end of the line in chain tick, it wasn't so good on the knees. Many a child needed lumps of grit gently easing from a wound with disinfected cotton wool, before being sent back out to rejoin the fray, bandaged and stiff legged.

One small section of the playground, opposite the Catholic Church, was high walled on three sides like a courtyard and here dodge ball or British Bulldogs was played. In dodge ball, boys would line up backs to the wall and the last to get hit had his turn as the ball thrower. In the latter game, all had to run to the safety of the far wall without being caught and lifted, by the lone catcher. Any thus caught, had to join in the catching until only the winner remained at large. He would then be the one in the middle starting the game off again.

When the game commenced it was like a cavalry charge, but at the end, more like hare coursing. Clothes were ripped and knees were grazed, but it was great fun. It was also useful in determining allegiances and physical strength of certain participants. If a particularly influential individual commanded the centre, it wasn't unusual for those seeking favour, to allow themselves to be lifted so they could all hunt as a pack. I've seen boys a tantalising finger tip from safety, but as it was against the rules to help, I'd have to witness them being dragged back and lifted to the cry of, "British Bulldog!" It was not always the heftiest that prevailed, for some of the smaller boys were incredibly hard to catch, side-stepping and wriggling free, perfect candidates for rugby, but alas, most went on to play football.

It was about this time the film, Davy Crockett was released, causing fake racoon hats to abound in the neighbourhood and boys never seemed to tire of playing the role, king of the wild frontier. Between the A and B playgrounds was a tall wooden gate made of braced open slats, ideal for restaging the siege of the Alamo. The aim was to invade the other playground by forcing the gate or climbing over it and the intense struggle could last the entire play period and would have gone on for much longer, had it been allowed.

A girl in the top year was called Maggie and if feeling fit and spry, a cry of "Maggie, Maggie magpie," would have her chasing you like the devil. You had to keep running and dodging mind you, for if she caught you, she'd knock the living daylights out of you. Standing breathless in our lines at the end of break, her threatening side glance could seem almost sexual and I quite missed her when she went down to the big school.

Occasionally Mr. Briscoe, the child catcher would march the length of our classroom escorting a fugitive through to the headmistress. His captive would often be a feral looking child few remembered seeing before. I recall one girl in a filthy ragged dress, sniffing a huge yellow candle of snot back into her dirt smudged face, as she looked around in sheer terror as if about to be caged. Most boys brought in had filthy faces and wore ragged over-sized hand-me-downs that had an acrid smell, the sort of aroma that could be achieved if drying smelly socks over a camp fire, but the school rarely held them long enough for us to find out who they were.

I realised I must have grown a lot bigger by the end of that first year, because in a competition to see who could piss furthest up the wall in the boy's toilet, only Geoffrey Tomkinson and myself managed to aim it through the airbrick at the top. A passer-by with coat collar freshly darkened put a stop to that, reporting the matter to the headmistress, who threatened corporal punishment should it happen again. Luckily she didn't attempt to identify the champion pissers and as the school was later closed and converted into apartments, Geoffrey and myself must reign as champions to this day.

Although tall for my age and quite a good assailer of trees, there were certain notable ones I still couldn't master, for the lowest limbs were beyond my reach. Being able to climb the apple tree at the bottom of the orchard, almost became like a rite of passage, but even though able to touch the lowest fork when taking a running leap, I still couldn't grasp one of the branches.

High in that tree an important abode had been constructed and you can imagine the frustration of hearing chatter and laughter as they beavered away, but me being unable to get up there.

# In a young man's mind

What do naked ladies look like? Can be high
On the list when not much more than seven.
Big kid Johnie from top of the hill, had said with a sigh,
"Not much to look at, but feels like heaven."
Most of the big kids were usually looked up to.
And so able, to roam with them far and wide,
Scrumping, exploring and do what they do,
Was enough to swell a young breast with pride.

Yet nothing more likely to cause frustration;
High antics in branches when upwardly gazing;
Listening, watching tree-house creation;
Exclamations heard, "Fantastic! Amazing!"
Discussions drifting, which piece should go where?
To share in their laughter would have been sublime.
It seemed incredible fun. Life just wasn't fair.
They'd constructed their camp where I couldn't climb.

As far as naked ladies went, there were of course those well-thumbed little books, providing Bernard from around the corner let you look at them, but apart from that the nearest thing to titillation was derived from the Brian Mills clothing catalogue.

I remember Copper knocking on the door one day, "Is your mum in?"

"No. Why?"

"Let's have another look at her Brian Mills catalogue?"

The pages of swimsuits, corsets and brassieres were turned over, but ever so slowly.

# The younger gang

One of the best things regarding living on a council estate in those days, was not knowing what the day would bring. Anything could happen, literally on a whim. Obviously latest films were an inspiration and sporting events could fire us into action, but often it might be nothing more than a chance occurrence.

A whack of stone with a stick, sending it unerringly into a nearby drain could have us all playing a form of golf, from manhole covers to drains at the bottom of the road, or Pete Clark announcing he'd got his Mobo scooter to go further than ever before, could have us all rattling down Clee View on pedal cars and go-carts. I say on the pedal cars, for we'd all outgrown them and I've known three share the same vehicle, the driver sprawled with legs on the bonnet, another perched on the bonnet itself, plus a third swept-haired voyager standing on the back. Obviously the all clear had to be given before taking the sharp right-hander at the bottom, lest an unwitting neighbour joined the crew.

Many of the older boys had obtained part-time jobs or had become more interested in girls rather than escapades we got up to and so our little band of ragamuffins was led by Roger. Obviously, there was nothing stopping older youths from joining us if they cared to and at times the younger ones were invited along providing the mission was not too arduous.

I had moved on from Mrs. Bodenham's class and was now in Mrs. Ash's, our number having been whittled down to 30. There were three rows of double desks with five in each row, so each group, top, middle and bottom had ten students. The top group, were mostly those held back for a year, while the rest of us were there by virtue of being likely candidates for the top class, where the imperious and revered Miss Perry held sway. If you could make it into her class, you stood a better than average chance of passing the 11+ exam to the Grammar School. I was now as good as any of my classmates regarding reading and writing, but my brain didn't seem to cope well with multiplication and long division. It wasn't helped by our monetary and measuring systems being so arcane and I knew if my reckoning was running into a second page, I'd slipped up somewhere. I had to pass that 11+ exam somehow and could feel the pressure building.

Before I go on, I'd better mention here how Copper fitted into the scheme of things. Even though he'd broken ranks and passed to the Grammar School, the older boys still respected him and he was never shunned with the usual sneer of, "Piss off Grammar dog!" He was just that bit older than any of us in Roger's little band and so wasn't usually included in the general business of the day, but because of his athleticism, always took part in running and bike races round the block and occasionally, the ideas he came up with when tinkering away in his washhouse could inspire us to such an extent, we looked upon him as a sort of mad professor.

He and his brother were constantly falling out, with Roger being called a Philistine for never having read a book and Copper being called a bighead in return, but you could tell Roger secretly admired his brother and wouldn't have put up with anyone else deriding him. In fact he often related the crazy things Copper had got up to in the past.

Long before I knew them, Copper had purloined his sister Jane's plastic headed doll with which to conduct an important experiment. All the council houses had Rayburn stoves and beside them lay a tubular poker for ignition, connected to the town gas supply. What could possibly go wrong?

Well, what Copper did after announcing the amazing forthcoming performance of the flame throwing doll, was to fill its head with gas and then strike a match. The blast left him with a bemused expression and a headless doll.

Not deterred by Jane attacking him for blowing up her pride and joy, he returned to his washhouse lab to think. The conclusion was, the human element had been missing and all were rallied once again to witness the never seen before, amazing mortal fire breather.

Once again, the coal gas, once again the grand striking of the match and then all watched mesmerized as the expression of triumph led to one of misgivings, closely followed by panic on realising his breath was giving out, but not the tongue of flame. When the whites of his eyes, amid black and smoke finally blinked with relief, his audience erupted into side aching laughter, for not a single facial hair remained, with even his fringe having gone.

A smoky, "Don't try this at home folks," had them almost wetting themselves.

Roger was the natural leader of the usual six or eight of us and so was obviously put out whenever witnessing his brother's interventions and madcap schemes gaining favour. Therefore, when seeing a massive roll of binder twine being produced one day, God knows where he'd got it from, he sneered, "So what the hell d'you hope to do with that?"

"Make a camp."

"Now he has gone mad! Whoever heard of a string camp?"

Nonetheless, we all followed down the lane to see what the mad professor had planned for the day. In a place with overhanging branches, we helped him hack out the undergrowth and nettles, held the branches as he tied them to pegs in the ground, then watched as the interweaving began. An opening was left for the door and he continued back and forth until a string and branch-walled chamber took shape.

"OK if you want a giant fucking mouse's nest," commented Roger.

"Hold your horses. I haven't finished yet."

In the Big Field opposite, the mown grass had been baled and collected, but some remained around the meadow perimeter, which was gathered for him to weave into the mesh and spread on the floor, giving all a cosy look. Looking at each other in amazement, we couldn't wait to give it a try.

Roger now took over, sending us in search of wood and after testing for wind direction, had a blaze going at a safe distance away from the camp door.

"You can sit by your fire if you like, but some of us still have work to do," called Copper, who started busying himself again with the string.

"Whatever's the mad bugger up to now?" asked Roger, shaking his head in disbelief.

We could see his brother beavering away, but left him to it, for even when questioned he didn't divulge his latest plan. He'd almost been forgotten, but suddenly a Tarzan like yell made all look up and lurching towards us was Copper, jerkily announcing, "The treetop walkway is now open."

Each step on the string supports sent him into a plummet as if trying to walk over waves and all winced expecting to see him caught like a fly, but finally with knees quivering in the attempt to remain upright, he beat his chest to let out a Tarzan-like yodel.

"Now you canna tell me that's normal," said Roger in disbelief.

The new camp served as a focus of attention for the next few days until one morning we found it wrecked. The string hung in pathetic strands and the hay had been mockingly strewn across the lane.

"Sandpits!" said Roger.

We held a council of war, interrupted by Tommie's dog Nip. His trick was to drop a stone at your feet and wait expectantly, eyes excited, willing you to throw it. To get rid of him, the stone would be hurled as far into the nearest field as possible, but seconds later you'd hear a plop and there it would be, back at your feet again.

Tommy lived five doors on from Pete and four on from Francie, just before Riddings Road took a dip down towards Rock Lane. He had relatives in the Avenue and as luck had it, one had told him of a camp the Sandpit's gang had constructed down at Tay's pond.

Although we all knew where Tay's pond lay, with its crested newts and frogs, the importance of the operation required a map to be drawn. Roger scratched one in the dust and central to all, a stone was dropped by Nip the dog.

"Fuck off, Nip!" said Roger flinging the stone away and then continued by sketching out the approach route. "We'll take them from the west and if they put up a fight, we can drive them into the ----."

The dog deftly deposited the stone, dead centre of the supposed Tay's pond.

"Thank you, Nip," said Roger removing it, adding, "Look Tommy, can't you do something about this flaming dog of yours?"

Exasperated at us seeing the funny side, he said, "It's alright you lot laughing, but this is a serious matter. Now let's all get mounted."

Armed with our trusty sticks, we climbed onto the imaginary steeds, and making suitable hoof-like noises with the tongue and giving ourselves the odd whack across the backside, cantered down towards Tay's pond. With me being the Indian scout, my mount was a Pinto pony.

At Roger's signal, we reined in and even though a glance was enough to ascertain the camp was deserted, I was sent to spy out the land. Behind I could hear ponies, frisky at the expectation of the imminent charge, having to be brought to order. I added a little drama by creeping up to the camp's entrance and after returning to deliver the report, remounted and waited. The air crackled with tension, with only the whinny of an impetuous pony breaking the silence. A glare from our leader restored calm and then with his dramatic pointing of a finger, we all thundered in, scattering the flimsy construction to all corners.

Satisfied we had exacted revenge, we cantered back towards Clee View, triumph tinged with disappointment at there having been no inmates to chase off. We had the most magical steeds, not requiring rubbing down, feeding or mucking out and when we'd finished with them, they disappeared as if never having been there in the first place.

Amongst some of my ancient scribblings I found the following regarding Nip, Tommy's persistent dog.

# Nip

If Nip, a mix of terrier along with border collie,
Happens along to present you with a stone;
Bright eyes say, 'Throw it,' but don't it's utter folly,
For from then on, you'll not be left alone.

Even hurling damn thing as far as you could;
Into hedge, bushes, swaying field of wheat;
Chuck it into pasture, deepest, darkest wood,
Turn your back, he'd be back to drop it at your feet.

Swear, shout or threaten; no good all part of game.
He could turn, dodge and had answer for ignore.
Turn of back was useless, to him was all the same,
Bark, bounce, scratching an interruption with his paw.

Stone, mid-marble-ring was his best party piece.
Instinct was to swear, chuck it down the street.
'Works every time,' he'd think, 'Wonders never cease.'
Bright-eyed retrieving, it would be back there at your feet.


With members of both gangs from Sandpits and the Airey houses having to attend the same schools, raids could almost be arranged by appointment and so we were well aware of a likely visitation the following Saturday and although confident we could resist the incursion, the news leaked through that a certain Jasper, newly released from whatever institution he had been held in, could be included in their number. His real name was Robert, but with him having a nasty streak he had also been given the local name for wasp. Few had ever seen him as he'd rarely attended school and had spent a good deal of his time on remand, but rumour had it he was an unpleasant piece of work to be avoided at all cost.

As usual, Tommy had advance warning of their arrival, plus the worrying snippet, Jasper was armed with a table leg. Roger gathered the troops and luckily we had Mick Woodcock's elder brother, Brian, plus Copper along with us that day. Even so, the youngest Woodcock, Robert, nicknamed Eecock was sent up to the Smout's house, top of Clee View and Pete was sent to the house recently vacated by the Greenhill family to ask if the new lad, Alan, would care to join our little band. Pete had already told us his elder brother Robert was off working with his father for the day, but avoiding any mention of Jasper, did return with the new recruit keen for action.

John Smout, however was readying himself for an assignation with a young belle he was due to meet that very afternoon and so Eecock, arriving red in the face and out of breath, blurted, "Smouter canner come 'cos he's off seeing some wench this afty!"

This was a mortal blow as John Smout was the only one considered big enough to tackle the infamous Jasper, but taking this on the chin and making the best of a tricky situation, Roger gave the instruction for stones to be gathered while Tommy was ordered to stand on watch further along Riddings road. The drama of occasion must have got to him, for instead of just waiting on the brow of the hill, he climbed a nearby tree.

"See anything, Tommy?"

"Yes, I can see Mrs. Hughes hanging out the washing."

"Don't piss about Tommy and get yourself down from there the minute they appear."

The stones were stacked in two piles either side of the road and on hearing Tommy's, "Here they come," we all ran and armed with nothing more than sticks and those stones grabbed from our ammo piles, we formed a line. Watching the enemy straggle into view, stood a bunch of kids, most of whom were not yet ten years old.

If you counted little Eecock Woodcock and my brother, the defending force was eleven and they numbered roughly the same, all with corresponding ages apart from one standing out like a bull amongst heifers.

"Look at the size of that breed," muttered Mick.

"Leave him to me," ten-year-old Roger replied, for which we were all mighty grateful.

Their initial approach was silent and menacing and although the blood chilling screams accompanying the charge prompted the notion to run for it, not one backward step was taken. Instead, we pelted them with stones as fast as we could throw them. The two youngest kept us supplied from the piles either side of the road.

A van coming up the rise brought a lull, but once the battlefield was open again, we found ourselves under fire from our own returning missiles and the whole affair turned into a conventional stone fight.

Then seeing the brute, fresh from an institution, rallying his troops with the obvious notion of taking us on at close quarters, Roger called, "Hey Jasper!"

The youth in question looked up.

Almost in a confidential manner, he continued, "Jasper, I heard tell, Alphie couldn't take it."

"Who told you that?"

"Dunner matter who told me. Is it right?"

Jasper approached, trailing his club almost as if a toy horse and said, "Honest to God, I inner joking, he cried like a fuckin' babby."

129

"That's what I heard."

"He was pleading with me, Jasper, Jasper, dunner let 'em get me. I told 'im, 'Dunt expect me to 'elp.' You knows as well as I does, what ee done to that wench dunner go down well amongst 'onest folks."

By this I assumed he meant, self-respecting brawlers, pilferers and other petty miscreants.

"It must 'av bin tough for you an'all," said Roger.

"I managed, mate, but I inner kiddin,' I dunner fancy goin' back there."

"Swinging a table leg, you might just manage it," yelled Copper, ever the diplomat.

"Shut up, our kid!" Roger snapped and then suggested, "Why don't me and you sit this one out and let the others have a go at one another."

After a moment's thought, Jasper said, "Ah, alright." and he and Roger stood talking quite amicably while the rest of us, apart from our two youngest, waded in swinging and thrusting sticks.

There were bruised knuckles, the odd whack on the head and the sight of Brian driving two of the raiders back down towards Rock Lane, but after no more than about eight minutes an honourable draw was declared.

Before they departed, there was even talk of a return fixture, but it never came to anything and walking back to the lane Roger said, "Not a bad kid really, providing you dunner get on the wrong side of 'im."

I mused, "He looked too much of a hard nut to be worried about wrecked camps."

"He told me, he never clapped eyes on the thing," said Roger, "He'd just got 'iself roped in to help. And fair play," he said, as he gave me an appreciative slap across the shoulder, "You didner do so bad."

I walked home a proud young man that day.

As with most examples of a tale being retold, the truth became stretched, but I didn't bother to correct exaggerations or downright untruths, for having taken part in what was becoming an epic, I now felt an equal to those who'd related details of previous battles. The besieging of their hay bale redoubt in the Big Field was a favourite and how they'd tied a captured youth to the aluminium utility pole halfway up Clee View was another. It had taken a posse of parents from the avenue to cut him free, as all other attempts had been driven off.

I suspected the battles from those years of yore, involving older participants, were of far greater savagery than our little skirmish, but it didn't matter, for even though I'd arrived as thoroughly green and maybe slightly precious, having now stood shoulder to shoulder with them, I was at last accepted. Sort of.

Apart from an incineration of a camp, end of lane, we'd long ago stopped using, we had no real trouble from our nearby rivals, but having said that, I still wouldn't have risked walking down Sandpits Avenue alone. It was bad enough being sent on the odd errand down to Briggs's shop, but if you went the back way via the allotments and Wheeler Road, the general store was then literally just around the corner. Getting served there could be a problem, mind you, for they'd be so busy gossiping, a small boy, with head barely above the counter, could be left waiting until another adult entered and then with luck Mrs. Briggs might say, "Oh, I think this young lad was first."

The shop door had a large glass panel, enabling one to check if the coast was clear, before scooting safely back around the corner, then up the short rise to the allotments and home.

So, things returned to normal and as usual, on a fine day we'd lounge on the bank opposite Pritchard's house while dreaming up the morning's activities. There would often be a background noise of Copper's tinkering in the washhouse and if the door was open and an ear was cocked, you could sometimes hear him talking to himself. "A bit more should do it," tap, tap, BOOM!

We'd all sit up, enthralled; watch him emerge through the cloud of smoke and then laugh at his unruffled explanation, "Bit of a teething problem."

Once the smoke had cleared and he'd disappeared muttering to himself, Roger would comment, "I tell ya, he's never right."

One little pastime we had when playing down by the lane, was for a few to slip up into the branches of nearby trees and then call Buster, Owen's mongrel, which from the way it ran, must have had a touch of greyhound in there somewhere. Seeing it sprawled on the pavement we'd call, "Here Bust. Here Bust," then watch the mad panic as the other children tried to scramble into our vantage points, before the brute savaged their clothing. We'd hinder their attempts at gaining safety until the last possible second, then haul them clear of snapping jaws.

Here's another bit of doggerel I wrote a few years back. Excuse the pun.

# Buster

A bow-legged, red bummed dog named Buster,
Often lay, legs twitching, dreaming of life's joys;
Called, he would gather all the strength he could muster,
Try to sink teeth deep into tormenting boys.

Red-eyed hatred, growling with each stride,
Back legs, a whisker from overtaking ears,
Forelegs together, in collision with backside;
Hackles raised, teeth bared, snarling up at jeers.


It was from down near our Buster refuge, we espied Copper one day, aloft on a new creation, a pair of stilts, with the added touch of calf-straps applied to keep him attached and looking as if trapped in a pair of mechanical trousers, he came stumping towards us down the hill. With the gradient increasing momentum and the realisation dawning there was nothing to stop him, other than the tall hedge at the bottom of the road, his normal nonchalant look turned to one of considerable concern, but with teeth gritted and eyes bulging, he managed to veer off to the left, where he gratefully sprawled on the banking, laughing maniacally.

Roger drew a deep breath of incredulity and aiming a meaningful sigh in my direction, slowly shook his head.

All offers of giving the stilts a try, were of course refused as were all offers of a trip aboard a new lightning-fast contrivance.

In the days before DIY shops, reclamation centres and auctions of general household goods, materials for home improvements and go-carts were hard come-by and men would often return home with a treasured little stack of wood under an arm, thus it wasn't unusual for the underside of shelves or box section of a cart to have part of the name Fyffes or Fray Bentos on display. Even though our racing models could be skeletal, the way Copper had stripped down a go-cart to such bare essentials, was considered a touch too cavalier. His theory of lying on a section of purloined draining board, lashed to an axle between two pram wheels, was fine until you needed to steer the thing, plus once oscillation set in you could break your nose on the pavement. Being so lightweight it was a nippy contraption and taking the tight right-hander around into Riddings could only be managed by a deftly yanking the wilful conveyance away from its natural inclination to pioneer a new way through to the football pitch. Even though the fastest piece of kit to ever descend from Woodcock's round to Lochbaum's, none of us would go near the thing.

The major achievement, that actually stood for years as testimony to his inventiveness, was the ghost train. On returning from the May Fair one year, he'd decided Clee View would benefit from having a permanent, rather than merely an annual opportunity for fun. The ghost train entrance was opposite our house and by spending weeks hacking out the centre of the hedge, a 30-yard arboreal tunnel had been created high enough to stand up in. A section, with barely enough room to squeeze through, was handy if being pursued by one of larger girth, for it allowed time to escape via the tiny egress at the top of the hill opposite Woodcock's house. Originally the creation had been bedecked with masks, fake cobwebs and bones, but by the time I'd moved there it had settled in as a treasured relic, where girls set up house for their dolls or where you could hide in one of those games children often play. It was still in use until 1959, but then that whole area towards the top of the road, was levelled for the construction of a huge water tower.

Our family still enjoyed the honeymoon period evident when first moving to the eastern extremity of Ludlow. While settling into the new home, it seemed parental differences so obvious in the latter days at Waterloo House, had at last been put aside. I suppose, having to fit all our belongings into a much smaller dwelling and needing to tackle the garden must have taken their minds off it. Or maybe they saw it as a new start. A clean sheet. I lived in dread of hostilities opening up again and with eyes tight shut and fists clenched in concentration, nightly prayed they wouldn't.

Isn't it strange, a nightmare for one family can be source of mild amusement for another. The walls between the houses were probably only one brick thick and so we could clearly hear the regular carryings on next door. It was always one sided; Mrs. Owen screeching about some bone of contention before trotting out all the other supposed misdemeanours of Mr. Owen's past. He was as mild mannered and pleasant a man as one could ever hope to meet and we wondered how he was able to take it. Their son Anthony would sometimes draw some of the flack, by growling in exasperation, "Ahh, shut up you old **bag!**" At which we winced, imagining him covering up beneath the flailing of slaps, as she screamed like a scalded pig in knickers. Gathering herself, she would then round on her husband once more and we'd ask, "How on earth does he put up with it?"

The neighbouring house one door up from us, had at one point six adults and a spoilt child living there. Old Mr Griffiths had been a volunteer fireman and his son in law carried on the tradition, cycling like crazy down to the fire station every time the old air-raid siren wailed up from the town. He was married to Pearl, who worked in the trouser factory down Old Street and Pearl's sister and brother-in-law also somehow fitted into the place for a while. Old Mrs. Griffiths had an unfortunate respiratory disorder, which you couldn't help but hear as she hunched her way around front or back garden, for it was a rasping snort, sniff and whistle every few seconds, only interrupted if needing to say something. One day she confided, as if it was something to be proud of, "Snort, sniff, whistle---Mervyn's mother works very hard and brings him home just the one good toy every day---snort, sniff, whistle."

This was the same Mervyn who had featured in the lane incident years before and although he didn't join us on our wanderings, he would sometimes be nearby if we happened to be in the orchard or down at the football pitch. Approaching teatime, his mother in curlers and headscarf, could often be seen sweeping the path, but if she stopped to scan before putting a hand to the side of her mouth, a hasty warning would be given. "Quick, grab hold of something."

You could almost imagine leaves and detritus being drawn towards her intake of breath and hamming it up we'd pretend to get blown by the tornado as "MuuuuurVIN!!" was screeched as loud as the siren that warned of a fire outbreak.

In late May to early June, on a sunny weekend, their radio was often turned up so it could be heard by those in the garden. The commentary and snarling engines, heard live from the Isle of Man TT, would spark us into organising bike races and having taped a stiff piece of cardboard to rattle against the spokes of the rear wheel, we imagined ourselves as Geoff Duke or John Surtees for the day. In order for me to take part I had to be particularly nice to Mrs. Owen, as I didn't have a bike of my own.

"You're only nice to our mum when you want something," Anthony would growl.

"What a cruel thing to say," I'd reply, gleefully rattling off down the road.

On Sunday mornings we'd rarely stray far, as Sunday lunch was more of a family taboo then church and on a sunny day, flocks of homing pigeons would wheel in the sky and from open kitchen windows chosen melodies of Two-Way Family Favourites would drift. Usually treasured songs full of longing; Love Letters in the Sand; Que Serra; Scarlet Ribbons, but times were changing and hits from Jerry Lee Lewis, Jackie Wilson, the Everly Brothers and Elvis Presley would soon be arriving from across the Atlantic.

"Great Balls of Fire!"

In those early days much of our time was spent playing in the lane. The trees either side could be ship's masts, wild borderlands, Indian territory, or Sherwood Forest, plus of course we built numerous camps. After a long spell of heavy rain, a small crystal-clear spring would well up near the old stile leading to the Big Field and by using clods of mud to hinder the flow down into Bache's pastures, a huge pool would form, deep enough in the centre to almost pour over the top of our wellingtons. Water pressing on the side of the footwear felt cool against the legs and the bottom of our creation, a carpeting of weeds and grassy fronds gave a surprising beauty to our new world.

After a deluge, nearby Morgan's pond would swell through the hedge into the next field and matting the surface in springtime and billowing mistily down into the blackness was what looked like wallpaper paste containing millions of black dots. One Sunday lunchtime my sister had announced, her biology teacher had offered the incentive of sixpence for every frog introduced to their newly created school wildlife project. I had almost forgotten this until walking with Fran one Saturday morning. We wondered what it was at first, for the grass itself seemed to be moving, then as they leapt and sprang at random all about us, we realised the ground was alive with tiny frogs each no bigger than a thumbnail.

Taking Fran by the arm I said, "You might not believe this, but we've just hit the jackpot."

"Why? They're just frogs. Millions of them, but just frogs."

I explained, "My sister can get us sixpence for every single one." As the notion sank in, his eyes betrayed a certain avidity, which was backed up by two emphatic words, the second of which was, "Hell!"

Fran, short for Francis, lived three doors along Riddings Road, having Pete and his family on the one side and the driver of the mobile library on the other. The latter had an organ in his sitting room and on a Sunday morning, the lusty hymn singing of family and friends, could clearly be heard in Fran's dining room. Although a year my junior and much shorter, he was somehow able to put his compact shape to frustratingly efficient use. I don't know how, but his arrows flew just that bit further, his knife cut more deftly and if putting his hand to making something, he made it look simple. I could easily outrun him, mind you, whether sprinting or long distance and although I say it myself, was much better at football.

His father, a native of Lower Saxony, had been in the German Navy during the war and after his second sinking, was taken prisoner and interned at a camp just outside Ludlow. It could have been the one out on the Sheet Road, I don't know for certain, but what I do know is, he and a local girl fell in love, got married and then took up residence with their two children in Riddings Road. They moved in when the previous occupiers, the owners of that only TV set mentioned beginning of the story, left under a cloud. Locals had always wondered how that TV set had been paid for.

Fran would get the odd taunt of, 'Jerry' when he got on our nerves and believe me, he sometimes could, but it was meant with no more ill feeling than, Taff, Jock or, 'Ya big Jessie!' He was one of the gang and his dad was a marvellous man. I often thought, we couldn't have gone wrong capturing a few more like him. He was hard working, diligent, stood no nonsense and within ten years of residence became production manager of a local light engineering factory employing at least fifty people. His wife kept the house, herself and if out visiting, her children spotless. The second child, Helen, was my brother Michael's age.

Fran's English grandfather would often take up residence for lengthy periods and if we became too boisterous for his liking, he'd pronounce us to be, 'little flamers,' but was much loved and known to all as granddad.

His passion was fishing and would fearlessly take out a wasp's nest to obtain the grubs, locally known as cake, for the bait. He seemed to have a mysterious supply of mint humbugs and rather than offer us the bag, would plunge a hand deep into a trouser pocket and produce one without the slightest hint paper rustling. The fact he'd had so many offspring meant Francy seemed to be related to half the town.

Anyway, back to the frogs. Fran and myself ran back to my house in such a state of high excitement, you'd have thought we had stumbled across gold nuggets. My stepfather, a keen cricketer, was out at a pre-season net practice, my mother and Ann were downtown shopping, which left us free to grab a basket, plus bucket the washing was boiled in and armed with these, we raced back to the pond, hoping the frog migration was still in progress. If anything, it had intensified and we laughed and whooped as we gathered them up, then on seeing our captives springing to freedom we used our shirts as restraining lids.

You know that feeling you get, that feeling when it all seems a bit too good to be true? Well, once we had a fair haul I called a halt, reasoning, flooding the market could easily reduce the value to a farthing a frog and back at the house, they were carefully transferred to cooking pots and Pyrex dishes. Not wanting them to suffocate, we had the good sense to leave tiny gaps between lids and bases.

I said to Fran, "Wait until our mum and Ann see these!" and off we went to join our friends for the rest of the day.

On breezing back into the kitchen around about teatime, I'd almost forgotten about our amphibian haul and was therefore puzzled why my mother should be looking so out of sorts, with back of hand to forehead as if about to swoon. Standing beside her was my sister, with a stompy look of anger.

"Here he is!" she said accusingly.

My mother looking at her wit's end, asked weakly, "John did you do this? Oh my God there's more! I can't bear it!"

Frogs were leaping across the lino, sliding down the windows, hopping about in the sink and lurking in any available crevice, including the shoes by the door.

"I thought I'd got DT's! What on earth were you thinking of?"

Feeling my bonanza was teetering close to bathos, I said defensively, "Ann said I would get sixpence a frog."

"Yes, for adult ones!"

"Give them time, they'll grow."

"Oh I think I'll go mad," said mother, hands in her hair as if they'd taken up residence. "Look, they're even on the walls. Get them out of here. I can't imagine what possessed you!"

Grumbling to myself, "How was I to know they'd make a break for it," I began the tedious task of returning all to the wild. There was one crumb of comfort, for at least they'd travelled further than their siblings back at the pond.

Now I'd better make brief mention of missiles. A cider apple from one of the trees in the orchard opposite, could fly miles if wanged off the end of a stick and if aimed properly could spark an apple fight. The farmer never bothered with them and they put fur on your teeth if eating them, so an apple fight was better than just letting them drop and rot.

A Western or a Robin Hood film shown at the local cinema could have us searching the hedges for just the right limb with which to fashion a bow and down the lane, the long straight growths of hazel were ideal for making the arrows. These were carefully flighted with cardboard, then sharpened and along the shafts of particularly good ones we'd etch patterns in the bark. Throwing arrows tended to be shorter and stouter and flew like darts a hundred yards or more if aided by a simple piece of string used for the launching. None of us realised this technique was as old as time, we did it simply because it worked. We all carried sheath knives, not as weapons, but as essential tools and took a great pride in the bows and projectiles fashioned using them. The older boys often made a bow extra to requirements to give to a younger brother. I still couldn't string that yew wood bow in our hallway, by the way.

# The Crow (a true story)

One day my brother appeared from the hedge;
Dark eyes, tousled hair, stained cheeks, runny nose.
Hazel bow mimicking his sad little shape,
With tummy protruding from hand-me-down clothes.

I smiled, placed comforting arm round his shoulder.
A huge tear welled. Sadly, he held up the bow.
Whilst aiming at things across in the orchard,
To his horror he'd downed a large passing crow.

Half out of pity and half admiration,
Wondering how the tragedy had come to pass.
"Where d'you shoot him?" I asked, scanning the field.
Mumbled, sniffled reply, "Straight up the arse."

More about the neighbours. The Pritchards lived two doors down from us and in addition to the two brothers mentioned, there were also two sisters, Jane, a year younger than myself and Helen, who as a baby had unwittingly starred in the evacuation drama from the smallest bedroom above the porch. Roger had jumped to safety from the imagined fire, but Copper's lowering of Helen in a basket was interrupted by their mother, yelling from the bedroom window, she'd cut their tails off if Helen wasn't delivered back to her that very instant. Being none the wiser, the baby was hauled back up and with his mother understandably preoccupied, Copper shinned down a supporting porch post and fled with his brother to safety.

Mr. Pritchard hailed from the nearby town of Leominster and the alarm shown at the merest hint of us bringing home game, brought the notion he could well have been a reformed poacher, still on the radar of the local law. He was an excellent gardener and the front of the house with wooden trellis and arch, was an absolute show in summer, especially when the roses were out in all their glory. Life seemed serenity itself behind the trim privet hedge, but there again, a neat little hole still evident in the small horizontal kitchen window light, gave hint there could yet be chance for chaos.

Every year, manure barrowed down the side passage to be dug into the back garden and allotment, invigorated the fruit shrubs to the rear of the house to such an extent they almost fought to be free of the netting, casting a gloom on the back lawn. After a wet spell, the rhubarb would bolt and wear the forcing buckets at crazy angles like party hats.

When he'd the time, his little gems of natural wisdom would be passed on to us boys, as with most healthy sceptics growing up, we didn't accept all as being gospel. We did respect all instructions given when he organised the bonfire nights, however, even diligently throwing our bangers in the fire, but that was in the early years. You know what young boys are like.

Mrs. Pritchard had once had a secretarial job in London and traces of her Cockney accent lent a certain warmth to her voice. She seemed able to somehow rise above the chaos her sons were constantly creating and when visiting, we never forgot a few sharp words were sufficient to bring us to order. When those eyes took on a steely glint through glasses, it was time to back off. She wasn't a big woman, but her presence was.

I've saved this little saga as an example. It actually happened when I was still in Mrs. Bodenham's class and I once tried to capture the detail in ballad form, but looking at that now, realise only a few verses deserve inclusion. Being so young at the time in question, you can imagine my shock at having such a momentous revelation blurted, especially when you consider I had been standing almost within earshot of my family.

I was just about eight when Copper appeared.
"Did you know fucking is true? Found this book
Our mum's medical encyclopaedia,
Even our kid, who reads sod, all had a look."

Being suitably amazed yet still in the dark,
Would look daft to ask, "Please explain more."
Hadn't realised the word had actual meaning,
Just bad swearing, sent early to bed for.

The plan was, for us all to assemble on the bank opposite their house just after teatime, when Copper would toss the book down to Roger waiting in the front garden. The little scheme had almost been scuppered by the latter, who as ever courting danger, had dropped a fairly obvious hint as to what they were up to.

Seeing him take up his position, we all got to our feet, keenly awaited developments. Suddenly, following an angry screech from within, the window of the small bedroom clattered open, out sailed the book, closely followed by Copper, who narrowly avoiding his mother's attempt to grab him, leapt to freedom from porch to lawn and as we headed towards the safety of the lane, I looked back to see Mrs. Pritchard with fist shaking, shouting, "You dirty little bleeders! Bring that book back!"

At a camp we'd made down by the stile, Copper grandly opened the tome and relishing every syllable, started to read out the juicy bits. His stopping mid-sentence and the way his eyes widened, gave hint of something unexpected being imminent.

His mother plus carving knife and white lipped rage
Had same effect of lobbed hand grenade.
All wildly scattered as she threatened removal
Of the very things from which life is made.

As I ran, my mind was in complete confusion, for up until that point I hadn't the slightest clue about the facts of life. They were simple times when sex was never really openly talked about, meaning most of those growing up remained completely in the dark until somewhere near the end of junior school.

So naughty bits took on a brand-new meaning.
Now I viewed everyone in a different light.
That waddling Mrs. Smock with twelve kids must mean,
They're always at it, yet fat, ugly, a fright!

Nice genteel ladies I'd admired from afar;
'Even them,' I thought, and you know what's worse is?
I thought they'd been doing, no more than playing
Occasional game of doctors and nurses!

I must admit the revelation really shook me, especially when thinking even my mum must have done it, at the very least, three times. There again, knowledge can mean power and I felt quite proud of knowing what none of my classmates did, when still in my first year at junior school.

Anyway, that had happened the previous year and I was now sailing along in Mrs. Ash's class, to such an extent she began to read my few lines of verse to the class. I don't know what sparked the notion to try my hand at poetry, was it after reading The Owl and the Pussycat, or Charge of the Light Brigade? I really don't know, but anyway, my classmates enjoyed what I occasionally dallied with in the evenings. Little did I know a change was imminent. A bit of a test.

With autumn approaching, Roger would announce it was time to start gathering wood for the November 5th bonfire. It was a huge local tradition with nearby neighbourhoods vying to build the tallest. Not much heed was given to Halloween back then, apart from a bit of hilarity ducking for apples and not much heed was given to poor Guido Fawkes who had been burnt alive all those years before.

The first and most essential item for our fire was a tall slender sapling for the pyre to be built around, which Roger would have set his sights on months before. His father owned a hacker with a keen blade and when Roger appeared with this, handle just visible from inside his jacket, we knew what the mission would be that day. A lookout was sent aloft into a nearby tree, entanglements cleared to offer a good swing and after a few deft chops the whole tree would start to quiver. Then with all carefully avoiding its likely point of arrival, a couple more strikes had it sneering into a slow topple, where thrashing the ground, its girth of trunk emphasized our misdemeanour by bouncing on the barbed wire fencing. All evidence of the tree having been there was covered up and top of the stump muddied over. After trimming, the trunk was hefted home and hidden in the allotment, while the younger ones dragged all the severed limbs for hiding in the lane.

The collecting of dead wood and branches would go on through October with all being stockpiled awaiting final collection. The actual fire assembly wasn't until a few days before the 5th and then a watch would be kept lest jealous rivals took the notion to ignite it prior to the big day. Any unwanted furniture, usually old scrub-topped tables and easy chairs, would be put ready for the assemblage and old newspaper and cardboard, kept stacked in the washhouses. The guy, made in readiness was pushed around the neighbourhood aboard an old pram or trolly and we'd knock on doors requesting, 'A penny for the Guy.' Takings were added to the money all had saved and then a small select party had the delicious task of choosing from the fireworks on sale at three outlets in the town. Also, each had a small box of fireworks bought us by our parents and in the early days all was handed to Mr. Pritchard for the grand display to be lit on the firework's table.

The edifice each year stood roughly 20 feet high and had to be scaled for the upper section, holding the guy, to be completed. All was rammed in securely to ensure no sections tumbled to roll blazing amongst the onlookers and very last of all, the paper and cardboard was added. On the great day, Pete would stagger round with his old comics, only allowed for incineration provided none of us tried to read them. His father could at times resemble a disgruntled Grizzly and would have been thoroughly wrathful had he known we all sneaked a few copies of the Beano and Dandy from out of the stack.

On the actual night of the 5th, the sight from our dining room window of thin beams of light around the fire, caused Mike and myself to bolt the rest of our meal. No-one, having helped build the thing, wanted to miss out on the actual lighting. Innocuous looking early flames seemed to disappear only to reappear all the stronger, curling and licking further into the twists of paper. The first crackling sounds told us it had caught. The dark red tongues roaring higher forced us all into a wider circle and above, lit orange, was the expressionless stare of Guy, lolling from where he'd been tied to the upmost spar. We stared transfixed, hardly noticing the parents, some with a babe in arms, who had silently drifted in to watch the spectacle.

Mr. Pritchard, reading by torchlight, announced the description of each firework about to be lit and the usual oohs and aahs accompanied the golden showers, silver cascades and rockets that rasped skywards. Although, all was well organised, it didn't stop an errant aeroplane from offering a baptism of fire by flying straight up the leg of my shorts. Thankfully, only a small portion of thigh required treatment.

Once the ferocity of the fire abated, the homemade cakes and mugs of lemonade were handed round, the younger ones, including Mike were taken home to bed, but I was allowed to stay with the others, roasting spuds in the embers.

That was how the first two bonfire nights on the allotment at the back of our house had panned out. The third was far more memorable, but for the wrong reason. It wasn't helped by the dreaded silences having descended on our dwelling once again. When my parents weren't talking to one another, it almost felt as

147

if you could carve out the atmosphere with a knife. I don't know why it is, but when one isn't feeling one's best, certain people tend to instinctively home in on it, never wasting an opportunity to augment the misery.

I'm not saying Pete's elder brother actually disliked me, but him and a chum of the same age, known to all as Cabbage, on account of having the surname Greenhill, had always been quick to put me in my place. Cabbage and family actually moved that year, which came as a relief, for he was no longer there to constantly sneer in my direction, but Robert Clark was still in residence and with money earnt from holiday jobs, he'd purchased an impressive looking leather jacket, plus a pair of prized leather gauntlets which unbeknown to me were to figure large in my discomfiture. It served as a good lesson in life; never take continued success for granted and although ever the optimist, it was at this point I learnt; always keep an eye out for a soft place to land, just in case.

I helped build that third bonfire, completely oblivious to the fact, that apart from the sacrificial Guy, there was also destined to be a fall guy that evening whose demise almost entered Clee View folklore. Again, never realising I would write about it years later in a book, I recorded the episode in verse form. I've included a few stanzas, but before continuing please imagine the late arrival of a massive box of fireworks and in pride of place on top, as if trumping all our preceding efforts, were Robert Clark's pair of brand-new leather gauntlets.

# A bad patch

Like gloom creeping phantoms around bonfire base,
Muffled voices, questions, 'Who's that? Oh it's you.'
We assembled fireworks, then on each torchlit face,
Up-shadowed features had a strange eerie hue.

Fireworks cascaded with usual 'Aahs and oohs,'
Home treats supplied; pies, toffee and cakes;
Large jug of lemonade, but no hint of booze;
Mr. Pritchard was in charge for all of our sakes.

Don't know if done for a bit of a lark,
For with firework confusion in the dark,
Large laden box-full owned by Robert Clark,
Was brought to life by an odd stray spark.

Went up in minutes, arsenal prized for the night;
Bangers, whizz bombs, snow fountains and rockets;
Hissed, fizzed, banged, flew; put everyone to flight,
Amid all came the wail of, 'Pounds out of pocket!'

We all laughed, not our money we'd just seen burn,
Then a gravel enraged, strangled cry came;
With smoking gauntlets held, done to a turn,
Rob rounded on me; it was I got the blame.

Protests of innocence didn't do any good.
Why my spark in particular, or stray match?
First this, then the sledge, I soon understood,
My life had entered a testing bad patch.


I'll explain the sledge reference a little later, but first more details
of home misery. I'll try and keep it brief.

The worst thing about any bad spell is the not knowing how long it will last. I'd see my schoolfriends running to the loving embrace of their parents and just yearned to be able to do the same, for the happiness seemed to radiate like a shield around them. During such times of silences, we three children would mooch about the house feeling blighted and then creep to the sanctuary of our bedrooms. Each night I would pray even harder than before, for the nightmare to end. With ears strained, I'd hope to hear laughter, not discord from the room below. Neighbours stopped calling, repelled by the atmosphere, for it was as tense as waiting for a bomb to go off.

"Is he in?" I heard one whisper before daring entry.

The bad times always seemed to follow a visit from my stepfather's parents and it was only years later I figured out the reason why. I might as well tell you now, however, as I don't want you thinking he was a totally bad person and in fact during the times when peace reigned, he couldn't have been a better dad.

Now, remember me telling you about a trip to Shrewsbury, when the kittens were killed and following our return, how Eric had slept with his rifle? Well, I'm pretty sure at the heart of it all was religion. The 'drop of vinegar on the razorblade,' Clun grandma, was High Church Anglican and my homely nanna, living in Shrewsbury was Roman Catholic. Listen to this. On that particular visit to the White Horse Hotel, Michael, without his father's knowledge had been slipped into town to be baptised.

It was years later I began to piece things together, for when mother told me the baptism had been slightly delayed on account of the Derby being run, followed by the priest quietly announcing to all, Gordan Richards had won the coveted prize at last, I was not only able to pin down actual time and date, it at last became clear Mike had not been given an Anglican christening. So no wonder my stepfather had looked angry enough to bite a six-inch nail in half the minute we arrived back at Waterloo. Imagine; he'd not only been excluded from his son's christening; his baby boy had been baptised into a faith his dear mother abhorred.

I'd probably not been taken to the actual event on account of one so young being likely to spill the beans. To no avail of course, for my stepfather obviously knew the minute we had all set off for Shrewsbury without him, what the likely plan was. In fairness, over the years, he never tried to vindicate his ire by explaining the reason behind it and it was only after he and my mother split up, that I eventually figured it out for myself. Undoubtedly, he could be a bit of an odd package, but you have to admire him for not involving us directly in the battle.

So things were not going at all well and no matter how much I protested my innocence regarding the firework debacle, I seemed to be the popular choice for the fall guy. Was it because, even though I did my best to be one of them and fit in, they sensed I was actually a bit different. I don't mean different in any superior way, just somehow different, whether good or bad. Perhaps Pete had told them about the poems I wrote. After all he was in the same class, but no, if that had been the case, they'd have taunted me, as they did regarding the fireworks, but I swear to this day, it was not my fault.

Why is it, when the pressure is on and you do your best not to err in any way, you tend to tighten up and become a blundering mess? Nothing seemed to go right to such an extent, I began to become quite withdrawn, not helped by the fact I now occasionally stammered. It made me afraid to open my mouth. Life had seemed to have been sailing along and then suddenly I was in a trough I had no clue of how to escape from. Then to cap it all my mother rounded on me, horrified by the fact, I was getting a Shropshire accent. Looking back, I was probably a convenient outlet for her frustration regarding the marriage breakdown and I remember thinking, 'What's wrong with a Shropshire accent? Better by far than the ridiculous one spoken by that lofty Mrs. Plum.'

With it now being well into winter, I decided to build myself a sledge. There were no cheap plastic moulded models in those days and so I banged one together out of wood. For runners, I used strips of galvanised metal bought from Rickards, the ironmongers, along with a bag of galvanised nails. I had no way of drilling the metal and so kept hammering away until a hole finally showed through. It took ages and many a nail was bent in the process, but eventually, I had my first sledge. Before telling you how it fared, I'll give you a few lines salvaged from the poem regarding the venue.

# Sledging track

Just after Christmas, was safe bet as a rule,
Heavy snowfall in silence of night.
New world explored en-route to school,
Having leapt from bed at first strangeness of light.

Dull avalanche thuds from trees shedding loads.
Dark straight-dotted tracks from early birds' feet.
Muffled car struggling, whirring up road.
But other than that, a virgin white sheet.

Soft fistfuls were taken from hedges in swipes,
Inevitably pressed into missile balls,
Aimed at each other or dull ringing drainpipes.
At school snowballs rained in thick free for all.

There was a huge nagging worry a young mind felt,
Longing for home-time and frantic race back,
Before unthinkable might happen, the snow should melt,
And not allow a night on the sledging track.

Long natural gulley, creased field, sweeping steep,
Before dipping away off a natural hump;
Most hurtled down over stomach-drop leap;
Local sledge version of mini ski jump.

Pushing bent-over, then the dive onto sleigh,
Sometimes two flopped onto prone rider below.
Sledging by moonlight brought more laughter than day;
Stooped figures slow-climbing for next turn to go.

Into all this I introduced my sledge. I ran bent over as described, dived full length, then nothing. I tried again; same result as if the runners had gone straight through to the grass. In fact they were too broad and with nail heads slightly proud, resistance was too great and it just wouldn't go. The firework pyromaniac was now the track blocker. The following day I tried applying candle wax, but the thing was as stubborn as a donkey, but then on the Friday night, with a halo round the moon, it flew at quite a respectable pace. On the Saturday morning, I couldn't wait to rush across to the sledging track once more, but the ice sheet of the previous night had started to thaw and once again my sledge wouldn't budge.

"Here, try mine," Robert Clark offered. Did I detect an arch smile? "But mind the pond," he warned.

His sledge was a low little speedster running on dual, thin copper pipes. It was by far the fastest in the whole area and for that reason, required deft steering. Well of course, having only ever had one evening's experience aboard a sledge that had kept to the natural gulley, with not the slightest danger of reaching the pond, I hadn't a clue how to steer. Hadn't needed to.

So off I flew on the racing model, took to the air over the dip, landed like a novice over Beeches Brook and ended up cruising serenely across the pond, until the ice cracked.

I stood up to my waist in freezing cold water, with youngsters, who had raced from every direction, assembled on the bank, splitting their sides laughing. All apart from Robert Clark, who shouted, "Here! Get my sledge back from under that ice!"

When I stumbled over a submerged branch, attempting to do this and then again when trying to get back out, the laughter became almost hysterical. If it hadn't been for that bonfire business I could have milked the situation, but they weren't laughing at an entertainer, they were mocking dismal failure and I trudged back towards the summit, freezing cold with the sound of their jubilation still ringing in my ears. With the track being so unique, it drew children from all over town and so in a matter of minutes I'd become infamous, dragging home a sledge that epitomized failure. Added to that, the wrist watch gifted a couple of weeks earlier as a main Christmas present, had stopped, giving an eternal reminder of the exact time of my demise.

# Biding time

I learnt two life lessons from these experiences. First it seemed, although of course everyone makes mistakes, for some reason certain people are allowed to get away with a fair portion of them, as I had done when avoiding Miss Holland's twelve-inch ruler and also not getting told off for knocking down damsons at Waterloo House. Secondly, when in a bad patch like the one I was experiencing, it was pointless trying to gain favour or moan about it, one simply had to be patient; never lose faith or self-belief; keep trying to do the right things for the right reasons and hopefully, one day luck would change of its own accord. All you could do, was stay true to yourself and sit it out.

I had immediate time available to ponder this, for getting the inside of your wellies wet in winter meant being housebound for at least two days until they dried. Meanwhile I was glad none of my family asked me the time, for I didn't dare admit my new watch had taken on water.

It was quite a dismal winter with the atmosphere so cold at home and then came news that shocked the country, the Munich air disaster. The sense of mourning was heightened by the fact so much amazing footballing talent had been obliterated. People often debated how much of an impact Duncan Edwards would have had, had he survived.

With Spring approaching, I suffered the misery of chicken pox and my brother was told to remain in the same bedroom to ensure he got a dose as well. The reasoning regarding most of those childhood illnesses was; better get it over and done with, for catching such things later in life would likely lead to far worse consequences. Even when the itching stopped, we still had to remain in quarantine and busied ourselves with Meccano, reading borrowed comics or doing jigsaws, while if we were lucky, the latest favourites were played on the radio, songs such as; Peggy Sue, Jailhouse Rock, Story of My Life.

Also, we sometimes contemplated the mysteries of life, such as wondering why people in Australia didn't just simply fall off the World? Why can't planes fly to the moon? Why did women in a cowboy film always mean the audience was in for of a boring period? Why do cowboys never need to go to the toilet? Where do flies go in winter? How come you never hear a cat fart and of course, how would certain neighbours sound when releasing wind?

There was a stiff, rather corpulent neighbour residing over the hill who rode an RAC motorcycle and I think we were still confined to bed when I asked, "Mike, what d'you think that Mr. Thomas would fart like?"

We experimented using palm of hand, bend of arm, really ripe ones against a bicep muscle and those produced by pumping air out of a palm cupped under an armpit.

"Never mind a kick-start, that would get the bugger going!"

"He'd be off down the road like Geoff Duke."

"Or what about that fat window cleaner? You know the one. That woman who cleans shop windows."

I made an explosive noise commensurate with her girth.

"No, listen to this one," said Mike, blowing the sloppiest raspberry he could manage.

"What about Mr. Pritchard? He'd be a no-nonsense farter. "Pruup! Take that!"

"No, I've got a better one. Mrs. Owen!"

"Oh, she'd be a happy, hysterical farter. Almost leaping about, like from one of those jumping-jacks. Whoo, perp! Oh my God, purp! Ha-ha this is the life!"

"That would get her polishing. Going at it, rubbing away trying to hide the ponk," added Mike.

"You're right. That's why her sideboard's always gleaming. You can literally see your face in it."

"Yes I know the dirty stinker! Hey, here's a good one,--- Mr. Clark."

"He'd fart in a man's way. Thruup! And shake a trouser leg, 'Catch that!'"

"What about Mr. Woodcock?"

"Bloody hell! Yes, he'd let one rip alright."

"Would almost be a pleasure to listen to."

"I dunno, depends on where you're standing. A deep moody growler."

"Then he'd blame Mick or Brian. Get yerself outside if yer gonna do that!"

"He would. You're right! He'd blame Mick. Get outside y'dirty bugger! Was he really a sergeant?"

"No, sergeant major. No farting in the ranks!"

"No wonder they're frightened of him."

"I bet every time he drops one, Mick has that flat-eared dog look, ducking under the table."

They say laughter can be the finest cure and with exploring such simple notions we'd sometimes end up aching with it.

"Mike, we've forgotten Suckum." He was a bloated, red-faced man, full of his own importance.

"He'd sound like a whoopie cushion."

"No! Once he let rip, he'd be a fluttering farter, like letting a massive balloon go without knotting it."

"We've forgotten Mr. Brown, how would he fart?"

"Oh, him! He'd let out a sneaky wafter."

"Yeh, the type that comes out in carpet slippers. And what about Janet?"

She was a sweet, smiling tiny two-year-old.

"Well, she'd hardly manage much."

With tongue and lips, we tried to make the quietest, 'dup,' sound possible followed by, "Pardee me." Then with both pulling a face, coughing and furiously wafting the air, we'd add with face averted, "She's the winner. Cough! Give her the rosette."

"No. Open that flaming window!"

So, with such simple hilarity we were bound to get better and with winter finally giving way to spring, the cold war between my parents seemed to thaw. The year warmed up, hand pushed lawnmowers whirred sending up the aroma of fresh cut grass, the first swallows swept high in their aerial ballet and still keeping my distance from neighbour's children, not yet tired of reminding me of two incidents I was keen to put behind me, I travelled to Saturday cricket matches with my stepfather.

A relative of his, a professional bat maker, had gifted me a proper cricket bat with a sprung handle, meaning the hands didn't sting with every stroke and I couldn't wait to use it, but had to wait until the application of linseed oil had sunk in.

My dad's club, the Dolphins, didn't have a pitch of their own and so every match was played away and with not having a clubhouse, the kit was kept at the New Inn, now long gone. All in the team were locals and the chatter and laughter, was in itself worth the trip as we rattled along in a small dilly hired from a local bus company.

There were always other children to play with and we relished the stop on the way back, where one of the parents would emerge from the pub to give us lemonade and crisps. It was before the plethora of flavoured crisps and you had to delve inside the packet for the salt in a twist of blue paper.

My dad, of course I called him that even though I'd not forgotten my own father, was obviously pleased I took such an interest in something so important to him. I helped with the teas and the Dolphin's scorer, Mrs. Hince, allowed me to complete some of the sections in the scorebook and on two occasions when she couldn't attend, I filled in for her, a fully-fledged ten-year-old scorer, which was like a dream come true.

I was perceptive enough to tell from my dad's expression when leaning closer for a quiet word with friends, but looking in my direction, he was proud of me and yet that perception still didn't provide the answer as to why all conversations on the home journey seemed more boisterous than those on the outward trip. It might sound a bit naive, but remember, with children rarely allowed inside pubs back then, none of us knew to what extent ale was quaffed or the full effect it could have, for with alcohol rarely being drunk at home beyond Christmas and New Year's Eve, those with a similar upbringing to mine seldom saw their parents worse for wear. Even if they returned from an evening function slightly tipsy, with our normal bedtime being at 9 o-clock, we'd not be up to witness it. Still tucked my teddy in, by the way. There! I've dared admit it.

Back at Clee View, I continued with my plan of keeping a low profile and even if managing to finally climb some of the most challenging trees, didn't brag about it and thankfully, when seeing me swaying atop one of the tall elms opposite the houses, my mother didn't shout for me to immediately climb back down. She admitted years later, it had given her 'kittens,' but knew she had to let, 'boys be boys.'

I had become much better at cricket, but when taking a wicket by spinning the ball out of the rough, never madly celebrated. I wanted to ease my way back in as quietly as possible and when those certain little episodes were dragged back up, I'd now often hear an answering comment, "Dunner keep on. Leave 'im alone, that was months ago."

In fact, most had started to see the funny side, in a way that was almost supportive.

"D'you remember how full of hisself Clarker looked when he arrived with that box heaped-up 'uv fireworks?"

"Dunner! He looked like the cat what got the cream."

"Yeh, but remember that look on his face when the whole lot went up! Desperate. Arms waving as if he could put a to stop it."

"Fat chance. And d'you remember? We'd only just bin told to chuck our bangers on the fire--------"

I know! That's what made it so funny. Cos straight afterwards, fuckin' World War Three broke out!"

"Never seen folk move so fast. Diving all over the place and I ooner forget-----I can see 'im now. Mr. Pritchard hid low in the sprouts."

"That's right! Then up he'd come----- like a rising moon!"

"I know. Like summat from a film. But each time he had to duck for cover, like some bugger was shooting at 'im!"

"What got **me** was;----------even **ee** was laughin'"

"I know, but not Rob. Remember that look ee 'ad. when holding out them gauntlets?"

"Steaming, like he'd overcooked the kippers!"

The feeling that, God willing, I was emerging from the bad patch, was endorsed when Mrs. Ash asked one of the prettiest girls in the class to sit by me for certain lessons. Even at that young age you could tell what sort of self-assured woman the little miss was going to blossom into. 'Rose, you've no idea what you did for my confidence.' I couldn't believe my luck, but still didn't let it show lest those forces governing our fate happened to be watching; rubbing their hands with glee at the thought of toying with me further.

What had helped my return to favour of course, was possession of a proper cricket bat. If they wanted to use it, they had to have me along as well. Also, after such an unpromising start, Roger and I began to hit it off as friends. I've noticed through life I've been a natural magnet for those with a bit of a wild streak. Don't know why it is. It's just the way it is and so when Roger came up with a mad idea one morning, I was eventually praised for being the only one to fully take on board the seriousness of the undertaking.

We had already risen to challenges, such as, how many ways could Ledwyche stream be crossed between the stone bridge and perimeter of the deer park, without getting feet wet. Shoals and logs were used, but also, we'd crossed by way of the trees that in places formed shading arches, but Roger's challenge on the day in question was completely unique and happened to be right on our doorstep. Could any of us, like a local Tarzan, traverse the hedge between the stile and Clee View, without putting a foot to the ground? A stretch of about 50 yards.

Two who went for the low route rather than swinging high through the saplings slipped out of contention early on, three baulked at the dense holly bush and then numbers dwindled further when summoned for Sunday lunch. With me ignoring my sister's calls, it left just Roger and myself on the final leg, which included a testing negotiation of shaky iron rods that supported two saggy strands of barbed wire, followed by shrubs so flimsy they almost required swimming across before being able to claim the accolade, in the relatively safe branches of an elder tree at the head of the lane.

Copper appeared, saying Roger's meal was on the table and the sound of the short altercation, brought my sister onto the scene, obviously piqued that I'd completely ignored her attempts at finding me.

"I've been calling you. Why didn't you answer? Now come on, lunch is ready."

"I can't."

"Why not and why are you standing in the hedge? Uhhh! Your legs are all scratched."

At my brief explanation she told me I was being totally ridiculous.

"No listen, it's not ridiculous. It's never been done before."

"Of course it's ridiculous." Then turning to Copper, "Have you ever seen anything so stupid, David?"

"Couldn't agree more," Copper replied, blushing slightly. "Look at our kid. He's not even in the hedge, he's standing on the ground."

"No I'm not. If you care to look, I happen to be standing on a lower limb of this shrub."

"But the branch is flat on the ground."

"Yes, but as long as I'm standing on it, technically I'm not on the ground. Them's the rules."

At this, Ann turned to go. "Oh, I give up! You're all as mad as one another."

As a parting shot she added, "I don't give much for your chances when Eric hears about this."

Even though on the home straight, I told Roger I'd better quit and that's why his record stands to this day. He managed to complete the challenge and as over the course of the next year all the hedges in the vicinity were cut and laid, to form neat, low barriers between pastures, an attempt at swinging like Tarzan through such an untamed local habitat could never be made again.

Instincts told me I was gaining the support of Roger and with him being such a powerful influence, I sensed I was easing my way back into the old pecking order. Mick still had the odd sour thing to say, as did his older brother Brian, but as the latter was considered something of a renegade, a loose cannon, he had remarkably little say in day to day plans.

Copper, however, our mad professor, always made ears prick up whenever coming out with a notion. Being older, he could sometimes slip into A movies without need of an adult escort and on one of the Pathe Newsreels he'd seen how men across in the eastern fenlands managed to cross dykes. We didn't have any of those handy, but did have the watercress stream that slowly oozed through nearby pastures owned by the Bache family. There was a wooden bridge that a horse and cart could rumble across, but it meant a bit of a detour and so if wanting to make a direct crossing on the way to the upper reaches of the Ledwyche, wellies were required, otherwise the rest of the journey would be in squelchy footwear. That's unless you took Copper's lead with vaulting poles.

We should have been satisfied that his idea worked remarkably well, but were so taken by this new way of crossing a barrier, a game was made of it and soon boys were sailing over the ditch and back in complete oblivion to the fact Bache's farm buildings were only half a mile away.

We weren't a destructive bunch, always keeping to field edges when crops were high; never leaving gates open and never letting our dogs worry sheep, but we didn't go about wearing team shirts and so to the Bache family we'd have looked exactly the same as those who didn't share our respect for the countryside. Consequences were, if you got caught when crossing their land, you stood a fair chance of getting your backside kicked, or at the very least receiving a clip round the ear.

My recent unfortunate incidents had made me wary in such circumstances and so it was I who raised the alarm when hearing the unmistakable sound of an axle squeak. I grabbed Roger's arm and standing on a raised section of banking, we could see a horsedrawn cart in the next field, rumbling straight towards us.

The man leaning into the reins to up the pace, turned to shout something cheerily over his shoulder to the two straddling a load of fence posts behind, meaning they obviously hadn't seen us.

All on the wrong side of the rill, vaulted to the home bank and we set off, running as if our lives depended on it. A challenging shout and crack of whip sent blood coursing cold through veins, but with no infants to slow us we made good ground and were soon homing in on the three-foot span of fencing that allowed the gamekeeper access through the high hedge. It might have been on account of having wobbly legs, or maybe it was the long impeding pole he carried, but for whatever reason, Pete became entangled, leaving those behind looking as if desperately waiting outside an occupied toilet facility. Prompted by the sound of our pursuers thundering across the plank bridge, Roger grabbed him, shouting "Come down from there!"

And with the ground vibrating to the drum of hooves, we three remaining fled the gap and if nothing else, such an incident proves, it's best stay calm and never flap.

It was when we'd swarmed across the next field to the safety of Small's ground, that Pete received a severe bollocking; "What were you messing about at, holding Clegger up? We'd have all got our arses kicked if he hadn't given the warning."

I was a bit stunned, almost as if I'd been suddenly promoted to second in command.

It was at that point, Mick asked, "Where's our Brian?"

We scanned the field behind and spotted him gulping for air directly below where our pursuer's carthorse, far side of hedge, was gnawing at the topmost fronds above his head.

Brian was quick over short distances, which I'd found to my cost when he'd taken exception to one of my wittier observations, but anything over about 80 yards he struggled for breath, wheezing as if breathing his last. He now had one hand to his mouth to dampen the sound of his gasping while the other was shaped into a threatening fist for us daring to laugh at him.

Once our pursuers had gone on their way, he loped across to rejoin us. You can imagine the animated conversation regarding how close we'd come to a kick up the backside.

Even when repatriated, I didn't always spend my time with those at Clee View, for of course, there were also school friends I could visit. Alan Dixon, the best footballer in the class, lived far side of the recreation ground mentioned earlier and I sometimes joined him and his mates for a kick-about, plus I often visited another friend, Leigh Northwood who lived way down in Warrington Gardens. It was at his house I saw a film portraying love between an outlaw and an Indian maid. The tragic conclusion saddened me well into the following day and to alleviate this I decided to construct a version of the temporary shelter they'd briefly dwelt in, a wickiup.

Trying to gain help for this was obviously likely to put my recent group reinstatement to the test, especially as neither Roger nor Copper were there to back me up, but deciding the notion was meritorious, I pressed on with the idea.

"He wants us to help him build a fucking wake-up!" summed up Mick's attitude, but at further urging they all dragged themselves into the task, probably relishing a humiliating failure. Long slender branches were cut and trimmed; thickest ends jabbed into the ground and then when all had been bent over for securing by use of willow osiers, it created an upturned basket shape. I could tell the idea was gaining favour, for can you believe it, when attempting sabotage by pretending not to understand instructions, Mick received jeers of derision. The Big Field had been mown and the grass turned ready for baling and enough was gathered to weave and thatch the wooden frame, with more being spread inside. There was a low half-round door plus a tiny window that offered a view of the lane.

I didn't expect any compliments, but could see by their faces the little project had gained favour. Even Mick seemed to have warmed to the creation, whereas his brother Brian, busying himself by picking his nose, sat brooding on the front axle of an old pram chassis.

"Got it!" he said, triumphantly holding up a wobbling lump of snot on a nail-bitten pinky finger. "Been after that bastard all morning."

Sometimes words leave my lips before I've time to stop them; "You'd have stood a better chance if you didn't bite your nails so much."

He drew a deep breath and with a sideways look asked menacingly, "Have you got yerself a decent dentist, Clegger?"

"Well, he's been quite adequate up until now." I was obviously on the point of fleeing the scene, but then stopped, for in his effort to launch himself, Brian slipped backwards to become tightly wedged between front and back axles of the pram chassis. He obviously felt a little foolish, but then with an almost blithe look, pressed down to free himself. He tried again, pressing harder. After the third attempt the truth dawned and glaring directly at bony knees his face began to take on a look of fury. He rocked and struggled, but no matter how hard he tried, he couldn't lift himself a single inch and the realisation had him, not only steaming with rage, but furiously kicking his legs like a child in a paddy. The sight had us doubled up, helpless with laughter, which maddened him to such an extent, his face turned purple. At Pete's reference to a pressure cooker ready to blow, our sides literally ached. The sight of such a dangerous adversary being so close and yet rendered so completely harmless, was obviously the magic ingredient that had touched the hilarity button.

"Pull me out you bastards!" With being in such a strange posture, even that sounded strained and weakly holding out a hand in Fran's direction, he pleaded, "I ooner hurt ya, Fran. Go on pull us out."

"You must be joking," said Fran, recoiling.

"Dunner be frit of us, Fran."

"I'm not frightened of you. Specially when stuck in a pram."

Through tears of rage, Brian screeched, "Yes and wait 'til I get free from it, you little bastard!"

"Now steady on. No need to get yourself all worked up, Brian," I gently admonished.

"Worked up? I'll fuckin' show you worked up!" Almost screaming, he said, "Can't believe I'm fuckin' stuck in a pissin' pram frame!" In desperation, he turned to Mick, "Pull me out. NOW!"

"I'll not be party to murder, brother."

Seeing Brian, now slumped, head on knees and remembering his respiratory problem, Mick gave a flick of head for us to make ourselves scarce, before finally extricating his brother from the trap.

He told me later, "You can thank me, that wake-up of yours wonner wrecked. If our Brian had had matches on him,---I inner kiddin,'--- the whole fuckin' thing would have gone up in smoke."

So even Mick was now on my side.

I'd better mention the prized sticks we always carried. They weren't just any old sticks, but those chosen for just the right girth, length and straightness. They obviously served as a spears, but also for thrashing a way through impediments, then above all, as a rifle. Roger bagged the best name for his, Betsy, the name of Davy Crockett's musket. Mine was called Carolina, but the prize went to Alan Dixon who I'd invited for a tour of our territory. When aiming at various things while walking, something we always did whether with spear, arrow or catty, Alan lost his stick on its maiden outing. We never, ever abandoned these, but with him being just a guest, all carried on without it. When on the home journey, it was spotted low in the grass, Alan instantly named it Louisianna, "Cos first I losed it, now I anner."

I invited a number of school friends to enjoy the paradise we existed in. Rose obviously caused a stir, but when a friend, Bob, who excelled at football turned up, he was declared to be a bit of a drip. For while we could run around in the tree tops as confident as monkeys, he became rooted to a massive limb, absolutely petrified it might break.

Cousin Nigel always accompanied us on his visits, but under sufferance.

"You inner bringin' 'im again am yer?"

It wasn't that they disliked him, it was because he tended to get a bit carried away. He'd been brought up in Cardiff and suddenly having the full extent our wilderness available engendered a rather over-enthusiastic release. We'd set out with him looking freshly pressed, hair combed and tidy, but would return with a young lad, you'd swear had been dragged through several hedges, then a swamp for good measure. I always got the blame when taking him home, but beneath the filth Nigel's eyes would gleam like those of happy hunting dog.

I've not said much about the girls in our neighbourhood, which is not really surprising as they weren't interested in our escapades and for what earthly reason would we invite them along? We'd begun to show an interest in the opposite sex, but for some reason rarely found those we'd grown up with attractive. The two girls who had moved into the Greenhill's old house, however, stopped a few in their tracks and activities were invented that might just be of interest to them. Their brother Alan was my age, but both sisters were way beyond my reach, being thirteen and fifteen years old. They were in fact half-sisters and if favoured I'd have chosen the younger one who had the same father as Alan. I'd realised they hailed from Birmingham, for I remember Alan's elation when running towards me one day, shouting, "Aston Villa have just won the cup!" Some of the stories we were told about violent city life could make your blood curdle.

Time had moved on from the Villa FA Cup triumph and word had obviously got out regarding our two lovelies to such an extent, youths we'd never seen before would turn up like moody tomcats, just to hang about at the end of the lane. We younger ones almost became celebrities by association.

The eldest sister had sometimes been paid to babysit when my parents were out and Ann hadn't been available and although feeling rather silly at needing a carer, the fact she was so close, in the very same room and actually showing an interest, talking normally for my benefit, gave me palpitations.

I've just used the word normally, for it indicates I understood what she was talking about. When in conversation with would-be suitors, however, the dialogue always seemed to run in such riddles, peppered with inuendo I'd completely lose the drift. But not that calm little miss. She always seemed able to laconically control the conversation, leaving no doubt as to who had the upper hand. Young bucks probed for weaknesses of course in the hope of gaining advantage, but for the most part were unsuccessful, unless for some reason favoured. In real terms, these young women were little more than children and yet gave the impression they'd been through it all before.

It was no good me trying to compete. My ears still burnt from the occasion I'd offered the eldest some of my books to read, hoping they'd help pass the time whilst babysitting. After flicking through them she'd asked disdainfully, "Haven't you any with pictures in?"

# Now a little old grandmother

Not much happened, idle talk, split the kipper
On town's football pitch, spread below road level.
Soft ball, like a honeycomb of old rags.
We'd one eye alert for the groundsman devil.

All looked up, pretty vision appeared.
Small girlish squeak negotiating gap,
Hips gracefully swung as she descended the path;
Amazing spell cast, plus glimpse of bra strap.

"What you dolled up for," one idly asked.
Tapping her nose, she then folded her arms,
Feigning insouciance, yet nervously checking
For lucky young man who'd captured her charms.

Attempting to tease, "Why breathless? Hands shaking?"
All emboldened by her distracted yearning,
Yet mindful, lest that quick native wit
Flashed fire to bring embarrassed burning.

Alarmed by the fact he may not show,
Yet scared by the thought he actually might;
This lot too familiar, hardly caught her eye;
She'd spent hours readying for Mr. Right.

There was resentment that our local angel
Could be lured away by a lad from town.
We'd probed, tried to guess who the youth might be;
Response, mere shake of head and frown.

"That's him," she said, suddenly upping away.
Tight jeans, collar-up, slicked hair awaited.
Eyes followed her gait, with handbag swinging,
Like our old soft ball we felt deflated.


The wickiup I'd devised lasted much longer than most of our camps and we often spent time in it mulling over what the future might bring, plus we even received guests. Some of the lads hoping to gain favour with the two belles of Riddings Road, would often join us adding a bit of spice to the conversation. They frequently bragged what they would do if given the chance, but apart from occasionally giving physical vent to their frustrations, it of course never came to anything.

Things at home, spluttered along with the odd fresh outbreak of hostilities, but thankfully all became harmonious with the trip to Morecambe beckoning. As money was tight and incurring debt was thought of as shameful, often the only way to enjoy a break from home was by visiting relatives. The attitude was, if you can't pay for it, you shouldn't be having it.

The whole trip was exciting from start to finish, for we were to go by train; I would be reunited with my three cousins and Mike had never seen the sea before. Very first afternoon, he found an old discarded spade on the beach and busied himself excitedly digging one hole after another. It was a joy to watch and with my parents walking arm in arm, they looked the happiest I'd ever seen them.

It was hard to believe, that I and my cousins would be allowed such freedom to wander the seafront at night, leap down from the sea wall onto the sand, explore the arcades and listen to latest tunes blaring, all just a five-minute walk from their house. Freight Train was still popular, but hits such as Rave On, by Buddy Holly and All I Have to do is Dream, by the Everly Brothers would stop us in our tracks, so we could listen to them in entirety.

One day while exploring rocks and pools below the Central Pier, searching for pennies that had dropped between the boards, a shower of copper fell on my brother and with arms raised, standing in a shaft of sunlight he shouted, "I'm rich! I'm rich!" They were tiny discarded bullet cases from a rifle arcade above.

The whole place to us, seemed like living in heaven and the thought of home was too depressing to contemplate, not helped by seeing on our return, the privet hedge had grown out of control to block access up the path.

The first friend I met was Pete, who showed not the slightest interest in where I'd been, keener in fact to tell me of visits to the Ledwyche river and how so much time had been spent with the two girls of such local interest, along with explicit details of the banter that had been exchanged. He hardly paused for breath, but remembering the mighty sweep of Morecambe Bay and conversations with my cousins, I could feel my heart sinking. Often we had talked deep into the night, touching the very essence of how I felt, needing only a few words to bring a picture to mind and cause laughter. With them it had felt like flying and yet now I had to endure life back on the ground.

I asked whether he ever went to the seaside. He told me about the day trips to Borth, but then my ears pricked up at mention of the Minsterley holidays, for an older cousin there had a massive pair of breasts and she let Pete play with them. Maybe with talk such as this, I could just about settle back into the South Shropshire routine.

Awaiting was the year to be spent in Miss Perry's class, followed by the dreaded 11+ exam. The pressure was mounting. Nearly forgot; I'd had one pleasant surprise at school, for when prizes were awarded for academic achievement, Mrs. Ash had tagged on one extra and I was presented with a book in appreciation of my poetic efforts.

Meanwhile, early in the summer holidays, we'd had a rather narrow escape. We were all on our way back from a trip to Bluebell wood and tagging along with us were my brother and young Eecock Woodcock. Again, years ago, I'd jotted down a few verses trying to preserve the memory.

# The chase

The main issue we'd had no doubts on
And always feared by each in the band,
Was an adventure we might just miss out on,
Being chased by those owning the land.

Hedges were followed to avoid detection
And though engine audible some two fields distant,
Was always best to check wind direction,
Or tractor could be on us in an instant.

Or dull wheeled rumble and harness creak;
Hooves drumming across the broad estate;
Often our saviour from narrowest squeak;
Hedge hopping act, as carts need a gate.

But farmer mounted on snorting horse,
Was by far the scariest scenario.
Beast, five times faster, yet even worse
Could basically go where we could go.

So precautions we took, plus being aware
Of farming schedules, it's puzzling how
We were caught one day so unaware
Shod heavy in large field, soft under plough.

Whip crack and scream! Beasts in our field!
Two youngsters struggled behind those older.
My brother's fate now seemed sealed
Until hoisted onto Roger's shoulder.

Flinging our bodies in last surge of fear,
Over rails and diving hedge and wire,
We resembled white-eyed fleeing deer
Escaping the rage of a forest fire.


I've omitted a number of verses and nearly didn't include the above, but after some consideration, decided its touch of melodrama suited young thoughts of all those years ago.

# Into the top class

Miss Perry didn't divide us into graded groups, for we were all now supposed to be of similar ability, but there was a division, with the girls sitting nearest the door and the boys located to the right, lined up in two rows beneath the big school window. I can't remember much about the curriculum, other than regular mental arithmetic tests and the slender text books, containing problems we had to solve. Once you'd completed all in one volume, you were handed another. With two to a desk, we helped each other, but before long, Fatty Hollingsworth and Mike Wall to my right were well into their second book before Leigh Northwood and myself had completed our first, meaning in certain subjects, we weren't really equal at all.

By today's standards, Clive Hollingsworth was not fat and in fact you wouldn't have called him fatty to his face, for he was immensely strong and would flatten you. He was in fact, little more than well covered, but as fat kids were a rarity in those days, he got called fatty when beyond earshot.

Way back in the early days, when boys with names such as Eggy, Icky, Cocky and Pompy ruled the roost, there had been much debate over who was Cock of the School, but now, with the toughest lads being in the top class of the A section, there was much less fighting. There was no real need for it. That's unless a certain someone started pushing his weight around of course.

His name was Richard. A large lad who had been kept back a year and because of his size, no-one had dared square up to him. The sense of power must have gone to his head, however, for one day he pushed his luck too far and Mike Wall, a butcher's son gave him a straight right that sent him into the nearest classroom in shock. Roughly two minutes later, obviously over the worst, he ran into the playground arms flailing, where Mike standing his ground gave him a bloody nose. The effect was almost seismic, for news that the self-appointed champion had been knocked off his perch, raced around the school in seconds.

It must have been an attempt to regain a semblance of dignity, that caused him to pick on me a few days later. Without going into detail, I went home a proud young lad that day.

Back on the home front there were great changes. All nearby hedges were thinned and laid to a height of no more than four feet and grand works were begun, levelling and digging out massive footings for the water tower at the top of the hill.

The Smouts, living on Clee View's crest, moved to Leominster, Muuuuurvyn and family decamped but were still within earshot, having only shifted location to Wheeler Road, while Aston Villa-Alan, plus his delightful sisters, disappeared to London.

Infuriatingly, with them having entered that bodily change towards manhood, both Mick Woodcock and Roger could now outsprint me.

More cars and delivery vans now used our road, which interrupted our games of cricket to such an extent, we were forced to prepare a small square in the orchard. We still sometimes played hit and run; over the hedge, six and out, in the street, if only to deter driving instructors who constantly brought creeping learners to practice three-point turns.

The man selling ice creams from twin tubs mounted above the small front wheel of his bike, was long gone, superseded first by the Messerschmitt car with a massive plastic ice cream cone on the roof and finally by a van that signalled its imminence by playing the Harry Lime theme.

The town football pitch was relocated to the water meadows beneath the castle and it was strange to see the field at the bottom of the road ploughed, harrowed, scuffled, then planted for the first time. Depending on the season, we used the nearest corner for football, athletics and cricket. We shouldn't have of course, but having played there for so many years, it almost felt like we had squatter's rights.

The birds still flew up, seconds before the blast from the Titterstone quarry became audible and the tank engine still hauled grit twice a week from Bitterley down to the main line, but I'd still come no closer to achieving my ambition of climbing to the summit.

My mother took on a nursing job at the local cottage hospital and one day, biggest news of the lot, Pete Clark informed me, "You've got a television."

I obviously thought he was joking.

"I saw them putting the aerial up."

I ran home that afternoon and couldn't believe it. On our chimney were two aerials, the H for BBC and the horizontal squiggly one to receive commercial ATV. The set was a huge bulky thing, taking up a whole corner of the sitting room and a man was still there tuning it in. Hawkeye flickered on the screen, then some boring woman talking, the whole process going on for another half hour, but eventually the set was ready for use, meaning I could now join in conversations at school regarding latest TV series. Also we had the usual requests, "Can I watch your Telly?" Copper was mostly interested in news programmes, Brian became a changed character in order to occasionally gain admission, but his brother Mick took things to extremes, playing with my little brother, half his age, to be on the spot the minute the programmes started. You can imagine what Roger thought of that!

That's why he wasn't with us on nighttime visits to Small's haybarn, intent on the latest project, tunnelling through the bales from one end to the other. We gained entry via a small wooden door high in the eastern gable end and by methodically rearranging bales to form a tunnel, we progressed forward. The working party consisted of Roger, myself, Francy and Rob Clark who had long forgotten the firework incident. Each was expected to raid their larder to provide something towards the little feast that concluded each evening's efforts. We must have been at it for at least a week and on the big night of finally reaching the far end, debating who was to have the honour of being first to descend to the farmyard, the decision was made for us by the sudden disappearance of Roger, as if swallowed into the night.

A stern voice said, "And the rest of you! I've been listening to your carryings on. Too big for rats."

Our inclination to double back was met with, "I've got the far end guarded, so best come out this end."

We didn't expect what followed for we were spared a thick-ear to remember and instead got a severe lecture regarding suffocation and the risk of accidently starting a fire. It left a lasting impression on all of us.

Another place where we shouldn't have been playing, was on the construction site of the water tower, but trenches dug for the foundations proved irresistible and we played attackers and defenders. For some reason there was a stack of aluminium billets, perfect for stick grenades and if one landed within three feet, you had to count to 100 before being allowed to continue.

Mr. Woodcock had been made unofficial nightwatchman to try and keep us off the site and to our amazement was backed up by his son Mick. There were no more invites to watch our TV after that, I can tell you, and he was openly called a sneak, by Roger.

Approaching bonfire night, he and I joined forces as a bazooka team, for we'd 'borrowed' one of the shortest of the construction site's scaffolding poles in order to aim rockets. None of us bought

Roman Candles, snow showers or golden rain fireworks anymore; it was all rockets and bangers. All rival groups lobbed bangers at one another, but our bazooka put us in another league, for with rockets whizzing overhead, all adversaries stayed well beyond range. Bangers in dustbins of reviled neighbours, I'll admit to, but we never did anything insane, like post them through letterboxes and on bonfire night itself, spent more time roaming the area than we did beside the fire.

None of it is acceptable today and rightly so. These scant details I've given are not in expectation of anyone condoning it, or considering us to have been nothing but little scamps, I've done it to briefly explain what went on back then. I certainly didn't allow my children to do what we did.

During the early winter of that year, it seemed to be just Roger and myself going on the longer treks, often accompanied by Judy, a tiny short haired terrier. Looking back, I can only surmise, Mick Woodcock was still estranged, Pete often helped his father with the printing business and Fran could be a nuisance to have along, forever moaning he wanted to travel by road rather than on country terrain. So it was just Roger and myself who roamed the upper Ledwyche that day in December, with the brown waters still in spate. It was hard to recognise the river, for rather than gravel beaches, musical rapids and deep pools on the bends, the raging torrent ripped bare-branch shrubs into such a frantic thrashing, it was amazing they managed to cling on. Debris along the field edge indicated the waters had recently been even higher.

Nearing the high fenced perimeter of Henley Hall Estate, we couldn't believe our eyes, for far side was the carcase of a young deer dangling from the railings. Immediately, Roger was keen to be across and at it, declaring notions of venison and a deerskin jacket, but the only way over was by edging along the hefty wood and iron grid that spanned the stream. We had often used it, but not in these conditions. The waters were that intense you needed to shout to be heard and daring to ease our way over, knowing one slip could be our last, we managed to safely alight far side. We examined our prize and being still limp, it was obvious the young buck must have broken its neck earlier that morning.

Sharing the burden, we struggled inch by inch above the raging torrent, almost losing grip of our dead weight on two occasions and on reaching safety, stood for a while, legs shaking and completely drained. I helped Roger heft the young buck; Judy was released from where she'd been tied and feeling elated, we headed slowly home. Of course, we couldn't take the most direct route, for if caught lugging home venison, it would at the very least have incurred a visit to a juvenile court, so our route was a bit of a zig-zag, having to use the cover of hedgerows and it was almost dusk by the time we reached Clee View.

With the coast clear, Roger shambled up the ascent and it just so happened his father spotted us bearing a thing of such great bounty along the garden path. He stood framed in the kitchen doorway, absolutely incensed, not shouting, but hissing, "What the hell have you two idiots been up to now? Are you trying to get me locked up?"

We explained the circumstances, even pleaded, but it made no difference. We were instructed to get rid of it that very night. Its last resting place was a small copse on Bache's land and if anyone stumbled across a deer skeleton, before the whole area was built on, this is exactly how it got there.

There was another significant trip late that year, but before that, I'll take you back to early Autumn. Again it was just Roger and myself and for some reason, Judy the dog wasn't with us. We often mulled over where our lives might take us and I'd admitted, instincts told me I'd not be staying locally, to which Roger asked, "Why go searching the world when we have all we want right on our doorstep?" He said, he'd probably work on local farms and if able to, would buy a small plot of his own.

I'd already professed my love of history and then dared admit a hope of becoming an archaeologist.

Following an utterance of, "You what, a life spent digging fuckin' 'oles?" his look said, 'Rather you than me,' but he then asked, "What about all that stuff you'm always writing?"

"My main ambition is to have a book published."

"If you get's to be famous, will you still come back to see yer old mates?"

"Of course I will," and I meant it.

We walked on over Ledwyche bridge, up to the pool where we leant on the Georgian brick wall, near the sluice outlet. The pool was twice the size back in those days and in winter regularly inundated the small wood far end. A pair of swans eyed us from over by the reeds, the abrupt honk of a coot echoed and forming a broad V across the smeared-glassy surface, was an industrious moorhen, with head bobbing.

Rather than take the trail up to Caynham camp, we headed further along Squirrel Lane and once beyond the brick cottage, for the first time ever, explored the land off to the right. We couldn't believe how untamed it was and how so much wildlife abounded. Partridges took off to glide, wings arched; pheasants clattered airborne from beneath our feet; hares bounded, ears, dark-tipped and upright and rabbits scurried white-tailed into burrows beneath banking where gnarled hedge remnants stood ragged with snagged wool.

We named it Wilderland. Well I was only ten. On our way home, cutting straight down to the river, we chanced on an enclosure where Christmas trees had been planted to grow in straight rows with aisles between. It gave us an idea, which leads us directly forward towards the Yuletide of that year.

In fact, it was the week before Christmas and there had been much rain. We of course wore wellingtons, but rolled the upper clumpy sections down, so they were more like walking boots. The Ledwyche was up again, water swirling like a Waltzer ride as it roared beneath the bridge and opposite the farm, a short walk away, Ledwyche pool was full to the point of near overflow into the lane. Our destination was the small firtree plantation off to the left of Squirrel Lane.

We crossed the intervening field unseen and slipping into the fenced enclosure, wandered the rows to select two small trees of right size and shape. Roger had his father's hacker and with me checking there was no-one approaching, he deftly put it to use. The trees had been planted so tight together, we left our two looking completely undisturbed and having completed the first half of our mission, returned home.

Under the cover of darkness, beneath clouds blown ragged across the moon, rain occasionally freshening our faces blew in from the west, necessitating a watch to be kept to the east, lest unheard, the gamekeeper intercepted. He was a particularly nasty piece of work, you wouldn't be wanting a meeting with in the dark.

We crossed the Ledwyche via the stone bridge, walked up the lane and passed the farm unchallenged, but at the cottage a dog barked with hollow insistence from an outhouse, causing us to pause. No-one appeared and so we continued to the gate leading to the field above the firtree enclosure.

We must have spent a good ten minutes trying to find the trees we'd cut. It was almost as if their trunks had rejoined themselves. To my relief, I heard Roger whisper, "Got it," and then by counting along the row, found mine.

The main danger point now, once having slipped across Squirrel Lane to the wild territory far side, was crossing the Ledwyche river. With it being in full spate, the only option was to use the bridge. It was a tricky circuitous route avoiding the lane and farm, but eventually, with the bridge in sight, we climbed into the briar and brittle, dead-weed tangled section, where old willow, birch and hawthorn grew in an untamed triangle below the lane.

Scrambling amongst this, we added our Christmas trees. We'd seen the lights of an approaching vehicle reflecting off the telephone wires and above the roar of water, the growling sound blown on the wind told us it was a Land Rover.

Directly opposite, it squealed to a halt and as a torch beam scanned down into our piece of wilderness, we ducked low behind the Christmas trees. The man seemed to be looking for us, for he shone his torch far side of the bridge, but then for some reason returned for a quick scan high above into the trees.

Finally, following a door slam and graunch of gearbox, the vehicle snorting at pace, headed up towards Ledwyche pool.

We quickly waded a small brook that ran through a culvert under the road, crossed the lane at pace, branches swishing and with relief, climbed the stile that led down to the pastures and our way home. We were midfield, quietly congratulating ourselves when on each lull of wind, we heard what was unmistakably a Land Rover, growling with each gear change as it approached at speed.

We ran to an ancient plank bridge that spanned a brook coursing way below and on the farm track far side, waited in the avenue of trees. Again, the vehicle squealed to a halt and again the torchlight probed, first into the small spinney we'd vacated and then slowly along the riverbank like a searchlight. The beam was played in our direction, but we were at too great a distance for it to pick us out. There was a door slam and engine roar. The occupant was obviously looking for us and had probably guessed wrongly, we'd be using the lane to link with an ancient track that eventually led to Small's pastures.

It was thought wise to take the longer route back, going across Bache's land and we reached the bottom of our road without mishap. Roger surmised, that somehow our presence had been spotted and on eventually realising the firtree anomaly in the patch of wilderness we'd hidden in, the gamekeeper had done a quick U-turn to come back looking for us.

I asked him why had the light been played in the trees above us?

"Pheasants," he answered. "Didn't you see their eyes glinting?"

I must admit I hadn't. We had been sheltering in a pheasant roost and luckily the gamekeeper had assumed, whoever it was, was after them.

Roger said, "In actual fact we couldn't have picked a worse place to hide if weeda tried."

"Then it was lucky we had those trees handy."

After staring for a couple of seconds and noticing my grin, he pronounced, "You daft bugger!"

More trips would be made for mistletoe and holly, but we'd secured the main prize and none of the others in our neighbourhood had a clue as to the source.

"See yah, Clegger," Roger said as he walked up his path.

"See yah, Rog," then nearing my house, "Hey, Rog?"

"What?"

"Merry Christmas!"

I imagined a shake of head preceding the word, "Dunner."

Dunner had various meanings depending on circumstance and inflection. In its simplest form it meant 'Don't!' Then, when the er at the end was emphasised, it was a shortened form of 'Dunnerr keep *on*!' The colloquial version of, 'Please desist, it's becoming tedious.' If said sharply, with hand raised for emphasise, it meant, 'Push your luck and you'll get one of these!' Said with a solemn shake of head it meant; 'I don't believe it.' A more subtle version of that was accompanied by a mystified shake of head and chuckle, meaning the listener shared understanding of how ridiculous the notion was. Preceded by a tut it meant, 'That's flaming typical.' It could also be the equivalent of, 'Tell me about it,' but in this case, considering what we had just been through and Christmas still being days away, it meant a subtle repeat of, 'You *daft* bugger!'

# A momentous time and other stuff

Christmas came and went and back at school we could all feel the pressure building as we headed for the test of our lives. Pass it and you had the equivalent of a public-school education for nothing; fail and your chance for gaining the passport of O-Level certificates was virtually nil. Out of interest no-one from Daddy Williams's class on the B side of the school, had ever passed to the Grammar or High schools and only one boy had ever progressed to college from the Secondary Modern. The latter scenario did improve, but back in 1959 the prospects seemed grim.

I was obviously now in the right class, however, which was in the right school, for quite a few of my classmates came from way outside the natural catchment area and I can only assume certain deals of mutual benefit must have been struck for them to be there.

We were allowed to listen to the commentary of the Norwich City-v-Luton Town FA cup replay on the radio, but generally the regime was necessarily intense. Norwich, by the way, had captured the hearts of the nation. It seemed unbelievable that a third division side could beat Manchester United, Spurs and Sheffield United, but on that particular afternoon, played on the neutral pitch of St. Andrews, Birmingham, the dream came to an end with Luton winning the semi-final replay 1-0.

The thing I enjoyed most of all when studying in that final year at junior school, was the free time where we could delve into whatever interests we had. Mine was history and there were books available that held such fascination, I'd stay behind after class, busily taking notes while the headmistress marked our work. One evening she'd obviously had enough of me, for she asked, "Don't you think it's time you went home?"

It was that year I struck up a friendship with classmate, Mike Wall and I'd often walk down to the family butcher's shop in the High Street. On a rainy day and stuck in the front room, we couldn't run about, as it was directly above the shop. I did a few meat deliveries for them; tagged along when his father went rough shooting; visited the old family home out in the country where Mr. Wall's mother slipped Mike and I half a pint of dry cider each. It might have tasted bland, but almost immediately, I realised why those exiting a pub could be completely different from the quiet folks who had entered.

On one occasion I helped when a heifer, led along the narrowest of passages, was slaughtered in the small abattoir to the rear of Quality Square and then could hardly believe that the meat hanging from hooks had so recently been a living animal

Mike was a keen angler and we'd often fish the reach between the Dinham and Ludford bridges and I've just remembered, in their house I was proudly shown one of the first twin-tub washing machines to come on the market. As the title above stated, it was a momentous time.

Meanwhile back at home, relations were deteriorating. Then things really came to a head on reaching the great epic, 'The battle of the bike.' My dad had been using it for years and so when my mother announced, with now working shifts at the hospital, she had an equal right to it, a tense stand-off ensued, not helped by my mother sticking a meat fork into the front tyre one morning. It sounds amusing now, but living through those prolonged silences was a nightmare.

At mealtimes with Eric staring darkly at nothing, he radiated such a sense of menace we used sign language if needing something passing and hardly dared chew lest it made a noise. We could masticate slowly through meat and two veg, but celery and crunchy apples were certainly not on the menu. That slight stammer I mentioned, returned and one day Ann was mortified to find a list on her dressing table, itemising her make-up and complete wardrobe. Nothing she had was a sign of excess, for apart from her school uniform, she mainly wore hand-me-downs my mother had altered to fit, or woollens she had knitted. Many invitations had been turned down, because school friends arriving in the latest fashions, made my sister feel a complete frump.

Not knowing at that point, the underlying reason for the initial breakdown in the relationship, I naturally sided with my mother, but witnessing the damage it was doing, she encouraged me to continue going to cricket matches with my stepfather. Strangely, once away from the house, he and I got along quite well and as mentioned, he never used it as an opportunity to have a dig at my mother. What went on at home, stayed at home. To be savoured by all in full.

My sister and Eric had never really got on, but at the end of the school year, having taken a part-time job at a nearby ladies' finishing school, she was more or less out of it and following that, a three-year Domestic Science course in South Kensington awaited.

Regarding brother Michael, the man was his dad, pure and simple and we all had to be mindful of that.

Going back to my sister, she might have thought herself to be a frump or thoroughly out of fashion, but in today's parlance, she could still pull 'em. They were all Grammar School boys, more hopeful suitors than boyfriends and in the period prior to her last year at school, when she did actually walk out with a young man, I remember two in particular.

One was a tall youth, and although still only fresh to the senior school, he was quite full of himself. Puffing his chest out, he told me of his rugby prowess and said I was just the sort of chap they needed in the under XV's. He didn't last more than one visit and I now know for a fact, even though huge, he never made it into the school's 1st XV.

The second lad, would have been in the lower 6$^{th}$ at the time and like the previous youth, was from a wealthy background. He entered our council house, however, as if having been granted an audience with the queen and to add to his unease, each question put to him seemed to be just after having taken a mouthful of food. To Mike and myself, his rapid chew and gulping discomfiture was hugely entertaining, made all the more enjoyable when he suddenly let slip a rasping fart. I've never known such an abrupt intervention bring such silence. The lad's face glowed like a brazier, and at the sight of Mike looking wide eyed as if to say, 'Did I hear right?' I burst out laughing. We were helpless, laughing until our sides hurt. Tears streamed and even though attempts were made to shut us up, they could have shaken us until teeth rattled, it would have made no difference.

I did try, with jaw clenched firm, but one glance at Michael with eyes ready to pop, started me off again. In the end we both had to go outside, literally falling about, thumping the lawn.

When daring to re-enter the house, the youth had departed and the clearing up had entered its final phase.

"Well," I said. "That didn't go too badly." My sister chased me from the kitchen flailing a drying-up cloth.

Both Mike and I teased her, making fun of her cooking efforts, but in actual fact she was quite gifted, not only cooking main meals, but topping them off with tasty puds.

With mother often away on nursing duties, both Mike and I became dab hands at rustling up quick snacks, but didn't venture beyond scrambled egg, beans on toast or fry-ups.

Now before I go on, I must slot this in. Thought I'd lost it, but searching for something one day, chanced upon a scrap of paper, detailing some of my sister's memories of the Isle of Man, way back in 1949.

'I was highly amused at seeing you rush to puddles in the main road outside our house. As mum went to grab you, you plonked yourself into the water. Your name for the large dray horses that worked the fields to the rear of the house, was, "Gee-gee ponk," on account of the noise a foot-stamp made. I missed winning money at the village fete as mum announced you'd disappeared. You had crawled through a gap in the hedge to be spoiled by a lovely neighbour.

I remember you wailing at your golly being left behind, but imagine how I felt having to leave my dolls, toys and complete doll's house. It felt like leaving part of me behind. All that, plus my daddy had been torn from me.

Anyway, back to my story. You could just reach my bedroom window and if I forgot to close it, guess what I found when returning from school? All my doll's furniture out on the path. You can imagine the outrage, but I still loved you, even though I had missed taking part in that race at the fete. I had so wanted to please daddy.

I don't know what happened to an Old English Sheepdog we had, but the mongrel that replaced it was really protective of you and would pin me in a corner. You can imagine my annoyance at needing my small brother to rescue me.

Daddy and I always drove to a baker in St. Johns to buy your birthday cake.'

Quite poignant don't you think? Four years of being told her father would soon be home from the war, then after a mere further three, losing him. Is it any wonder she didn't take to her stepfather?

In the spring of my last year at junior school, the water tower had taken shape and even though the first rung of the access ladder was way beyond reach, we still managed to clamber up there, much to the annoyance of Mr. Woodcock. He could shout all he liked, however, for we were unassailable high up in our fortress.

In what had been the town football pitch, a deep trench had been dug to take the overflow pipe and heaped up alongside was a high ridge of clay. What crazy notion made us negotiate its length, I've completely forgotten, but suffice to say we all became stuck. It was funny at first, for with wellies sunk deep we couldn't even fall over, but then reality set in, that we were all stuck as if in some macabre tableau.

Pete was only inches from safety, but even he couldn't free himself and so when instructed by Roger, to run and fetch his brother, he replied, "I can't, Rog. My wellies are stuck."

Said with a sigh, "Then pull your fucking feet from out of them!"

"Oh ahh."

We watched our shred of hope hobbling off to bring Robert to our assistance. The sight of us dotted over the muddy tump, made him roar with laughter and then in a business-like tone, he said, "Come here, let's get you out."

"Don't step in it," yelled Roger.

Too late. With a lame look, Rob Clark said, "I can't move." He struggled a little more, "Nuh. can't move a flamin' inch."

"You don't say," Roger replied from the summit, completely exasperated.

With the sun going down, we all began to feel quite chilled and as a last desperate ploy, Roger sent Pete to fetch Copper. He appeared, shook his head at our stupidity, then returned home to fetch a spade.

Dark had fallen by the time we'd freed not only ourselves, but essentially our footwear, for with wellies being such a valuable asset, we couldn't afford to abandon any. It was Roger's trusty right wellington that proved the most obstinate.

The assault team of four crawled in their socks to the small oval void near the summit and by excavating a narrow entry shaft in the west facing slope, to expose the majority of one side of the boot, they were finally able to wriggle it free from suction. Use of the sliding technique, then enabled a swift return to basecamp where the freshly rescued wellington was reunited with its partner.

Absolutely exhausted, the entire team then climbed the short rise to the road, where they assembled like ghouls beneath the strange orange glow of the street lamp and on realising only the smallest of orbs on their personages still shone clean, after much wide-eyed pointing, they fell into helpless mirth.

Our generation was probably the last to witness the annual trek of a Romany family, down to their traditional camping ground in Darkie Lane. We upped stumps, an old wooden cider crate and watched in silence, broken by plodding hooves, the creaking of the two gaily painted vardos and the grating of wheels, that sounded like barrels slowly rolling down towards Riddings Road. Both men at the reins, wore blank expressions, probably tired of being stared at, but the young woman walking alongside the second cart, fired me such a glint of eye, it pierced right to the pit of my stomach, just above, 'you know where.' When I dared look up again, I noticed her long black hair was tied back by a colourful headscarf that revealed small gold coins dangling and with head nobly erect, the way her faded frock flowed with each stride, seemed to bestow special status. From the carts' rear awnings small dark faces peered and you wouldn't have been wrong in thinking all had magically ghosted from a previous century.

As indicated above, we still sometimes played cricket in the road and I remember one interruption very clearly.

# Growing pains

A hard contested mid-road game of cricket;
Normal rules, ball over hedge, six and out;
Must field before bowling straight after innings;
Was stopped dead by wild, animated shout.

Looking red in the face, Copper arrived.
"Just seen Busty Edwards lying on her back!"
He spluttered, voice cracking and finger pointing,
"In the long skinny field by the sledging track."

"What hurt?" asked Pete. "Does she need kiss of life?"
"He'd got her knickers off. Saw dark brown hair!
Doing more," said Copper, "than just kissing her,
Sneaked up on them, didn't know I was there."

"He'd lobbed them both out. Killed me if he'd seen me!
Huge!" Eyes stared, but none wider than Copper's;
As slowly he described shape with his hands,
"I've dreamt," moaned Pete, "of those bouncy whoppers."

"Seems," said the teller, "he might have hurt her.
She was scratching, making funny little sobs.
Bloke's face was wet, like he'd just been scalded.
He was," laughed Copper, "sweating bloody cobs."

"Why sweating?" I asked completely puzzled.
"Well wouldn't you, when doing that to her?"
Rather than admit, I'd not the faintest clue,
Thought best, nod wisely and simply concur.

But this put a whole new slant on doing, **it**
And as regards an ever-pregnant neighbour;
What I'd imagined as a warm, tender affair,
Now seemed tantamount to manual labour.

Not quite as easy as it appeared, growing up.
Might seem all offered could appear alluring,
Yet I sensed many pitfalls lay awaiting
Along the tortuous path towards maturing.

We never missed going to the Mayfair, usually starting out as a group, but back then, there was such a tightly packed, surging throng, chances are you'd be split up and not meet again that night. It was pointless wasting time even trying. There was usually a new ride everyone had been talking about and on meeting families taking their small children home, the pace would quicken, passing those with massive lollypops, candyfloss and goldfish nosing about in clear plastic bags. Beyond the cordoning off rope by the Butter Cross, music coming from the first attraction, whirling and streaming colours and lights in the gathering dusk, beckoned from the end of the High Street. It did something to the system as if compelling a hastening into its embrace. The smell of hot dogs and onions cooking; slap of pellets on metal; latest hits, such as Eddie Cochrane's 'C'mon Everybody' belting out, lured you on and then when hearing the throaty, "Ava go on the darts, love!" you knew you'd arrived.

I'll give more details of the fair later, but meanwhile, almost forgot, must tell you this bit. Two years previously, a few of us had cycled to Leominster and after a two hour wait, saw Queen Elizabeth's hat as she walked between the eager throng lined up either side of the walkway leading from the Royal Train to the awaiting Rolls Royce. With all then racing to where her car went gliding past, we were just in time to see a white glove waving.

Now listen, for on one particular day lay the promise of an even more exciting trip, if only I could lay my hands on a bike, for believe it or not, Copper had heard tell of a shop in Tenbury, that on a Saturday sold the largest Chelsea buns you'd ever wish to see, for only thruppence!

"I know why you're being nice to our mum again. You want her bike," said AnTHONee. His low, slow, huh-huh-huh, laugh was the sort a giant might let rumble when crushing fingers in a handshake.

Having promised heaven and earth, to have the bike back by 2pm, I was then joyously free to join the throng. Once beyond Bluebell wood all was new territory, almost feeling like a new land and people we cheerily waved to, found it infectious and waved back. Beyond one hill crest you could almost imagine the sea beckoning, well that's what it felt like, Tenbury's nowhere near the sea, but it was all incredibly exciting, different and so when careering, carefree over a bridge of the Ludlow to Severn Valley railway line, we all skidded to a stop, narrowly missing collision with the hedge far side of the T-junction. We could easily have been flattened by a passing truck, but we weren't and so laughed about it.

When riding down main street, people stopping to stare made us feel like visiting celebrities. Local beauties laughed at our observations and then there in a baker's window, packed in a tray, were the buns that had lured us there. They were huge, fruity and had a sweet succulence that intensified right into the final twist at the end. It had been a long road, but worth every push on the pedals.

All that was now required, having spent at least an hour exploring the river Teme, was the energy to ride home and then find something to placate Mrs. Owen, who would have been forced to walk to her shift as a nurse at East Hamlet hospital. The handlebars were fronted by a small wicker basket, into which I crammed purloined flowers, but it was those artistically arranged in the hole in the saddle that won the day. The simple soul found them hilarious.

I could now swim, by the way. I had managed a few strokes at Penarth, when down there staying with my aunt and uncle. Nigel had still marvelled at how we unerringly knew our way around the territory of home, but I said it was no different to him knowing his own neighbourhood. My stepfather wasn't with us on that trip, so we must have slipped our moorings during one of the 'silences.' Now I think about it, the way mother looked so nervous until the train at last pulled away, must have meant she'd left him a note.

There wasn't much opportunity locally as regards learning to swim, as the pools in the Ledwyche weren't broad enough, the Teme was considered too dangerous unless accompanied by an adult and the nearest public pool was at Leominster. We biked there one time and in a game of tick, I skidded and knocked myself out on the wall. To bring me round, my good friends slipped me into the deep end. I remember flailing until they pulled me back out. A braining followed by a near drowning.

As part of the school curriculum, we were annually bussed up to an openair pool at Nash Court and no matter what the weather, in we went to try and master the breaststroke, practiced while lying on a bench at school. Even though blue with cold, we relished every second and returned to school tingling and famished enough to tackle the school meal.

Dinner, we called it, on account of the dinner ladies who served it. Apart from sloppy fat in the stew, I suppose the main meals were alright, but I hated tapioca, 'frog's spawn,' and would spread mine under the oilcloth table covering. I remember one day, my friend Mike Wall, barging me out of the way to get to the school bins. He'd been made to sit until all his main meal had finally been eaten and so ramming all the fat into his mouth, he'd fled the table to spit it all in the bin before it made him sick. And remember, he was a butcher's son.

Before leaving the subject of swimming I'll slip in a remembrance slightly out of sequence, going forward in time, as it happened at the very end of my time at Junior School. The summer was particularly hot and we were all wilting from the want of cool water. It was only at Copper's assurance that he'd look after me, that mother allowed me to join the others in a trip to our nearest holiday resort, Batty's Island.

There would have been at least fifty of all ages there that day, some arriving by boat, but most walking, carrying swimming gear and picnics. Nibbling sheep always prepared the best surface to lie out on and the ever-changing river pattern had prepared for our enjoyment, an island for all sorts of pirate adventures and far side rapids flowed at such speed, you could float on your back to be carried twenty yards to a pool, deep enough to swim in. Wearing ancient footwear, we were able to chase across shingle and take possession of the island without thistles and stones causing pain or impediment.

With the river having potential to claim young lives, we had lessened parental concern by promising to be home by a certain time, but it was a huge wrench leaving those water meadows, especially as late bathers sped past us down the path from Burway Lane with tightly rolled towels under an arm. The lane itself was hot and dusty, making it hard to resist the temptation to turn around and join them.

Another location that drew us away from our normal territory was Whitcliffe. For those not familiar with the area, I'd better explain. Over the millennia, the river Teme had cut a way through quite a significant hill and across the narrow valley from Ludlow and its castle, was a wooded piece of prominence called Whitcliffe, on account of sheer limestone cliff that remained after stone had been quarried for buildings up in the town. It was the perfect place for all escapades young boys get up to and we ran harum-scarum along the paths, climbed a sheer stone wall up from the Bread Walk, slid down into the dingle on cardboard, explored along from the Donkey Steps, to finally recline beneath the pines above the cliff face, marvelling at the view across to Whitbatch and Brown Clee.

There's a road that runs from Dinham Bridge, up over Whitcliffe, down to Ludford Bridge and at the summit far side, the building still there, was once a pub called the Bowling Green and when drinking lemonade bought from a side-hatch, we would gaze down onto the town and castle, then scan all our territory as far as Titterstone Clee. One of the finest views in the country, making us feel like privileged Kings of the World.

As regards athletic prowess, nature seemed to have decreed I was to be a stayer rather than a sprinter, which took some getting used to, but I did make the centre-half position in the school team, my own. I remember one match played was against Clee Hill. I'd never known one player dominate to the extent their centre forward did. He completely controlled the game and I've often wondered what happened to him.

One match I should have played, was just before Easter, the annual fixture against the old boys of the previous year. My sister had been confined to bed with mumps and so I knew what the sharp pain below my left ear meant. When I told Daddy Williams I'd probably be unavailable he looked truly mortified.

On the day of the match, I could hear cheering drifting across from the recreation ground, but was in such pain with one side of my face bulging fit to burst, I couldn't have cared less. Mike caught it as well of course and I remember, during our recovery, we'd tap out tunes on the headboard for the other to guess from the rhythm what the title was.

We kept it simple; old favourites and easy to recognise melodies.

"Hey, Mike. How about, 'Tap-tap; tappa, tap-tap; tap, tap-tap-----TAP-TAP?"

"We did that one yesterday; How Much is that Doggie in the Window."

These days some try to claim there's no difference between the sexes, but let's face it, have you ever seen girls daring to dive from the protective rail around a swimming pool, over the tiles and into the deep end and have you ever witnessed them try to conquer every tall tree in the area? No, and as regards the latter, they would never even have appreciated the magnitude of the mission we had decided to undertake.

There were two quite notable local trees that remained stubbornly unassailed. This was on account of the fact a ladder was needed to reach the lowest limbs. One fine day, Roger announced it was time we put an end to their legendry status and so we all trooped down to an oak growing just beyond the Willow Tree. Having surveyed the task, Roger set out on the eastern face, with me close behind. Remaining roundels from old severed branches and summer's new sprigs offered enough to cling on to and scrabble over on our way towards the first main branch. Faces below looked up in wonder and I heard gasps at each foot slip, but first Roger and then I gained the safety in the spreading arms. The rest of the climb was simple and we received a small cheer when giving a celebratory wave from the top. Then the feat of jumping down from the lowest limb, even though it brought a bit of a murmur, was no greater than the leap from bedroom window to back lawn, which we occasionally did just for the hell of it.

This left just one tree in a virgin state of never having been conquered. It was another oak, but by dominating the hedge between the skinny field and sledging track, right next to what was known locally as the Easy Tree, it seemed to mock, for the Easy Tree was a low limbed beech, even a four-year-old could climb.

This oak also had new growth, but it looked worryingly meagre compared to the previous conquest. As before, Roger went first, but his desperate scrabbling left very little to cling to and at about fifteen foot up, with victory in sight, I fell backwards staring at sprigs of greenery in my right hand. A holly bush broke my fall, a barbed wire fence ripped my shorts off and so I emerged from the clump of nettles in just underpants and a ragged T-shirt.

"Are you alright?" brother Mike asked, visibly concerned.

"Well, I suppose so, but our mum will kill me."

"You did a backward swallow dive," said Pete.

"Just like a stuntman," Fran added.

"Didn't half look good," murmured my brother with a look of awe.

The pool that had provided the staging of my sledging debacle was only about 50 yards away at the bottom of the field, but by comparison, my latest accident would have scored a maximum had my audience been a panel of judges in a diving competition.

Once home, I got a good telling off as expected and was sent straight to bed, scratched and itching with nettle stings.

When stupidly trying to conquer a sapling conker tree at the bottom of the hill, my descent again tore the shorts off me and ripping apart my effort of stitching them, my mother then laid into me with a leather belt, so I had welts on the back of my legs to go with yet more nettle stings.

Out of interest, corporal punishment always came courtesy of my mother as my stepfather had only ever delivered one sharp smack when I was about nine years old. When the family was beset by the silences, we endured a mental menace, not a physical one.

On a lighter note, with Mick Woodcock repatriated back into the gang, the following happened one day.

# The gap

Was the gap in my teeth that started it.
We were in Pritchard's house, parents away;
Guzzled water and flopped wherever we could
Hot, red faced, having played football all day.

These days I'd be made to suffer teeth braces,
But actively worked to keep mine apart,
To such an extent I could squirt between them,
Thin jet of water, true as a dart.

With thirsts satiated, just seemed to happen.
Zap! "How d'you do that, right in my eye!"
Each quickly arming with gulps of water,
Soaked their shirt fronts having a try.

Stung by frustration and my well-aimed jet,
The avenger missed, I'd hid behind chair,
But Mick, not as quick, sitting just beyond,
Received cold face-full fair and square.

He ran from sink with large pot brimming,
Aimed, swung at target scrambling for hall,
An arched back soaked, plus half the room,
From that point on, mad free for all.

Echoing shrieks as from municipal baths.
Pots, pans, bowls and even a bucket.
Stairs thundered. No sides, the whole thing was mayhem.
If stalking, door meeting, just yell and chuck it.

Stopped more from laughter than sense of guilt.
We thought, boys will be boys and have their fun,
'Til hearing ominous drip-drip-dripping;
Enormity dawned as to what we'd done.

Even though envisaging absolute shock
When parents finally darkened the door,
Just couldn't help it, few flicks and a splash
And battle raged madly, worse than before.

Normally considered apt cause to leave home.
Even bold Roger wore a look of dread.
We mopped, wrung the place out, best we could,
Then left two to their fate; rest of us fled.

Back home lying low, hoping storm would pass;
Attempt at concealment was a hopeless flop,
Mother, following damp trail to the bathroom,
Was convinced that she'd been tracking a mop.

When trying to explain my half-drowned state,
I narrowly averted impending smack,
As screeching commotion drew us outside.
"What's that?"--- I answered, "Pritchards are back."

"What d'you mean, his teeth started it?"
"Look! Walls, ceilings!" We heard, "Man overboard!"
Roger jumped ship through a bedroom window.
My teeth became straight of their own accord.


With the dreaded 11+ exam looming large, even though not a
natural, I did have the reassuring feeling I was now much better at
maths and had made up my mind, if I failed to gain a place at the
Grammar School, I would run away to sea. I'd be like a cabin boy,
or midshipman in those tales of old.

The delivery boy who worked for Briggs's, our nearest shop, didn't help. He was an upstanding, sensible chap, who often enjoyed the chance for a chat and one day imparted the view that gaining entry to the Grammar School was difficult beyond compare, for even though he'd answered every single question, he had still not gained admission.

"All depends on what you put in the answers," Copper said, with what I considered, an unnecessarily callous laugh.

Thankfully, things on the home front had become bearable and with both parents working, Mike and I had far greater freedom to come and go as we pleased. Our sister took on much of the cooking and cleaning duties, which was truly admirable, but she lacked a certain flair for diplomacy and so when needing our help, rather than using feminine guile appealing for it, she would simply demand it. To be truthful, her new responsibilities tended to bring out a bossy side and when dealing with a brother possessing innate stubbornness, it didn't tend to end harmoniously. Then when my old gym shoes got chucked out onto the lawn, it awoke a natural aversion to injustice.

"What did you do that for?"

"They're old and stinky."

Old, I had to concede the truth there, but not stinky. They were the ones used on river adventures and so were constantly receiving a thorough cleansing. Although ragged, with holes in the fabric, they were superb running shoes and were comfortable to the point of being old friends.

When she barred my way to the back door on a rescue mission, I simply changed tack and jumped out through the dining room window. It was on trying to regain entry that the unfortunate accident happened.

Ann grabbed the handle to close the window; I grabbed the frame and then both stared in shock at the sight of large shards of glass falling into the flowerbed. Not a good outcome when the relationship between our parents was so brittle.

I spent the afternoon worrying, dreading having to explain myself. With money being tight it was a very serious matter. If there was to be a thrashing it would have come from my mother, but it was father's ire that I truly dreaded.

Mother was first home and simply said, "Well, you'll just have to explain to your father."

I suspect the day was a Saturday and he would have been returning from a pre-season net practice. I think Ludlow Cricket Club allowed the Dolphins to use their facilities, but anyway, on seeing his approach I decided to meet him at the back door.

Leaving my sister out of the tale, well I did owe her one for that popgun lie years before, I simply said I'd accidentally broken the window while trying to gain access through it to the living room. Following a long silence, then inspection of the damage, he simply said, "I should try using the door next time," and thanked me for my honesty.

I must have said a prayer of thanks at least ten times that night before drifting off to sleep. I also wondered, even though I was largely ignored during the 'silences,' did he actually genuinely like me? I know he welcomed my interest in the Dolphin Cricket Club.

I have many memories of matches played on village and small-town pitches, but will only tell you briefly about two that stand out. The first was against Buildwas, a works side that played in the grounds of the large power station over by Ironbridge. To my knowledge, the Dolphins had never beaten them and for some reason, my dad had been promoted up the batting order to fourth man in. To everyone's surprise, he took root as if a top order veteran and with wickets falling about him, became the nucleus of the innings.

I heard home supporters asking, "Who is that bloke?"

It gave me a thrill, for I thought, 'He's my dad, that's who.'

The Dolphins won and of course Eric was man of the match, but took the accolade quite bashfully, almost as if needing to explain his unexpected golden touch. "In the end, the ball looked as big as a football," he offered by way of an excuse.

The other memorable result could have gone any one of three different ways. All depended on the final ball, which my dad shuffled up to deliver. With the sight of a stump knocked back, the Dolphin's supporters were ecstatic. Mick Crump, roughly my age, punched my shoulder in celebration. The very shoulder, stiff and sore from a recent immunisation jab, but I laughed through the pain, hardly able to believe my dad was yet again, hero of the day.

I said to him later, "He only had to snick the ball and they'd have won."

"But the point is, he didn't," was his simple reply. Although the atmosphere at home could be at times almost unbearable, we were quite close at times.

The chapter heading stated this to be a momentous time and plans don't come much more weighty than the following. Having discovered the Ledwyche joined the river Teme just before Tenbury and that the Teme then flowed into the Severn at Worcester, the notion was mooted that we ought to undertake an exploratory trip, for there was nothing really stopping us sailing through Gloucester and on into the Bristol channel. All we needed was the right craft. North American Indians used birch bark canoes and this was discussed at length, but in the end, with Copper championing the idea, we settled on building a raft. It needed to be a sizeable affair, mind you, for it would be carrying seven crew members.

A day was spent cutting and trimming the right lengths and tying all together, but it soon became obvious, even though the craft would float, it wouldn't carry all the shipmates without flotation chambers. Even so, it was worth taking our seats to imagine how it would feel when cruising through Worcester. Things were a bit cramped, but by budging up a bit, it seemed feasible.

"Shift up, Mick!"

"I already 'ave. If I shifts any more I'll be in the bruck." (Bruck was a corrupt form of the word brook, which in the dialect meant, large expanse of freshwater, such as a river)

"What about you, our kid?" Copper asked.

"I inner budgin'," Roger replied. "If I does, I canner steer the thing." (As you've probably guessed, 'inner,' was the South Shropshire dialect word for, I will not, or won't and canner could mean, 'can't,' or in this instance, was a concise way of saying, 'I won't be able to.')

Words and phrases I'd found so indecipherable when first moving to Clee View were now as clear as the water we were proposing to embark on, but before realising that dream, we first needed to locate some oil drums.

It was when undertaking this seemingly simple task, that reality began to sink in. Local garages didn't sell oil from large drums and if they had have done, they were too valuable to be just given away. We had to satisfy ourselves with gallon cans. We thought, 'Cans? Drums? What will it matter if we have enough of them?' About thirty were gathered in all.

The next problem came when first shouldering our craft of dreams. Staggering under the weight, Mick gasped, "'Kin-ell!

Weeda done better building this closer to waiter." (Kin-ell was a shortened form of swearing, 'weeda,' meant 'we would have,' and obviously waiter, meant water.)

We staggered along the lane and manoeuvred it over the fence into Bache's, the first field on our trek towards sea trials. Copper had reasoned it would be best to put the craft through her paces and get used to handling it, before venturing out into the Bristol Channel. Only when ready would we take on board sufficient supplies for the big trip.

Five of us bore the weight, while two retrieved the cans that dropped off along the way. Copper had said, it was pointless tying them until we'd assessed the balance of the ship and once that became evident, the flotation chambers could then be positioned and secured to level things up.

Rests were required, so more than an hour must have passed before our launching site hove into view and on a sheep nibbled stretch of banking, our craft was at last tentatively offered to the water ready for her maiden voyage.

"It was my idea, so I'll go first," said Copper. "But once I've got the feel of her, the rest of you are welcome aboard."

The oil cans were shoved beneath the timbers, but left untied, for Copper had reasoned they were bound to require re-adjustment.

"Right, hold her steady, lads!" he cried out and to avoid wet feet, took a giant stride to midships. Here, crouching in readiness, he said almost in a whisper, "OK boys, time to shove off."

As we pushed the raft towards midstream, Copper stood to loudly proclaim, "I name this ship----ooha--- bollocks!" With arms out wide for balance he added, "I'm not kidding, it's like trying to stand up in a hammock. Bloody hell! That was a close one. Nearly in the drink!"

Then, with his weight forcing the aft end beneath water, cans escaping from the prow sent our navigator into a backward sprawl and lying there grinning he said, "Only a few teething troubles, shipmates."

He did get to his feet, but the attempt to stay upright had the raft in such a dramatic see-saw wallowing, it loosened the bindings and looking up from his sudden unexpected sitting posture, he called grimacing, "Ooh, right in the goolies! But it'll be alright once I find my sea legs."

The sheer anticlimax of it all had his supposed crew, rolling about on the bank laughing, clutching their sides in agony.

"Never mind Worcester," shouted Roger. "You'll be lucky to make it to the other side of the bruck!"

The desperate attempt to snatch at errant cans, had more bobbing up from beside him and as he lunged in a half-submerged retrieval, he shouted through bubbles, "It's like being a blad bloody goalie on the losing side!"

Seeing our grand plans sinking into the Ledwyche River, we were absolutely helpless, begging him to stop, but with a shout of, "Can't get much wetter," Copper sploshed downstream to dive on three cans sedately making a break for it.

Back on shore, his earnest reasoning that it was obvious a few adjustments needed making before embarking on the next attempt, had us in such side-aching agony, Mick Woodcock pissed himself.

Once having recovered sufficiently, everything was gathered up and we returned with our burden for Copper to undertake the necessary tinkering he'd spoken of. Needless to say, nothing ever came of it and the ship was eventually broken up for her timbers to be incorporated into one of our residences in the lane.

The secret ingredient, leading to such climactic hilarity, seemed to be our sheer earnestness and self-delusion. Another venture, having not the slightest chance of success, was a fishing trip to our beloved Ledwyche. Although fun was had as usual, I also remember the angling notion being set aside once we'd started on an exploration of a brook that babbled merrily down into the main stream. With the verse written years ago having a stanza that came to me in a dream, I've included it.

# Fishing trip

The trip started with high expectations.
Straight fishing poles cut from the Willow Tree.
Cotton reels held the green twine through staples.
Four set off dreaming of fish for tea.

Our swimming hole, Tarzan jungle river,
In summer, was no more than babbling brook.
Trout weren't on offer to young splashing boys
Dangling kitchen chord and Meccano hook.

Plus patience was not our strongest virtue
And sheer luck not with us, patently clear;
"We've more damn chance catching fish," said Roger
"If I used this rod held like a spear."

Along secret branch bridges to exploration,
We followed dark brook's meandering weaves.
Sat feet dangling from old boarded crossing,
As life's constellation glinted through leaves.

And like day hour dreams weaving laced patterns,
Shaded dark star-pools flickered soft sunlight;
Mythical visions danced near our bower,
Edged on reality just beyond sight.

Fractured glows rippled up branches, faces;
Breeze gently stirred, green orange and gold;
Mesmerized, hoping for glimpse of the future;
Proclamations made of what life might hold.

Farmers, soldiers, explorers wandering?
Maybe an author? Another a vet.
"None," said Copper, "will end up fishermen.
Nothings for certain, but that's one safe bet."

"You'll forget about us," writing them stories,"
Said Roger, "Not one thought, he'll bloody give."
"No you're wrong," I muttered; staring far-eyed.
"I'll remember these days for as long as I live."

You might be wondering, what happened to those gallon cans we went to such trouble to collect and the answer is, I don't really know. One was kept as a target for catty practice, but I suspect the rest went for scrap. At least once a year, copious plastic bags would be left tightly folded to hang from front doorknockers. They were for old clothing and rags, but when the collection truck came round, they'd also take away small items of scrap metal and I suspect this was how the cans were disposed of.

Talking of cattys, when Tommie's dad, Mr. Preece spotted Roger and myself one day, each with a catapult tucked in our belt, he beckoned us over. We knew from previous conversations, he'd probably been quite a dab hand at providing meat for the family pot in his youth and so were rather defensive when he laughed and asked, "What the hell d'you call those?"

On hearing our reply he said, "You dunner want anything that big. Not unless you intends to club 'em tu-death." Spreading thumb and forefinger, "That's all you needs. Nothing that big, like what you got. Come 'ere." He led us to the hedge opposite and pointing to a small Y shape in the branches asked, "D'you see that? That's all you needs. Summat you can tuck in y'pocket."

We thanked him and he called after us, "Keep y'thumb out the road, mind!"

Obviously, you'll have gathered from the way he spoke he was a native of the locality, but you'd be wrong in thinking all in the vicinity spoke the same way. For instance, you only had to go the end of Sandpits Avenue, a ten-minute walk away, to hear a completely different method of exchange, staccato with gypsy words thrown in. We knew what the words meant, but because of recent conflicts didn't tend to use them, not unless being an amusing one such as gormer. It wasn't actually Romany, more a Sampedian way of saying, a gormless person. And yes, we called their earnest exchanges, Sampedian.

We would also throw in other phrases we heard locally, more in a slightly mocking way, for it wasn't usual to greet each other with, "How bist surreh?" Or, "How bist, butteh?" These, plus words such as, sniving; (writhing with) sklemmed; (incredibly hungry) and nesh. (bitterly cold) were heard in more rustic settings such as, Peaton and Bromfield, at least a fifteen-minute bike ride away. A bit beyond the pale, for after all, the fact we were living on the outskirts of Ludlow made us almost urbanites.

Our form of greeting, if not having seen each other for a while, might be "How am yer?" but the one used on a daily basis was simply, "Ayah." Then if hailing a member of a different gang, the sort that would come to your aid if needed, the greeting could well be a friendly, "How y'doin', stink?"

If Rod Stewart's 1977 hit, 'I don't want to talk about it,' had been available in 1959, our version would have been, "I dunner wanner--- talk about it;--- 'ow 'er bust me 'art."

It's actually quite difficult to spell some of the dialect pronunciations, for there isn't an English equivalent of the French, un. So you need to remember that when reading, spun (spoon); poon (a sharp wallop); I ooner (I will not). Whereas, I oodna (I wouldn't); we didner (we didn't) and they canner, (they can't) are quite simple by comparison.

Not so long ago, when talking of such to a friend from South Wales, he said they'd also used some of the words I'd mentioned. Later I emailed him the following to illustrate how the dialect was used. I promise, it's totally fictional and keep it to yourself, for I don't want to be 'no platformed' by the Woke mob when next trying to board a train.

# Oozle

Back then girls used to go round as a pair;
Miss Dumps plus friend, pretty with juggly ones.
My mate made a habit, in those days rare,
Declaring, which was handy, he'd have the ugly ones.

We were Shropshire lads and so spoke a bit rural;
Phrases like, canna do this and munner do that;
Woman was ooman and wenches if plural;
"Inner touchin' that 'un, squeaky stockings and fat!"

Then usual happened a few weeks hence;
M'mate pulled Miss Dumps and I pulled the stunner,
But after a kiss by 'er garden fence,
Recoiling away, she hissed, "Hey dunner!"

Took 'er out to the flicks, even out to dinner;
Like a gent, olluz walked 'er to 'er 'ouse;
But soft, subtle hints always brought, "I inner!"
There seemed no way inside that blouse.

Then asking m'mate, how he'd got on?
"'Er 'ad whoppers. Lord ahh! Each one a plateful!"
"But she was plain," I said. "Must have weighed a ton!"
Slowly smiling he said,---------"Thaim olluz grateful."

I said, "All I got was a kiss by her gate;
But as ever, she hissed, "Get off! I wooner!"
Leaning close he confided, "Just remember, mate,
There's them oozle go and them uz ooner."

So we're finally approaching the crunch time of that year; the 11+ exam, but first conditions at home. They were bearable, but the patched-up fracture, ready to split at the slightest onset of pressure, had us nervy and on edge, whether reading, studying, eating in silence, or alone in the bedroom imagining the dreaded raising of voices again. I once heard what I thought to be opening salvos in the resumption of hostilities, but was then amazed to hear it was laughter. Creeping down to listen outside the living room door, I felt such relief for they were not arguing, but actually enjoying a joke together. I raised tight closed eyes to heaven and thanked God. But how long would it last?

Not long was the answer. It was really bad this time. The fact they were both working gave the odd oasis of calm, where Ann, Mike and myself could restore some sanity and talk about how we really felt, but for the most part, I spent as much time as possible out of the house, which was possibly part of the reason so much time was spent on that history project I mentioned.

By this time, I was getting good marks for English comprehension, essay writing, the Friday IQ and mental arithmetic tests, but still struggled with some of the mathematical problems.

I've already mentioned I was in the school football team, but better than that, in the final term I was made cricket captain and up on the rec, removed two of the opposition top order with successive deliveries. Being on a hat trick, I unfortunately stiffened up and sent the ball slightly too wide down the off side. The batsman swung, snicked it and my friend Leigh Northwood, dived and caught it in the slips. I was mobbed by my team mates, but actually didn't feel overly elated, for with a fairly poor final delivery bringing such success, I wondered could it be one of those lessons in life?

I received another soon after, that brought home with a bang how fate and luck can be so fickle, to the point of leaving your whole future hanging as if by a thread. The incident began with nothing more than yellow six-inch ruler that had snapped in half. The snapping had left ragged upturned edges and in an idle moment, with the headmistress not in the room, I interlocked these to see what would happen if I flicked one half, by use of the other.

Three inches of yellow metal flying straight across the classroom was the answer. Even though it brought a few gasps of wonder, I held hand to mouth, for I'd not expected such a successful outcome and when lumpy Richard declared he would tell Miss Perry, I knew I was in serious trouble.

Even though I owned up to being as surprised as anyone regarding the flight of the ruler and others urged him not to snitch on me, you could see by the sanctimonious look his mind was made up. As soon as the headmistress returned, up shot his hand. The fact she didn't notice at first increased the tension. The boy sitting next to him, tried pulling his arm down, but he wrenched it away and in a sickly voice said, "Please miss-----"

I had got on well with Miss Perry, but not to the extent she'd put up with a ruler being flicked across the class and I was told to stack all my books ready for taking next door to Mr. Williams's. I was to be expelled from the top class and would miss out on the final preparations needed to undertake the biggest test of my life, the 11+.

As the afternoon dragged, a ray of hope began to glimmer and when class was dismissed, I sat awaiting my fate. Did stay of execution mean a reprieve or did the delay mean I was to be formally handed over to the B side of the school?

Miss Perry carried on marking, but then, peering over her spectacles; she would have made a marvellous Miss Marple; she quietly told me to put the books back in my desk. As said before, everyone makes mistakes and of course sends down the odd bad delivery, but if you don't push your luck, these mistakes are sometimes forgiven. I apologised once more and then thanking the Lord, vowed to make the most of the chance given me.

On the big day in question, we all walked in crocodile formation down to the Grammar School, to join the massive throng assembled to take the exam. The allotting of desks was done with almost military precision and I sat near a window, with Pete Clark directly in front of me. As I rushed to beat the clock and answer all the questions, I noticed him looking quite untroubled, at times even staring through the window.

He'd told me he didn't want to pass and was certainly being true to his word. Roger and Mick Woodcock had said the previous year, they thought the Grammar School to be only for snobs and going there would be tantamount to betraying their mates, but on top of that, hated the thought of giving up 'futter,' as they called it, for at the Grammar School they'd be forced to play rugby.

Back at school one afternoon, a list was read out. It contained the borderline cases; those selected for an interview. The rest of the class had to wait until these were conducted, before knowing whether they'd achieved a straight pass, or had failed. What a terrible ordeal at such a young age.

Prior to walking down for the interview that would determine the rest of my life, mother gave last minute instructions to ensure I told them of the prestigious job my stepfather did; the fact my sister had done well at the High School and on no account was I to put hands in pockets.

The actual interview went quite well, with them being quite taken by my ambition to be an archaeologist. That is until I was asked to spell the word and hearing me struggling, I was handed a large dark tome, the Oxford English Dictionary. It seems unbelievable now, but none of us had ever been taught to use a dictionary and seeing me floundering mid-book a panel member kindly took it from me. The fact the interview didn't end there and then, was a good sign, but I was still deeply worried.

On the day all the passes were announced there were a few shocked faces and many tears. One poor lad, who came from a particularly bright family, sobbed in snotty floods as if his life had come to an end. My mother had been on such tenterhooks, she'd walked to meet me from school. I can see her now, waiting with a concerned look at the end of what we called the Flats.

After a disconsolate look and shake of head, I announced, "I passed," and her face lit up like the sun coming out. She was absolutely thrilled, but for me there was a sense of relief rather than elation, for some of my friends, either academically equal or in one case far better at maths, had failed. Quite inexplicable. I found it hard to look them in the eye, let alone offer consolation and felt almost guilty regarding my good fortune. In fact, when end of term came, I was mightily relieved.

# Part Three

# Secondary education and
# another bad patch

At family gatherings, you will have noticed how certain reminiscences can be greatly relished, to the extent of even drawing hilarity when having been heard many times before. Funny anecdotes and comical things children do, being requested time after time, but you've probably also noticed, not only can some listeners be reminded of things they had clean forgotten, but also, how raconteurs can be completely unaware they are relating events in completely the wrong order. Of course, it's exactly the same when writing, for unless there's a hit song or major event to exactly pin down recollections, they can easily be described out of sequence.

For a start, although my brother and I certainly did pass part of one term of confinement following an illness, trying to imagine how our neighbours passed wind, reading back through it, I suspect our little comic sketch happened a year or two later. I've left it where it is, however, if only to illustrate this point.

However, when recently talking to Copper and realising an event of far greater significance, his running away, well cycling away actually, happened two years before the slot at which it rested in my memory, it prompted much needed alteration of the text.

He told me, that back in 1959 he had been incredibly unhappy and yet I remember, on his return from the two-week sojourn, he'd regaled us all with what an adventure it had been. Having cycled as far as Evesham, about 50 miles, and realising he was less than half way, he hid the bike and hitch-hiked through the night to London. You can imagine his aunt's shock at seeing him on her doorstep and having heard his story, she immediately informed the police of his whereabouts. That's how the message reached his parents.

His brother had been less than enamoured by tales of the exploit, however, for having directed the police to a camp we'd recently constructed way over by the Ledwyche, the discovery of Copper's abandoned school satchel there had led to an extensive search, where Roger and his father had had to partake in the macabre night-time act of directing police frogmen to likely spots in the river where a drowned body might be found.

Out of interest, upon his return he continued at the Grammar School until leaving in July 1962, furnished with sufficient O-level passes to see him on his way in life. A bit of a rough diamond, you might say, but talent shines through in the end.

So, my first term at the Grammar School was only weeks away, but meanwhile I had one last summer of freedom before that shackled feeling of wearing a school uniform. I can't remember the visit to the outfitters in town that supplied all to the right specifications, but can remember my mother being aghast at the cost. Oh, I've just remembered, how dispirited I felt when trying on the school cap, but nowhere near as bad as when tugging on rugby boots in Ross's shoe shop. They felt horribly stiff and restricting, plus the way they covered to above the ankle, put me in mind of something of a surgical nature.

That last summer of feeling unbridled, was the year of the Rome Summer Olympics and boys crowded into our front room to watch the most prestigious events on television. We of course had high hopes for our competitors, but had to settle for just two golds; Don Thompson in the 50 kilometre walk and Anita Lonsbrough's, 200 metres breaststroke triumph. Then in the blue riband men's 100 metres sprint final, although only gaining a bronze, when all were closing in on the tape, Peter Radford was actually the fastest on the track. If only he had a better start or a thing boys often wish; if only the course had been two metres longer.

As in many sports, certain people transcend national partisanship to reach world-wide acclaim and Abibe Bikila managed this, breasting the tape to win the marathon bare footed.

What really made those games memorable, however, was the fact the overflow pipe from the recently completed water tower must have become jammed, for the entire contents ran down the far side of the road into Small's field, to even reach as far as the Willow Tree. Suddenly we had games of our own, racing suitably trimmed sticks to simulate pairs, fours and eights and although running alongside shouting encouragement was of course entirely unavailing, it didn't matter for we had tremendous fun. The races went on all day and we even devised our own medals' table.

The water was still flowing the following morning, but was only sufficient for a few stick entries for kayak and canoe events as far as the bottom of the road and so we then held running and bike races around the block, with commentary coming live from the top of an elm tree.

Rather than all hurtling off together, heats were arranged with two setting off in different directions and on certain parts of the course the competitors could be briefly glimpsed by the reporter aloft, excitedly announcing who had been first to reach the halfway point, Stead's shop. Where our two roads met at the bottom of Clee View, was the winning post.

Having got into the swing of things, the 100, 200 and 400 metre races were next, held on 'our' corner of Small's nearest pasture, followed by the field events. We of course didn't have an adequate piece of equipment for the pole vault and so used a 6-foot staff for the result to be measured horizontally rather than vertically. A flat stone was used for the discus and a round one for shot-put but when it came to the hammer, Copper insisted on us using the real thing.

A coal house was raided for the needed item.

And as none had yet witnessed actual event,

We started by running to fling the old lump,

Until Copper said, "That's not how it went!"

Continued, "It was more of a swirl, yell and chuck.

Think the hammer was bigger, as in sledge."

He bounced, bellowed and gave huge backward heave

And all laughed at its perfect arc to the hedge.

No points for direction, derision at style;

Lump hammer's loss and the worry this posed,

But search as we might, with darkness descending,

Tool stayed hedge-bound; games officially closed.

This was the end of the fun time for a while, for three reasons; firstly, things at home had become unbearable; second, I'd soon be entering into a new regime with homework every night and third, a girl called Carol came to stay with her relatives who lived over the hill.

I won't describe the return of the 'silences.' I bet you're already sick of reading about them, so suffice to say, it was obvious it couldn't go on for much longer, for we all had the feeling something had to give.

As regards the Grammar School, Copper had shown me some of the maths problems he'd solved, which of course was impressive, but with their complexity being way beyond my comprehension, I was worried in case I might not be able to cope.

On the final matter of Carol, her arrival coincided with Neil Sedaka's hit record of the same name and as if taking that as a sign, four of my friends went down with the same blight, Carolitis, hanging around, doing nothing in particular, just hoping to catch sight of her.

I found it most mystifying, for although not particularly attractive, in fact her nose looked as if she might have once accidently trodden on a rake, she seemed to somehow cast a spell over them. The new Clee View Queen did take the bestowed status in her stride, mind you, there's no doubting that, playing one off against another and then if deciding something on a whim, reigned supreme as all followed vying for her attention. Unfortunately, Roger became the most besotted and seemed totally oblivious to how ignominious it appeared. Of course, they rounded on me for not becoming a devoted courtier, but even if I'd have found her irresistible, I'd not have demeaned myself as they were doing.

I can't remember what I did as an alternative, but do remember collaring Pete Clark on his way to the Court of Carol one morning. I'd been meaning to ask him for ages; why had he looked almost in a dream, that day while sitting the 11+ exam?

"I told you. I didn't want to pass."

"What a waste. Even though only half-hearted, you still got an interview."

"Dunner! Couldna believe it."

"Your interview was just before mine."

"I know and mighta done you a favour, acting as thick and ignorant as I possibly could. That did the trick."

"How did that do me a favour?"

"Well youda come across like a buddin' genius, after what I gid 'em."

It almost made me feel like an imposter, for not only had my three best school mates been denied what the whole class would have felt to have been their due, also, with a different attitude, Pete would have sailed into the coming challenge of the Grammar School.

Unfortunately, I didn't. Obviously things at home didn't help, but it can't have been the entire reason why I was so all at sea.

First, I'd better set the scene. It was an unusually hot Indian Summer that year and I found wearing tie, cap and jacket, particularly stifling on the mile-long walk back home, but if reported for not being in full uniform, it could bring two strokes of the cane, or at the very least detention. The school at the bottom of Mill Street was hundreds of years old and had ancient traditions hanging over it like a spectre. Obviously, once back home you could wear what you liked, but going to, or returning from school you had to be fully attired and heaven help you if you lost your cap.

There was no first form, well not by name at any rate. The years ran, Second, Third, Fourth, Remove, then the Fifth form, when O-levels were taken and for those staying on to take A-levels there was the senior school of Lower and Upper Sixth. There were roughly 240 boys and apart from the caretaker's wife who was as wide as she was tall, there was not a woman in the place. The junior classes had 32 boys each, but with our year being the most bounteous 'bulge' year there were 44, split alphabetically into 2A and 2B. What also swelled the ranks was a higher than usual intake of sons of those serving in the military. I can remember at least six in our year and as they had not the remotest connection with the vicinity, they were accommodated in the boarding section of the school, at Dinham Hall, a place I was soon to have a grim experience of.

When I think back, it was like a light had gone out inside me. We went straight in at the deep end with French and Latin and I found my ignorance in chemistry lessons so frightening, I actually dreaded the double lesson on a Thursday. With algebra I was all at sea and even in geography, sat diligently listening, but nothing seemed to sink in. I felt horribly out of my depth and was petrified of demotion down to the Secondary Modern. Meanwhile the homework piled up and trying to complete it in our living room, bristling with such bridled tension, was like being expected to compile a nitpicking military report when expecting a bomb to go off. Then it got worse.

Ann disappeared to temporary accommodation with friends down the far end of Clee View; my mother escaped with Michael to stay with my aunt and uncle in Morecambe and somehow, she managed to wangle me a place in the Grammar School boarding block, at Dinham Hall.

There was the main entrance opposite the castle gardens but also a handy access through what had once been stables, halfway up Mill Street. The seniors 'dormed' here, while the dormitories for the fifth form and below were in the main building. There were two common rooms, junior and senior, a large dining room and a dungeon of a boot room, with open cupboards and hooks for all school shoes, sport's kit and coats. The boiler, spud bashing machine and laundry room were also down there. Junior boys had the duty of keeping the boiler going; providing the daily quota of peeled potatoes by loading and cranking the handle of the ancient peeler, then cleaning up afterwards, but also each had the task of polishing the shoes of an allotted older boy. As I had not the remotest chance of pocket money, I undertook extra shoe cleaning for threepence per pair, per week. On many a morning, with time obviously tight, some of the comments regarding my rushed efforts were disparaging to say the least.

I shared a bedroom with two boys a year my senior; more of that later and the only access was via the junior dormitory. There was a further exit, however, by use of the fire escape tackle hanging in the window. Fire drill was practiced once a year.

Any boy caught using the housemaster's main stairway, or wandering where they shouldn't at night, was caned, as was anyone caught with food in the dormitory. For minor misdemeanours there was what was called jankers; weeding the garden, spud bashing, general tidying etc and for late returns or if caught straying beyond the bounds, one was gated.

By today's standards it sounds frighteningly grim, but in actual fact our housemaster, Johnnie Jones, was a genial old cove with a ready wit. Peter, his faithful retriever plodded beside him everywhere, even into classes, where he'd obediently lie beside his master's desk for the duration of the period. Johnnie, as we called him out of earshot, had an encyclopaedic knowledge of cricket, was a master at chess and had taught boys, maths and geography all his adult life. Knowing what they could be like given the chance, he ran a tight ship and always took the trouble to explain exactly what each punishment was for and would even occasionally apologise for the caning about to be administered, saying the boy's actions had left him with no choice.

With quite a few of the juniors in my year being from military families, they joined their parents at each vacation in far flung outposts such as Hong Kong, Aden, Malta and Cyprus and it was fascinating, on their return looking bronzed, to hear tales of their experiences. Not so the little martinet I shared my bedroom with.

It happened like this. As said earlier, I don't remember my very first day at school, but I do remember, with particular clarity, my first day at the Grammar School. There must have been a staff meeting that lasted the whole morning, for all us new boys were told to wait, standing with our backs to the wall bars in the gymnasium. A prefect watched over us, but that didn't stop a small inspection squad from entering during the morning break. They were led by a boy, who made up for his lack of stature by assuming a chest-out military manner and I was surprised at the school handing such authority to one so young. He pulled jackets into line, barked orders to stand up straight, but on nearly throttling two boys with their ties, it dawned on me, he had no authorised duty whatsoever, he was simply playing at soldiers.

During my life, I've noticed the uncanny way my mind sometimes envisages what will happen next. I would have been one of the tallest boys there that morning and instinctively knew he'd take exception to the fact. He stared me up and down, hatred at first sight and with a sneer writhing, made a grab for my tie. When I parried this, his attempt to push me against the wall bars was not only anticipated, my retaliatory push rocked him backwards. Absolutely incensed, he hurled himself at my middle region and the ensuing scrap required the prefect to separate us.

So you can imagine my feelings, first day at Dinham Hall when shown to my sleeping quarters, I found the martinet and his main henchman waiting. The latter was a ginger-haired dolt who although older than me, was actually in my class, for he'd been held back a year. Almost a repeat of the lumpy Richard scenario, but this one was more solid and as yet had not been challenged in his role as enforcer. The pair of them pointedly ignored me when in the room and when out of it, made sure I was excluded from all games and activities. Any boy trying to associate with me faced a good thumping from the dolt, or the threat of being sent to Coventry, as I had been. The worry of the broken home was bad enough, but coupled with my struggle academically and now this, I began to feel like a non-person. If there was any inexplicable mishap in the boarding house, the culprit wasn't looked for, the little Hitler simply blamed me. It's no wonder I started each day feeling rather seldom. (By the way, the use of the word seldom in such a context is a quirk of the South Shropshire dialect I find wonderfully enigmatic)

Feeling so beyond the warm balm of friendship, helps explain two silly mistakes. Regarding the first, I must have been feeling particularly seldom, for I didn't see a trap coming. Little Hitler had taken most of the juniors off with him, foraging up Whitcliff to drag back wood for the November 5th bonfire. They held their efforts in such great store and yet in reality they were absolutely pathetic when compared to the grand edifices I'd help build. I had been excluded as expected, but strangely one of my classmates hung about in the junior common room and was being unusually friendly. Didn't care for him much, but felt so trapped inside, any form of company was a blessed relief.

Like all boys that age, we were starving hungry and he said he'd the perfect solution. Opening one of the small wall cupboards, he prised open an old biscuit tin to produce a jam tart. When I pointed out it was not his cupboard, he laughed through the crumbs and said it didn't matter as the house policy was, 'To share and share alike.' Well, that was fine by me and repeating his words ate two of the tarts.

Well you can guess the rest. When the others returned, the owner of the tarts went straight to his cupboard, loudly declared a thief had been at work and my knew found friend pointed saying, I was the culprit

Little Hitler, with a smug look, grandly turned to his audience and asked, had he not been right all along to insist on my exclusion from their gentlemanly activities? In cockney parlance, 'I'd been stitched up like a kipper,' but then had to suffer an exaggerated show of boys secreting personal items whenever I was near, as if I might have been about to steal them. Word got about and some of the older students began pronouncing my surname like something they'd just stepped in.

It doesn't take long for this sort of treatment to destroy a person's self-confidence and resolve. I asked a lad, who was one of my best friends when down at school, if he could ignore the peer pressure, for just one ally would have helped banish that feeling of complete isolation. He said, although he would truly like to, he didn't dare. What would I have done to have had Roger with me? Together we'd have soon put an end to such nonsense.

My room-mates from hell weren't in the common room the day a biscuit tin lid was being spun from one to the other bringing sounds of revelry and timpani and feeling obvious elation at being included in one of their activities at last, I put a little too much zest into the lid's flight, to the extent the receiver fumbled it. Following the resulting clatter as it hit the floor, the door flew open and there, right on cue, stood the housemaster asking who was responsible.

Well, we all had been, but reasoning he'd hardly be likely to cane all six of us, we remained silent. With hindsight, I made entirely the wrong decision. As I'd been the final thrower of the projectile, I should have taken the punishment for all, but left it seconds too late, for when just on the point of owning up, we were all marched up the forbidden stairway to receive three strokes of the cane.

Grimly waiting outside his office door, we stood in a diminishing line hearing the dull thwacks coming from within and being last to go, I'll never forget those glistening accusatory looks as each boy emerged holding his backside. Once the seniors got to hear about the incident, they were aghast that a boy hadn't had the decency to own up and I now had total pariah status. One even mooted the idea of reviving the tradition of Dinham Benching, where a person of such loathing is bound to a bench to receive a plimsole blow from all in turn. I'd had a few lows in my life, but this easily beat the lot of them.

It must have shown, for the headmaster summoned me up to his office one day. Wrapped tight in his gown and with piercing stare intensified by thick lenses, he resembled a huge omniscient black owl.

"You don't seem happy, Clegg."

I was quaking, wondering if I was to be sent down to the Secondary Modern School.

With head atilt, he genially asked, "What's the matter old chap?"

I could feel the muscles in my face twitching, lips quivering and so didn't dare reply, because just one word would have broken the seal holding back the flood. Besides that, the school omerta decreed, no matter what the circumstances, you never named names. Not owning up, as in the tin lid episode, was bad enough, but to have accused my room mates of psychological bullying would not only have invited a debagging, my trousers would have flown from the school flagpole in an ultimate display of humiliation.

The headmaster reasoned, considering recent home conditions it was understandable I should be a little below par, but then also divulged an interesting morsal I would not normally have been party to. Even though feeling numb at having been summoned to his study, I still managed to discern the fact, his mention of touch and go must have referred to the 11+ interview and that his convincing the board I'd be a late developer had been the magic ingredient that had tipped the balance in my favour.

Utterly dazed, I thanked him and relieved I was still a Grammar School boy, soldiered on through the term in survival mode, keeping a low profile until my luck would hopefully change. As said before, luck, good or bad can come out of nowhere to leave your life dangling as if by a thread and so the only thing one could do during a bad patch, was to keep believing until something happened along to turn things around, plus I now had a duty to not let the headmaster down.

Regarding the piece of luck, it's quite comical really, for remember that jam tart episode that brought me so low? Well would you believe it, in a round-about way, another jam tart would actually come to my rescue. It was one of a little batch my sister had baked, bless her, for she'd had the perception to realise, with having no pocket money there was no possible way, other than scoffing another boy's tuck, to actually acquire such dainties.

The tart mentioned, happened to enter the scheme of things the very evening Johnnie Jones had decided to undertake a spot check of all the dormitories. Having been down in the boot room, cleaning shoes to save myself the task the following morning, I blithely entered my bedroom to find the housemaster and head prefect staring at a large unsightly smudge on my bottom sheet. It was a complete mystery to me, but peering close I was horrified to see it was a squashed jam tart, obviously from the batch my sister had made. Well of course I wouldn't have wasted a tart by putting it in my bed and squashing it, but apart from plead complete ignorance, didn't dare reveal my suspicions, for accusing others with the possibility of getting them caned, was thought of as the biggest sin you could commit at boarding school.

On being led to my fate through the length of the junior dormitory, I noticed a few nudges and heard a few murmurs and almost felt as if I had a rope around my neck. Luckily, I was still dressed. A caning when in pyjamas stung like the devil and left welts right round to the upper thigh region.

But anyway, being fresh back from having had four severe strokes administered by a whippy bamboo cane, I burst into the bedroom and yelled, "So which one of you two bastards was it?"

An arrogant stare was returned by the Hitler youth, but the wavering look from the ginger dolt told all and I raved at him, "It was you, y'bastard wasn't it!"

"Own up if it was," said the Hitler youth, obviously dropping his henchman in it, for now I come to think about it, the whole sneaky affair must have been done in accordance to his bidding.

I wasn't in the frame of mind to be sorting out such fine details at the time of course and so laying into the dolt, I released every ounce of misery, sadness and frustration I'd endured and then told him, if he so much as even looked at me in future, he'd get, "Another fucking dose!"

Figuratively speaking, that lanced the boil and I had no further trouble from either of them. I'm not in any way condoning violence and I was too lanky to be a fighter, but when needs must-----.

That Christmas, all the boys were expected to contribute a little invention to the breaking-up party. I still had to take things cautiously, not appear obtrusive and so when not invited to participate in schemes devised by others, it left just myself and the original tart sneak without a partner. With him about as imaginative as a slug and only having one day to go, I wrestled with notions that might be considered entertaining.

The following afternoon things went well; funny poems and short sketches that made what I'd dreamt up seem frighteningly lame by comparison, plus there was the burden of knowing I still probably carried a degree of stigma regarding recent events.

There was one more act to go before our little attempt, which happened to be a rendition of Red River Valley on the harmonica, performed without any hint of seepage, by the boy who had once farted in our living room.

He was given a hearty round of applause and then came our turn. Beneath large borrowed dressing gowns, we had padded ourselves out with bolsters and massive balloons, making our energetic efforts to box almost impossible and we bounced off one another like two sumo wrestlers. I was amazed at the hilarity it brought. All were absolutely roaring with laughter and when hidden pins popped the balloons, sending us recoiling onto our backsides, we received a standing ovation.

As things had still not been resolved on the home front, I spent the vacation with the family of my friend, the one who had avowed, he would have stood by me in the bad times if only circumstances had allowed. With his father being stationed at RAF Shawbury, we had an amazing time exploring cliffs and caves in Hawkstone Park.

Life was a lot easier through the spring term, but my work was still not up to scratch, for I still suffered from that feeling of the light inside refusing to switch back on, but then came the news my stepfather had taken a job in the south, meaning the house lay vacant for our return. It was then I realised how much I'd missed my family and walking into the kitchen that first day back, felt as if waking up from a bad dream. With it almost seeming too good to be true I busied myself with a few household chores, until my mother asked wryly, "How long do you think you can keep this up?"

Roger and I were obviously glad to meet up again, although of course neither showed it. I had only been absent for two terms and yet it felt like two years. With him shortly to be saddled with a Saturday job, we hit on the idea of having one last grand tour of all our old haunts, but before giving details of that I'll provide a little more background material.

With Eric now gone, it meant I had to look after the garden. Safe to say, I'm not a natural, either in ability or volition, but someone had to do it. Mike was supposedly there to help and would enter the fray with enthusiasm, until declaring he'd not be able to continue for a single second further without a drink of water.

"Well don't take all day about it."

"Course not, I'll be back in a minute."

That would be the last I'd see of him until hunger drove him home.

Another chore was to fetch eggs from the baker in East Hamlet. They were thin shelled, which didn't matter when the man used them in cake baking and those surplus to requirements were sold off at the amazing saving of thruppence less than normal per dozen, about 1p in current money. I know it doesn't sound a lot, but back then it would have been enough to buy a pound of potatoes. The problem was, being weak shelled, if one broke the bag got wet and you lost the lot as brother Michael found one day when looking forlornly at a row of yellow bombs dropped along the pavement.

"Didn't you think of taking a bag to carry them in?" His glowering response indicated, obviously not.

With my sister Ann, again taking up the offer of helping with the catering at the Caynham finishing school, it meant I had to do the occasional Saturday shopping trip down town. While my friends were off exploring, I had to haul home all the things we couldn't order from Stevens' the grocer. There was a bonus, however, for I was occasionally invited to stay overnight at Caynham Court Finishing School for Ladies and it felt like I'd died and gone to heaven. A treasured memory was when leaning on the bannisters one evening, gazing down from on high, I was witness to excited girlish chatter and laughter echoing in the hallway, which brought further intrigue, for a young beauty then went into a demonstrative, unbridled version of Edith Piaf's memorable song, Milord. Drawn by her suggestive manner and raunchy delivery, acting out the part of a lady of pleasure, all the surrounding girls seemed on the one hand, nervous of being caught and yet on the other, were obviously compelled to keep looking at the saucy piece of theatre, while above I had the privilege of witnessing what young ladies can be like when no males are present.

On the home front, perhaps, because the family had been through so much, my mother relented and allowed Mike and myself to have a dog. Mick Woodcock said he knew of a litter of pups on the point of being weaned and returned one day from his part-time job in the Clee Hill quarries, to empty his bait bag on our living room carpet. Out wriggled a friendly little morsel that on examination was male and almost certainly, 80% border collie. Shep had arrived.

We taught him to sit, lie, stay, jump through a hoop and carry an egg in his mouth without cracking it. He took food from hand in a gentle manner, could sit up and beg, stayed at heel when walking through fields containing livestock, but we couldn't cure him of his overexuberance when greeting other children. He'd wriggle and squeal in a way that could frighten those not used to him, but those that were, would sometimes knock on our door and ask if Shep could come out to play?

There was no real worry regarding that, as he didn't chase livestock, had learnt to avoid traffic and also, the dog and cat killer, Benno, a greyhound cross from up the road had gone on to meet his maker.

# Shep

We had a sheepdog whose passion was moles.
Never known to have caught one, just loved the chase.
Dug up miles of tunnels, sniffed down the holes,
Bum stuck in air, muddy smile on his face.

Loved rolling in rot, when out for a walk;
Plus stagnant immersions to stink for a treat;
Downtown he'd once stolen huge joint of pork;
Low-tailed flight, chased by butchers up-street.

Would stay until called, could sit up and beg;
Jump smiling through hoop, catch a ball when thrown;
Mouth carried, so gentle, a new laid egg;
Passionately whimpered when given first bone.

Also remember his very first fight,
Six-week-old puppy, whimpering fluff ball;
When Benno attacked, he'd cowered in fright,
And the overshot Long Dog got brained on the wall.


Before telling you about that bit of a final tour Roger and I
undertook, I must slip in this little gem. It happened one sunny
afternoon when I happened to wander into mother's bedroom and
found her in a state of deep reverie, looking at old photographs
spread on the bedcover. She said she was just remembering old
times; pictures of her father, the house on the seafront at West
Kirby, picnics across on Hilbre Island, the cottage they'd had in
Wales and then I noticed a photograph of a handsome man in
officer's uniform. I don't know why I'd picked that one out from the
hundred or so images splayed on the counterpane, but I wanted to
know who he was.

"That my dear, is your father."

After staring at me and obviously weighing up the situation, she asked, "Would you like me to tell you a secret?"

I of course did and so was told, "Your father's not really dead. He's alive and living in the Isle of Man."

Seeing I was somewhat shocked, she took both my hands in hers and said, "I'm sorry darling. It was wrong of me to tell you what I did." With an earnest look she continued, "It really hurt me to do it, believe me. But I was under a lot of pressure."

"Does Ann know?"

"Of course, she's known all along. Can you forgive me?"

"Yes, but I don't know what to say. I can hardly take it in."

She told me how they had met during the war. It was in the early days of moving to Shropshire, when my mother had helped run the Unicorn Inn near the northern extremity of Ludlow and a mere bike ride away at Bromfield, was the massive ammunition dump my father had been assigned to. There was instant attraction, a whirlwind romance, five weeks of married life and then he was shipped off to India.

That was the last she saw of him until he returned from the far-east in 1946, a major with an MBE, in what they called the 'forgotten army.' Meanwhile the young slip of a girl was now a mature woman with a three-year-old child and she said, it was like getting into bed with a stranger. Of course, all his Manx family were also strangers and leaving all those she knew behind, she helped set up home in Crosby, my birthplace.

My father had worked in the bank before the war and I don't know what level he'd attained, but it would certainly have been much higher than the cashier's job he was offered on his return. So, from organising supplies for his beleaguered regiment on the Arakan, he now worked in little more than a cupboard, in the bank's tiny outposts at Peel and Castletown. Enough to turn a man to drink.

My mother said, he would regularly disappear for whole weekends and return falling all over the place, sometimes messing himself and would often sway over my cot sipping at spoonsful of steaming soup.

She would grab me to her bosom, petrified I'd be scalded. It must have been a living nightmare, for even when meeting him from work, or asking for her father-in-law's help and on one occasion hiding his teeth, it only delayed the inevitable. It's no wonder I remember that shouting on the stairs when I was two.

Then valuables she had brought from England began to go missing. Walking down a main shopping thoroughfare in Douglas one day, she spotted her antique dinner service for sale in a shop window, some of her rings disappeared, but with a sad look she told me, it was almost impossible to get the truth out of him.

Noticing the effect this was having, she tried softening the blow by explaining it was all down to drink. When off it, you couldn't want for a more charming and beguiling man. She had stuck it for three years, but when he broke her nose, she decided enough was enough and thus my memory at such a hurried departure when my golly had been left behind.

With a wistful look she said, "He still drinks they tell me, but at least he's trying to do something about it. It's a weakness really. Would you like to meet him?"

Well! As you can imagine, I was stunned. On the one hand I still had a father, but on the other, he had been a liar, a drunkard, a wife beater and to cap it all was weak. You can imagine the worry, for with me being his son, did it mean those traits would emerge as I grew to maturity? I had just rid myself of one stigma at school and yet might have had innate candidates for scorn lurking just below the surface.

The grain of hope was the MBE. Those weren't dished out to liars and drunkards and he had also been mentioned in dispatches for life-saving work, organising food for those starving in Hong Kong after hostilities had ceased. Back then, there was no help for those trying to settle down after the horrors of war, for when you think, Post Traumatic Stress Disorder wasn't even recognised until 1980 and so returning combatants were supposed to say nothing and just get on with it.

Even in the early 1960's there was still an incredible amount of ignorance. Sexual matters were not discussed and there was limited understanding of gambling or drinking compulsions. So is it any wonder I held a deep dread that alcoholism might be something not only innate, but something the sufferer had absolutely no control over; almost like a congenital disease. It was all very perturbing.

Anyway, moving swiftly on. On our last tour, Roger and I first headed out to the Ledwyche. We passed the time talking of past adventures, sport, what people had done at school etc. You know the sort of thing, but I didn't go into detail regarding my recent difficulties, but simply explained I'd had a bit of a problem to sort out.

"But you sorted it?"

"Yes, they don't bother me now."

"You'm too soft sometimes, Clegger. You 'av to fight yer corner."

"I did Rog, but in the general scheme of things at the Grammar School, resorting to violence is largely frowned upon."

"Huh! Some of them Grammar dogs are that big 'eaded, makes y'sick just to look at 'em."

"The one in question would certainly have made you sick, but most of them are fine."

"Dunno about that, but anyway, that one you had the problem with,---you knocked him off 'is perch."

"Not him exactly, the dull lump who always did his bidding. Strange thing is though, since the trouble's been sorted, they've both become almost nobody's."

Coming from a mixed school, Roger's snippets of information were more of a sexual nature; such as, what one of Francy's cousins had had the cheek to do, flat out beneath his desk not minding that girls were watching and how a certain fourteen-year-old was that overjoyed with what nature had endowed, if you asked her nicely, she'd let you witness the marvel for yourself.

Between Ledwche bridge and what we called Shaky Bridge, there was a small waterfall, a sight to behold in winter, but on our tour was just a copious torrent. Shaky Bridge was named after a wooden crossing that had preceded the rivetted iron structure that shielded the Elan Valley to Birmingham water pipeline. We would often open the inspection hatch and descend the steel ladder to sit with feet dangling from plank walkway. With the flow of water below, it was the ideal place to talk of life's meanderings. Many a core from scrumped apples had bobbed downstream from that little safehold.

Our tour took in Bluebell wood, plus the area beyond where Copper had launched his truancy two years earlier. On another day we walked to Caynham Camp to perambulate the ramparts and see if our initials were still carved in the beech bark. Yes, RP loves CP, (Carol) was still there. RP hadn't been altered to BB as had his inscriptions on Ledwyche bridge. At Ledwyche lake, the swans still flew low across the water, before spreading feet to send a threatening wave towards where we stood. Our Wildeland was as wild as ever and if chancing on wild flowers on the homeward journey, we always picked a bunch for our mothers. Yes, you read it right. We might have looked a little unkempt, but never forgot our mothers.

Even on inclement mornings we stuck to the plan and it was decidedly iffy when heading off towards Whitbatch one day, going by way of Rock Green. Actually, we always called it Rocks Green and we'd take a cut-through between the final cottages which led down through pastures and orchard to the haunted house. If lucky, we'd see the steam train hauling Dhustone to the mainline and on hearing the tell-tale thrumming when putting an ear to the rail, would stay and wait for it. There was no train that day and sadly not many more in the future.

The haunted house, by the way, had been a small Tudor mansion, Dodmore Manor that fell into decay and was then destroyed by fire in the mid-50's. Also, another piece of history, in the lower reaches of Whitbatch wood, we'd found an abandoned hamlet and mineshaft. Had the community once mined for lead? The whole place had quite an enigmatic feel and we often wondered what it would have been like when full of bustle and children.

The tour would not have been complete without taking in Batty's Island, Whitcliffe and Ludlow castle and regarding the latter, by way of a secret portal, we gained free entry and knew ways to climb up into the towers not open to the public. As you can imagine, that brought a certain sense of exclusivity, when watching baffled tourists vainly searching for a way to ascend.

On the final day of the Easter holiday, we'd planned to head off for a sloping meadow where two rows of barns formed what looked like an abandoned street, reminiscent of a ski resort in summer. Needless to say we called it, 'Little Switzerland.'

Easter was early that year and so the annual soccer match against the old school had been tagged on to what was almost the start of the cricket season. It was always played on the recreation ground to the rear of our houses, but being engrossed in our tour of old territory I'd clean forgotten about it. The sight of a team member running over the hill, fully kitted out except for boots, suddenly jogged my memory.

I explained the dilemma to Roger, who after a moment's consideration said, "Nuh, this ooner do. You give us yer word to visit every single place and you'm gonna keep to it."

Any further reasoning on my part was nipped in the bud by being wrestled to the pavement and then having Roger sit on my chest.

"Are you coming or not?" asked my teammate.

"No, ee's stayin 'ere along uv me," cut in Roger. "Ee gave 'is word and ees gonner stick to it."

"Look, we'll be kicking off in ten minutes!"

"Well in a perfect world I'd be joining you," I said.

"But this is ridiculous. How am going to explain our centre half would like to partake, but has someone sitting on his chest?"

"Well do you fancy removing him?"

"No fear!"

In the end Roger reluctantly let me go and I've not one clue regarding the result of the match, but I do remember feeling bereft, as if having betrayed and broken the spell of our magic Neverland.

It was all bound to end soon of course, for nothing ever stays the same. To give you one example, Ludlow Swimming Baths opened down at Dinham and so on hot days the focus of attention was to somehow scrape together enough money to gain entry. It was initially an open-air pool and in the early days we clambered over the fence, but in fear of being barred from the place we then needed to raid piggy banks, do odd jobs, or pick fruit, for if you couldn't raise the shilling required, you couldn't join the fun and have a chance to impress the girls. Yes girls. As I said, nothing stays the same.

In fact, Roger became so besotted by a young filly living next to the Nelson pub, he had us all troop down in our wellies to loiter around Rocks Green, hoping she'd make an appearance. He obviously realised it would have looked thoroughly weird had he idled about there alone, thus the reason for us being pressured into acting as stooges, but it was a thoroughly dull way to spend one's free time and so in the end I refused to go. Obviously, I can't remember what I did as an alternative, but do remember seeing Pete one morning, reclining on the bank opposite Pritchard's house.

I knew why he was hanging about and so suggested he break ranks and do something else for a change. At first he wouldn't hear of it, a Roger stalwart to the end and regarding any suggestion of an alternative itinerary, he said, quite truthfully, we'd been to them all before. It was on looking towards the horizon for inspiration that the idea struck me, "What about Titterstone, then?"

Pete stared at me for a while and then said, "You'm fuckin' jokin' incher?"

"No, Pete. I know it sounds mad, but if we set off now, we'd be back by teatime."

"Mad? Well you inner wrong there!"

"But Pete, just think,---we'd be the first to do it."

It was as if a light had switched on. "D'you know how to get there?"

"Yes, up the railway track."

So did we go? Sorry you're not going to like this, but I've got a bit ahead of myself and have left out some intervening details. I'll try and be brief. For a start, I have to admit that in the preceding term, my school work hadn't improved by much and following the summer holiday, I found myself in form 3B. We were told that our curriculum would eventually converge with that of 3A, but as they were being fast-tracked it didn't make sense, meaning it had been nothing more than a bit of soft soaping. Amelioration to cushion the blow we were all now in the duffer's class. On being told, top performers in the B form might gain promotion to join the high-fliers I decided it was about time I got my act together. I needed that internal light to come back on.

Another thing that requires a brief mention, is how a West Indian fast bowler put an end to my cricketing ambitions. In the MCC's 1959/60 winter tour, Charlie Griffith on his debut for Barbados blazed a trail through our top order, dismissing three legendary doyens in a mere two overs. Then in the 61/62 Indian tour, Nari Contractor had his skull fractured by a Griffith bouncer, that not only ended his career, but mine as well, for Charlie Griffith was later cited for throwing, rather than straight arm bowling the ball. It gained him such international notoriety anyone with a suspect action was banned from bowling. There's nothing really wrong with my arms, other than a suggestion of a misaligned crook to each elbow and although only slight, it was enough to put an end to any ambition of bowling for a school side.

So what else happened that year before the attempt on the west face of Titterstone Clee? Oh, I know, with now having no breadwinner in the family, my mother became an Avon lady. She was a dab hand at getting rid of the stuff; the tricky part was getting paid for it. Mike and I acted as the delivery boys and money collectors and not wishing to sound misogynistic, will stress the fact that I'm fully aware there are females perfectly capable of seeing the sense of bundling together all deliveries to one area, thus cutting down the number of journeys required, but sad to say, mother was amongst those bereft of any such gift in that regard, which forced me to take over the logistics.

Copper became a nightly visitor to our house, for it offered a peaceful sanctuary where he could complete his homework. He said, his place was a like a madhouse where even trying to read something brought on a headache and he wasn't the only friend to feel at home in our mother's, 'take us as you find us,' way of keeping open house. Thinking back, it became quite Bohemian and fun.

In the early autumn of that year we had a plague of Jehovah Witnesses. Having been brought up to respect my elders, I found it incredibly difficult to get rid of them. In fact it took my mother's intervention, "Not today thank **you**," as she closed the door.

Fair play, Tommy Preece had the answer. His mother had foolishly offered them admittance and then felt almost as if being eaten alive by their constant pestering. Having put coal ready on the washhouse roof, Tommy allowed ascent to halfway up the path, then peppered them shouting, "Fuck off and leave our mum alone!"

Although couched in the art insidious persistence, Tommy's more direct approach won the day.

One bonus of being in the slow stream, 3B, was to witness the arrival one morning of a fresh-faced young lad.

"What's your name, boy?" asked the form master.

"Joe."

"Joe what, boy?" he boomed.

"Joe Reece."

"Joe Reece, **what**?"

"Sorry, it's just Joe Reece. I don't have any other names."

Almost quivering with rage, the master lent down from his dais-borne desk and slowly enunciated, "You address me as **sir,** boy!"

From that moment, I instinctively knew master Reece and myself would be getting along. In actual fact, he's been a friend for life.

The form master, by the way, was the only one not having earnt the right to wear a black graduation gown when teaching. A master's gown in those days was rightly revered, for with there only being roughly 20 English universities at the time, a person gaining a degree was quite a rarity. In fact, back in those days it was considered such an accolade, every Ludlow Grammar School pupil to graduate had his name inscribed on a large oak wall plaque in the schoolroom.

So finally, back to the Titterstone saga. It was with a fair deal of enthusiasm that Pete and I set off across the fields to the stile leading onto the Ludlow to Clee Hill road that autumn day, for we were two young lads hell bent on creating a piece of Clee View history.

We took the usual route down to the haunted house and by way of a five-bar farm gate walked onto the rail track farm crossing. Behind, the line led to the world, but up ahead it led to the summit of a childhood ambition. Of course, technically speaking both Pete and I were still children, but in actual fact, as in every stage of our lives up until that point, each had had young thoughts of a man.

The railway sleepers were aligned too close together to take a normal pace and too far apart to take two in one stride and so it was at a sort of supressed lope that we set off for territory totally new to us. Even the nearby familiar places seemed wonderfully different when looked down on from a rail track and so our lofty view when crossing the Middleton road brought a certain frisson and sense of superiority.

We lorded it when crossing culverts and above rutted trails used by farm vehicles, but we did deign to descend for a sampling of local produce and made a note of certain orchards for future reference. Even something as simple as peering into a workman's hut, with its buckets, tools and lanterns, held a certain excitement, made all the better by the fact we were the pathfinders. We couldn't wait to tell the others of our bold venture when returning home.

It was one of those fresh autumn days of high scudding cloud and incredibly warm long-shadowed golden periods when the sun breaking through made it too hot for jackets. These we removed and tied round our waists. Beneath a lofty road bridge, we crept beyond and then stood staring, for a whole new exciting vista lay before us. Looking as deserted as if from a ghost town, was Bitterley Station and immediately to our right was a water tower, just like those seen in ancient shots of American railroads. Pulling on a chain, we dragged its canvas pipe mid-track and laughing, held out cupped hands to catch water to cool our faces. In a siding, stood open trucks, plus one of those rail maintenance handcars that gave the feeling we'd entered a deserted filmset for a Western.

The main line terminated just beyond the station building, with an offshoot leading to a large stone-walled engine shed and directly ahead, I finally saw the solution of how a rail line was able to make the ascent to the summit; an incline counterweight system, where laden trucks pulled the empties up for filling.

On leaving the station, we took the demanding ascent to the village of Bedlam, feeling fairly certain not many took the trouble, for net curtains were pulled aside and some householders even came out onto the raised walkway to watch us pass. The road terminated at the end of the village, with not a single car in sight, making it feel as if we'd reached a forsaken outpost. Beside a green corrugated iron chapel, was a cut-through leading towards the summit and once out onto the slope of the common we could see the mighty crag now at last within reach. Having quenched our thirsts from a cool clear rivulet, we clambered across a rocky barrier, totally oblivious to the fact it had once been a granite wall to a mighty Iron Age hillfort. Nearing the summit, we actually upped the pace and on spotting the theodolite marking the highest point, both broke into a run attempting to be first to the top. It was a dead heat and at last I had fulfilled an ambition held since first spotting the dramatic profile of Titterstone Clee when viewing from near Waterloo House all those years ago.

Hair streaming, we shouted to one another above the roar of the wind and held open like wings, our fluttering jackets to see if the buffeting gale would support us.

"Wait 'til the others hear about this!"

"Look that must be Ludlow."

"What?"

Pete yelled behind a cupped hand and with eyes streaming pointed, "Ludlow. Way down there."

I was just in time to see Saint Lawrence's church tower, so tiny and aglint in a patch of sunlight, before the cloud pattern changed and it was gone.

So then the long journey home. It was actually way beyond teatime, by the time we two pioneers finally made it back to Clee View, obviously weary, but buoyed up by the tale we now had to tell our friends.

I won't bother to describe the impact, you can imagine that, so suffice to say, even lovelorn Roger abandoned the quest for his fair maiden to lead the second expedition to the summit of Titterstone Clee. There were four in all; Roger, the two trailblazers, plus Francy. Our early departure allowed more time on arrival, to explore the quarries and ancient workings, where an engine house and scattering of huts were dwarfed by the sheer 100-foot cliff face beyond and at the bottom of a further excavation was the broad curve of an aquamarine pool. We found, a huge rusting boiler, small empty offices, more huts and joining all, a confusion of railway lines, weaving, interconnecting, some on pillared supports, leading down in a fascinating myriad to the vast hoppers for loading stone on the trucks we'd seen on the incline. Once, hundreds of men had toiled across the industrial complex like ants, but now all lay ghostly, in rusting abandonment.

From a poem written years ago, I've extracted a few verses, opening with us walking along the *only* road in Bedlam.

Four boys walked down Mainstreet, proud line abreast.
Their sticks became rifles slung low in hand.
Curtains twitched, dogs grumbled, faces peered,
Curious at sight of the intrepid band.

Took path leading out to spread of the common;
Hopped over rills silvering west;
Cupped hands relishing clear crystal water;
Summit in blue sky their own Everest.

Below lay their world like a patchwork blanket;
To explore and follow to where fortune led;
Dreams seemed boundless and all seemed possible.
They tried to imagine what lay ahead.

They all felt mighty, pioneering giants;
Small quilted fields seemed theirs, their land.
Life though simple was the time of their lives;
Yet dark silhouetted stood a small ragged band.

# Into long trousers

Strangely, although entering the third academic year, many boys were still not yet particularly fashion conscious and in fact didn't relish the confinement of long trousers. One would have thought, for sheer warmth in winter they would have been welcomed, but no; even when cold enough to scratch one's name in the frost on the bedroom window, somehow, wearing a coat over shorts and long woollen socks kept out the bitterness.

In 3B and then the first term in 4B, the light inside must have switched back on, for at each end of term exam I'd come top. Not in maths and I still had no clue regarding French, but my overall average put me in top spot, but with still no sign of promotion to the A class. In fact, two new boys I'd bettered were promoted while I still languished.

I don't know if it was a side effect of long trousers, but something I'd busily been experimenting at, on the quiet I must add, suddenly took over my body one morning, to the extent I lost control and with my mind having spiralled on such an exhilarating ride, I needed to lie there for a while in a state of complete amazement. Having recovered somewhat, I felt such elation, I couldn't wait to tell my friends and also couldn't wait to do it again. My admission of the mighty landmark having been reached brought a flurry of activity and soon we were all doing it, with Pete bemoaning, he'd become so addicted he'd rubbed a sore spot on his.

Again, it could have been the long trouser effect, but I noticed boys at school no longer thought of girls as tell-tales or spoilers of rumbustious games and having donned the long pants for over a school term, many started to become quite fashion conscious, attempting to train hair into looking how the TV pop idols wore it, swept back at the sides with a moody roll at the centre.

The school cap was worn as far back on the head as could be managed and the school tie was Windsor knotted for it to hang like a rat's tail. Money was saved in the hope of buying a pair of winkle pickers, leather jacket and jeans. The sullen look was all the rage.

So imagine how I felt when my mum made me take my winkle-pickers back to the shop. It was so embarrassing, but I did manage to procure a pair of jeans which sort of hit the mark when attempting to do the twist, which believe me was a cutting-edge activity that year. If only I'd had a pair of stylish shoes. I ask you! How can a young lad be expected to kick with the fray in a pair of sensible round-toed school shoes of the very type Rupert Bear wore?

I went with Pete to the Mayfair that year. He had three times as much money as I had, but with winning a little on the slot machines and pacing myself, had just as much fun as he did. In fact on one attraction, the rotor, you couldn't have paid me to have got spun around when stuck to the wall, especially when for next to nothing you could watch all the fear and trepidation from above.

At the dodgems, we noted which was the fastest car, but with no attractive females to bump into accidentally on purpose, we moved on to the Waltzer, which at the time was the rite of passage ride. I'd risked it for the first time the previous year without any side issues and so was not in fear of possible ignominy this particular year, yet still didn't climb up to join the youths lounging on the rail, in their leather gear and winkle pickers. Not in my round toed Rupert Bear school shoes.

Two youths slightly bent at knee as they rode the waves of the ride, collected the money and span the girls, who screamed as they hung onto beehive hairdos and when all slowed to a halt, that's when the big test came. Could a nonchalant exit be made from the ride? Any with ghostly white faces or showing signs of dizziness risked embarrassing ridicule from those onlookers lounging on the rail, looking so grown up and 'with it.'

Back at the dodgems I recognised two girls who had been in my final class at junior school and couldn't believe the change in such a short time. A little makeup, pretty hairstyle and the way womanly curves now filled out the simple shifts they wore, had changed them beyond all belief.

The fastest car became available and Pete and myself made a dash for it. To the sound of Dion's, The Wanderer blaring out, we rumbled and rattled across the metal flooring and aiming straight for the car containing the two lovelies mentioned, I veered away at the last moment. It brought the thrill of a, 'You just dare,' look and on another circuit, when delivering a deft little bump from behind, it jerked both heads back and this time the prettiest pointed and mouthed, 'I'm going to get you!'

Oh, if only, but when the cars slewed to a stop I slipped back into the crowd in my embarrassing Rupert Bears and Pete and myself went about the last action of the night, winning a coconut. Couldn't go home without one of those.

With Roger now working part time, I spent far more time with Francy. When down at the swimming pool, I got to know quite a few of his school friends and as he had a natural flair with the ladies, there was a natural spin-off, for I received an instant introduction into their company. Plus lest I forget; occasionally a mature cousin, who was massively well endowed, would glide up the pool drawing many an admiring look at the bow wave and I'd ask him to beckon her across to where we stood waiting. Even though we chatted away at our angelic best, she must have known. Course she did; for women with such assets have an inbuilt radar, sensing a lingering glance from a distance of fifty paces, let alone being ogled at from above.

He had two other cousins in a rock band and we'd walk down to St. Julian's Hall for the occasional Friday night dances, pace quickening when catching sound of the music. Yet another cousin was so accomplished at the jive, the floor would clear for him and his partner to give an impromptu display. Try following that in a pair of Rupert Bears.

The cousins in the rock band, by the way, had been brought up in the nether regions of Sandpits Avenue, contradicting the rent collector's avowal that all living there had been problem families.

We met a further cousin of his in the castle gardens one day. She was in charge of two much younger cousins, both pretty as kittens, but the one with the amazing big brown eyes, for some reason particularly drew my attention. I wasn't to know that many years later, on a return to Ludlow we'd meet again. The girl I had been drawn to that day by the castle, would one day be my wife.

Another unexpected meeting that year was on a raw cold day in Wellington. My father had been at an infirmary there and it would be my first sight of him since having left the Isle of Man at the age of two. He'd been receiving specialist treatment and of course, with this being my big day at last, I was understandably in a state of suspense and high expectation, for ahead lay that meeting I'd dreamt of for all those years.

I was introduced to a man slightly shorter than myself, who filled a well lived-in suit, for he was alarmingly bloated, especially around the jowls and to find refuge from the biting wind we entered the nearest café, a greasy spoon sort of dive. We ordered snacks, but my mother asked the waitress to delay their delivery on account of the disappearance of my father. Something forgotten, he'd explained with a smile.

I wondered if he'd reappear with a pretty bouquet for mother or small gift for his long-lost son. But no; about fifteen minutes later he returned looking thoroughly refreshed and struck up a conversation with my sister. Mike was given a friendly cuff under the chin and following the meal, with talk now going nowhere, we went back out into the cold.

In one shop window was a card, which had written upon it, 'Pretty assistant required. Apply within.'

"Just the job for you," my father said, causing Ann to blush. She was of course thrilled, for even if only briefly, she had her daddy back.

Nearby was one of those small glass-fronted gob-stopper vending machines and having a penny in my pocket, I put it in the slot, turned the knob and being at the perfect height Mike grabbed the sweet. Popping it into his mouth, he said, "Unwrapped sweets lose their flavour."

My father, who had obviously heard those same words as part of a TV advertisement, chuckled merrily and by way of congratulation gave him a friendly pat on the head.

We mooched about, with none of us saying much in particular and finally, when time came to say our goodbyes, with a repeat of, unwrapped sweets lose their favour, he gave Mike a squeeze and was gone.

A little later that year, I was amazed to find two bikes leaning in our coal shed, an early Christmas present. They were from my stepfather. It was something both Mike and I had longed for and we now had the freedom to roam for miles without troubling Mrs. Owen or anyone else for that matter for at last we had a bike apiece.

Before we leave 1962; in the October of that year the world held its breath as the Cuban missile crisis played out and early in that same month I heard a sound unlike anything I'd heard before, 'Love me do,' by the Beatles. I instinctively knew they were going to be a sensation. Sadly, however, this was also the year our beloved Clee Hill Junction railway line was dismantled. These days it would be a magnet for tourists had it remained open.

Just before Christmas, when school broke up that year, I was told of my promotion to the A stream. I had a lot of catching up to do, but at least I was aboard the fast train and now only had to work my way up to the front by way of the carriages. Oh, nearly forgot. I could now string that yew wood bow in the hallway and so it was now mine. It inspired others to purchase proper bows, but all that was fast coming to an end.

It was unusual to have such heavy snow before Christmas and with it being bitterly cold none of it melted, nor any of following blizzard that blanketed the country and when the wind blew all into blinding flurries it blocked major roads never mind our local winding lanes. I longed for the first ride on my bike and remember bringing it into the kitchen to check tyre pressure and breaking mechanisms. It was only second hand, but to me a thing of rare beauty.

Once the weather settled down, I joined others outside testing our machines' ability to cope with the snowscape. A gentle application of the back break and slight alignment of front wheel allowed a graceful slide through the right-angle bend at the bottom of the road. Then when realising Ledwyche pool would be a vast skating rink, we organised an exploratory mission to see if we could pioneer a route through the lanes. Below is another piece of verse written years ago.

# That Winter

Intense winter cold had frozen the pipes.
For weeks zinc pales had been hauled from next door
For washing, flushing, would cold never end?
Hard to imagine when chilled to the core.

All recent snow still lay pristine;
Fantastic for sledging or long slide at school.
One day, tentatively testing our bikes,
All headed for Ledwyche to skid on the pool.

We edged down road, rear brakes set ready.
Most bikes second-hand, Christmas gifts;
Keenness to ride, but care not to wreck,
In snow blocked lanes and hedge high drifts.

Yelps and laughter, near multiple pile-ups,
Down glassy ruts where a tractor had been.
Exploring thigh deep on sculpted hedge tops;
Flurries soft-powdered the arctic scene.

Villagers like charcoal sketch on paper;
Dark clad boy raised an arm to greet
Us hesitating on white-walled cycles,
Before slow-wheeled crossing of pale blue sheet.

Friendly folk in a strange winter world,
Assured us ice was too strong to break.
To prove it a tractor rattled to centre
As we explored amongst trees far end of lake.

Weird riding amid petrified coppice;
Laced limbs in agony from clenching vice
Of frozen water and breaking the silence,
We could hear eerie creaking of the ice.

Shards when hurled rattled the surface.
We'd wet clear licks, from frozen icicles.
Competing pool length for longest skid;
Wild-scarved speedway kings on bicycles.

Sun-glinting surface, burnished faster;
Then game was pointless; none could outrank,
The sideways skid of leading bike,
Gliding to summersault on distant bank.

Homeward, with faces glowing at dusk,
Hot, carefree, all waving and calling
To inching man, arms spread for balance,
Amazed at how close he was to falling.

The thaw didn't arrive until early March and when it did, all the rivers full to overflowing ran so wild, the weirs appeared as if mere undulations along the mad carousel. Bridges shuddered from the impact of stricken trees, that leapt to freedom far side, to be swept further along on the wild ride downstream.

Of course, the extreme conditions didn't mean schools were closed and we all attended as normal except for the fact cross-country runs took the place of rugby. Not exactly cross-country of course as we only ran along the lanes that had been opened.

By this time Copper had left school and from his first job, now had much more money to satisfy his experimental whims. Roger and Mick had part-time jobs and I could sense our age of innocence fast coming to an end. For instance, when the old gang was back together, on a pleasant evening we'd sometimes walk across the fields to the Nelson where the eldest would go inside to buy quart bottles of cider. As we swigged our way down to a state of merriment, talk became more outrageous, everything seemed funnier and if a joke was timed right, a listener got the nose-fizz from the cider they'd been unable to swallow through laughter.

Inspired by the harmonica playing on the first Beatles record to enter the charts, I dug an old fluff filled thing from out of a drawer and gave it a go. Before long I could play quite a number of melodies and found that down at the Nelson it was amazing how much the cider helped. It could of course also loosen the tongue and we received a number of glowering looks from locals using the outside facilities.

Back at school, a good mate was the under XV rugby captain, but I still had to prove myself worthy of selection and that young man, Brian Griffiths, has been a friend for life.

At lunchtime a number of us would set off to join all the others assembling in an old chapel down at Temeside where school meals were dished out from huge aluminium containers. We would sometimes take a left below Broadgate, cutting through via Saint John's Road and could hardly believe living conditions people still had to endure. It felt like stepping back into another century and apparently it hadn't been that long ago, living in Lower Broad Street had been akin to surviving in a rat warren. You'd need deep pockets to buy a cottage there now, mind you.

Going back to Copper and his fads, before his purchase of a temperamental scooter and then the ancient, hefty motorbike, model planes were his thing. He ordered all the necessary from the Gamages Catalogue and first to make an appearance from the washhouse was a balsa framed, paper covered aircraft of such an impressive size, word got about and quite a few gathered to watch its maiden flight, launched from the crest of the mound of garden waste near the entry to the lane. Powered by a thick elastic band driving the propeller, it took a worrying dip in Bache's field, before gaining height to head off serenely towards the Ledwyche river. Shading his eyes to follow the flight, Copper stood in wrapped admiration, until suddenly realising the plane's first flight could well be its last and he set off across Bache's pastures in hot pursuit.

All waited, curious as to the outcome and a cheer went up when he reappeared, carefully cradling the plane like a goose with a broken neck. It was patched up after each flight, but it was a battle of diminishing returns and on its final flight he put a match to it and all watched the dramatic glide into sad incineration.

The next planes were feisty little fibreglass models he'd put together along with a small motor mounted on the nose. Held in check by a long cord they snarled and dived round in circles until he got fed up with them and as I said, then came the motorbikes.

Nearly forgot, near the end of that year there was a cameo performance courtesy of his mother's hearing aid. First he purloined it for rigging up an intercom system in the house, but then came the realisation, its powers of communication were only limited by the length of wire used and so his house then became the beleaguered outpost, while reception was taken in the control centre way down across the gardens in Francy's washhouse. Tony Hancock's humorous test pilot record was hugely popular at the time and we laughed as Copper's voice came down the line, "Hancock to control tower. Are you receiving me?"

There were a few further exchanges and then we heard, "There's a strange knocking sound coming from outside the cockpit."

There certainly was, it was Copper getting thwacked around the ear accompanied by his mother's, "What the hell d'you think you're doing with my new hearing aid?"

Fran and I leant closer to the device, trying to decipher the intermittent transmission, "Ouch!" was followed by what sounded like static. Then, "Ow! Hancock to control tower, come in please."

"I'll give you ruddy, Hancock!" screeched his mother.

"Hancock again, are you receiving me?"

"Give me that flamin' hearing aid!"

Along with the sound of a scuffle came the strained, "We have a slight problem."

Following a few more thwacks, "Hancock signing off now. Ouch! Under attack!"

That summer all the talk was about the Great Train Robbery. It dominated the newspapers and TV and although the train driver had been badly beaten the gang almost achieved Robin Hood status for their audacity.

Later, came the breaking news of what became known as the Profumo affair, that brought down the Tory government, but also left us the legacy of an iconic picture of a shapely, but slightly vulnerable looking Christine Keeler astride a chair, plus the memorable phrase from her friend Mandy Rice-Davies, "Well he would say that wouldn't he," which is oft repeated rather than refer to someone as a bare-faced liar.

As far as us schoolboys were concerned, the main topic at the time was the banning of the 18th century novel, Fanny Hill. A well-thumbed copy did the rounds and I remember reading it in our dining room, disguised beneath the cover of a school book. My long pullover was necessary to complete the disguise, lest a certain something gave the game away.

Late that summer came an encounter with wasps and the notion of using grubs from the nest as fish bait.

# Wasps

Sagas of past deeds grew in retelling;
'Remember the time,' often the start line.
Laughter main effort for us on the bank,
Letting day drift by, happily supine.

We mused about fun vagaries of life,
Learned philosophical views.
'Just think, you could have real smelly eyebrows,
Yet not realise the fact unless somebody told you.

'Do wrinkly old people still kiss?' I asked.
'Not pecks, real smackers I'm talking about.
Would you swallow the fang or just hand it back,
If kissing so hard sucked a tooth right out?'

The number of wasps overhead was noted.
'We could dig out grubs then fish for a laugh.
Bet there's a nest, big as a football!'
'Must be directly under the flight path.'

We tracked down one to a hole in a bank.
Angry activity caused sudden halt.
Smoke would be needed before digging them out;
Calming them down before the assault.

Copper aimed spade, then ran for his life.
We attacked in turn, words choice and loud.
Circling the nest, like raiding Indians,
Whooping and thrashing, yellow angry cloud.

As we flailed for protection, wasps wreaked revenge.
Full war escalated from bit of fun;
On Roger's chest, a long line of stings;
'One of them critters owns a machine gun!'

Dense billowing smoke made the scene surreal.
Laughter at Copper's wild running wide-eyed
In panic, back arched, legs turning like wheels;
Sharp angry dot just inches from backside.

Wasps' dense ferocity held us at bay.
Brian turned up, uttered verdict candid.
Surveying his brother's and other's raw stings
And bank as if incendiary bomb had landed.

He who'd punched cousin Pat in the face;
Took delight at spit balls dropped on the prone,
Said, 'Serves you all right. What threat are poor wasps?
Harmless if you lot just left them alone.'

Next morning, Granddad from around the corner
Placed large trout on offer with calm pride.
He'd managed to scoop out 'cake' from the nest,
With wasps soundly sleeping from cyanide.


1963 turned out to be quite a year, for underlying everything was the extraordinary success of the Beatles, with their three number one hit singles. Not only did it spark an outbreak of talent across the country, it made teenage fans feel they were not only in control of what was heard on the radio, almost as if all having been their invention, it also led them to feel in control of their own destiny. If four lads from Liverpool could make it, it implied with enough dedication, anyone could. It would have been a major reason why Francy and myself had such certainty of being able to found a successful youth club.

School friends warned us not to waste our time, for many before had tried and failed, but we told them ours would be different, for with anyone over the age of 16 not being allowed to join, it would cut out potential for the young feeling threatened and general yobbish behaviour. You'd have thought, with our contemporaries not being keen, we'd have lost faith, but truly convinced we pursued the idea with vigour, searching for a venue and someone of authority willing to run it. Also of course, we needed money, but before giving more details I'd better explain the reference to Brian in the above poem.

Yes, he did punch my cousin Pat in the face, which earnt him pariah status for a while, but also there was another side to him I'd better describe and thus give a fairer picture. For a start, he was the regular delivery boy for Stead's grocery store, located far side of the recreation ground and never got orders muddled, plus he could be trusted behind the counter, even though his entries in the leger sometimes brought disgruntled mutterings. For example, writing in the sold column, '3d for bag of suck,' didn't go down well, but at least he could be trusted with the money.

Another feature; even though he could be a nasty piece of work, surprisingly he hated cruelty to wildlife, not only the wasps mentioned, but there had been another occasion years before where his disgust and anger at us shooting arrows at mating frogs across in the orchard, caused us to immediately cease our barbarity.

The punch incident came about on account of me bowling him out in a game of cricket played in the orchard, long before the water tower had ever been thought of. A chequered metal washing machine cover acted as the wicket and so there had been no mistaking the fact I'd bowled him first ball. He refused to walk, however, insisting he had another go. It was the first season we'd used the proper cricket bat I'd been given and tapping the ground with menace he awaited the next delivery.

At the unmistakable, 'ding,' of ball striking metal, he turned and slammed the bat down on the wicket, putting an ugly crease into the edge of the blade. I flew at him in anger, but on the very point of expecting a punch in the face, cousin Pat who happened to be staying with us, intervened and yelled, "Leave him alone you great big bully!" At the sound of his punch connecting with her jaw, everyone stood mouths agape, as if she'd just been shot.

So you can imagine my terror in the year of 1963, when Fran and I happened to be cycling home from town one Saturday morning. Turning into St. Julians Road, we espied Brian marching at pace in full uniform, obviously home on leave. I'd only meant to deliver a friendly tap to accompany the greeting, "Aya Brian," but misjudging the pace of the bike knocked his beret off. Not only was I aghast regarding the consequences, his screeched words of venom must have brought startled faces to front windows on both sides of the street and so rather than stop and apologise, Fran and I rode on down into Livesey Road, then up the rise to dismount at what we all called, 'The Well.' It had been an ancient source of fresh water for the town, but probably back in the early 1900's, had been given a low pitched-roof sealing of stone.

Well, there we were, blithely pushing our bikes up the short, left-hand stretch that circumvented it, thoroughly relieved we'd ridden beyond Brian's ire, when I heard rapid pit-pats, hardly touching the ground. Turning, I saw it was Brian close upon us, not with wheezy breath we'd all become accustomed to, but with lupine face set grim to carry out an act of unbelievable savagery.

Fran and myself ran, leapt on the bikes and standing on the peddles, both desperately tried to gain momentum. Bony fingers made a grab for my saddle, but a hard downward thrust took me a whisker clear and then again at his next lunge, until with the rise levelling out, I was able to ride from the certainty of having to wear the bike home, rather than ride it.

Our legs were still shaking when reaching the sanctuary of my garden and I made sure I didn't show myself anywhere in the vicinity until quite sure Brian had returned to barracks.

So that's cleared that little matter up.

Everyone is meant to remember where they were when hearing of President Kennedy's assassination. I know exactly where I was, inside Ludlow Buttercross. Fran and I were downtown collecting rummage in an effort to raise money for the opening of the youth club, when one of his friends ran up with the news. Like most people, we found it almost impossible to believe. At school the following Monday, the flag flew at half-mast; the first time such an honour had been provided for a foreign national.

The youth club, by the way, was a success, lasting long after Fran and I had outgrown it. Mr. Bill Jeffs, the town mace bearer was the official figure we needed, Friary Hall was the venue and both the MP, Mr. Jasper More and the lady mayor were present at the opening, but that's a story for another time.

Just like anyone writing an autobiographical account, it's difficult to give a conclusion, for God willing, life goes on. Also, it's incredibly difficult deciding what to leave out. There were school trips; an incredible six weeks spent in Killybegs, County Donegal; more visits from our cousins; two sad deaths in the family; our grandmother parking herself on us for weeks on end; enchanting girls brought back to stay from my sister's college; innumerable school anecdotes; Fran and I building an underground cabin, complete with hearth and chimney; the young ladies we invited there for visits; glorious kisses from Rose when returning from the Nelson; escapades my brother and Eecock got up to, but with this being mainly a story dedicated to those I grew up with in Clee View, during the years 1956-1963, I had to leave a vast amount out and not stray into later teen years.

If the above little saga is well received, I might write a follow-up, but for now will sign off with the short verse below.

# Bridge of Dreams

Four ragged boys leant on the mossed bridge rail;
Gazing into brook's soft lilting flow.
From under bank-hollow, fanned a fish tail.
In clear cool pool of soft brown glow.

Far shoal sparkled, and dry, littering shrub tops,
Matted twigs, fronds, raging winter's traces.
Then alit dancing like meadow buttercups,
Patterns rocked,--- rippling, branches, faces.

They talked, laughed, hoped on the great tomorrow,
White blooms and bluebells stood in damp, deep green;
Each grasped a bunch next to bow and arrow
And stared into water, into their dreams.

One retraced those steps, his old heart gladdened;
Told tales to kindred spirited daughter;
She, eager to hear, he then slight saddened
By memories, echoes, ghostly laughter.

With words not required, they let thoughts run.
Birds sang, patterns dappled as of yore;
With life's myriad track now almost done,
His children's happiness he now dreamt for.

# Epilogue

With numerous references to what life might have had in store, it seems only right to add the following.

Brian Woodcock had a successful military career.

Mick Woodcock's first job was with Clee Hill plant hire, before working for the Midlands Electricity Board (MEB) as a linesman.

Rob Woodcock, (Eecock) started out as a wool grader at Marston's Mill, but then, in the employment of the MEB, became a linesman foreman.

Francis Lochbaum also worked for the MEB, before spending years as a qualified electrician. He had a spell in Australia, built houses in Clunbury and Bucknell and in the 70's became famed for his shop, Bubble boutique in King Street, Ludlow.

Tommy Preece, who by the way had not a bad bone in his body, entered the army but unfortunately suffered a debilitating injury when knocked down by a military vehicle, while out on manoeuvres.

Robert Clark spent most of his working life at McConnels agricultural machinery manufacturer, Ludlow, before finally moving to Kennedys blade sharpening plant at Craven Arms. All his life, he owned a motorbike and almost certainly had fine leather gauntlets to suit.

Peter Clark spent his years as a car salesman before taking over the manning of the Woofferton Junction signal box.

When David Pritchard (Copper), left the Grammar School, his first job was with Henry Wiggins of Hereford, where he met his wife. In 1964 he joined Vinatex, a company in South London, gained a degree, plus membership of the Royal Institute of Chemistry and then worked for ICI until 1974.

On joining Angus Fire Armour, he was sent to the USA in 1977 as a technical manager, to help set up a company in Raleigh, South Carolina, where he rose through the ranks to become plant manager and finally Senior Vice President.

When the company was bought out in 1994, he left to help set up Highwater Hose Inc, which must have done fairly well, for when he sold his shares in 2019 he retired to live a millionaire's lifestyle.

Roger Pritchard spent years working for the MEB, plus running a rented smallholding at Stanton Lacy. He also achieved the ambition of owning his own patch of land, nine acres of virgin hillside up near Hayton's Bent, Shropshire. Remember how wild he was? Well, he has been a school governor, a parish councillor, plus he and his wife Eileen, have fostered 160 babies and children. To my mind, worthy of an OBE.

My brother Michael? I'm afraid I'd need another book to relate everything he got up to.

My stepfather, Eric Sciville gained a prestigious job, searching out land suitable for commercial development, before spending his final working years as a security officer at the Royal Court of Justice. In my undergraduate years he occasionally drove me from London to Shropshire in his MG sportscar and during my early antique dealing years, stayed in the family home on a number of occasions.

My father, Cyril Clegg, passed through his wet phase and worked as a quantity surveyor for a major building company on the Isle of Man. On the numerous occasions I took my family there, I discovered a man known for his one-line quips that hit the mark like a low flier, a man respected as an impromptu financial advisor and a man my 10-month-old daughter fell instantly in love with.

Waterloo House, by the way, remembered as a mighty stone bastion holding out against the wilderness, seems to have shrunk in size, for on a recent visit I saw a modest Georgian stone farmhouse, with barns only half the size I remember and sad to say, the wilderness has now finally won.